BEST LOVED INDIAN STORIES OF THE CENTURY

VOLUME II

Indira Srinivasan, educated in Delhi, Waltair, Chennai and Plymouth, is an English teacher with twenty years of teaching experience at the high school level. A resource person for teacher training programmes all over India, she is involved in the production of training materials. She is associated with the British Council's Business English programmes and is a trainer in Business English courses for various corporate houses in Chennai.

She is the author of several textbooks, including the *Connect* series, and is presently compiling another English textbook.

She is married and lives in Chennai.

Chetna Bhatt, educated in Chandigarh, Delhi and Plymouth, has been teaching English in a public school in Delhi for nearly twenty years. She has conducted teacher training workshops all over India for English teachers at the secondary school level and is a resource person for CBSE and the British Council. She is also associated with the British Council as a trainer for the Business English programmes and is a course writer for Indira Gandhi National Open University.

She is the author of *Interactions in English* and several other English textbooks for high school students.

She is married and lives in Delhi.

Indira Srinivasan and Chetna Bhatt have also edited *Best Loved Indian Stories of the Century (Volume I).*

PENGUIN BOOKS

[illegible] STORIES OF THE [illegible]

[illegible]

[illegible] educated [illegible] and [illegible] teaching experience [illegible] teacher training [illegible] She is associated with the British Council's Business English programme and [illegible] courses in [illegible]

[illegible]

[illegible]

[illegible] teaching [illegible] teacher training [illegible] English teachers [illegible] the British Council [illegible]

[illegible]

[illegible]

BEST LOVED INDIAN STORIES OF THE CENTURY

Volume II

Edited by

Indira Srinivasan
and
Chetna Bhatt

PENGUIN BOOKS

PENGUIN BOOKS
Published by the Penguin Group
Penguin Books India Pvt. Ltd, 11 Community Centre, Panchsheel Park, New Delhi 110 017, India
Penguin Group (USA) Inc., 375 Hudson Street, New York, New York 10014, USA
Penguin Group (Canada), 90 Eglinton Avenue East, Suite 700, Toronto, Ontario, M4P 2Y3, Canada (a division of Pearson Penguin Canada Inc.)
Penguin Books Ltd, 80 Strand, London WC2R 0RL, England
Penguin Ireland, 25 St Stephen's Green, Dublin 2, Ireland (a division of Penguin Books Ltd)
Penguin Group (Australia), 250 Camberwell Road, Camberwell, Victoria 3124, Australia (a division of Pearson Australia Group Pty Ltd)
Penguin Group (NZ), cnr Airborne and Rosedale Roads, Albany, Auckland 1310, New Zealand (a division of Pearson New Zealand Ltd)
Penguin Group (South Africa) (Pty) Ltd, 24 Sturdee Avenue, Rosebank, Johannesburg 2196, South Africa

Penguin Books Ltd, Registered Offices: 80 Strand, London WC2R 0RL, England

First published by Penguin Books India 1999

15 14 13 12 11 10 9

Typeset in PalmSprings by SÜRYA, New Delhi
Printed at Rashtriya Printers, New Delh

Contents

Acknowledgements

Grateful acknowledgement is made to the following for granting us permission to reprint copyright material:

Dhumaketu and the Sahitya Akademi for 'The Letter', from *Contemporary Indian Short Stories* (Sahitya Akademi); K.P. Poornachandra Tejasvi and the Sahitya Akademi for 'Tabara's Story', from *Modern Indian Literature* (Sahitya Akademi), ed. K.M. George; Ranjan Chopra and Mala Dayal for 'Tai Eesree', from *Land of Five Rivers* (Orient Paperbacks), ed. Khushwant Singh; K.K. Mohapatra, Leelawati Mohapatra and Sudhansu Mohanty for 'Maguni's Bullock Cart', from *The HarperCollins Book of Oriya Short Stories* (HarperCollins), ed. K.K. Mohapatra, Leelawati Mohapatra and Sudhansu Mohanty; Visva-Bharati and William Radice for 'Kabuliwala', from *Rabindranath Tagore: Selected Short Stories* (Penguin), ed. William Radice; Pritam Singh and Navyug Press for 'The Bull Beneath the Earth', from *Mahindi and Other Stories* (Navyug Press); K.K. Mohapatra, Leelawati Mohapatra, Paul St-Pierre and the Sahitya Akademi for 'Rebati', from *Indian Literature*; Krishna Sobti and the Sahitya Akademi for 'The Encircling Clouds', from *Anthology of Hindi Short Stories* (Sahitya Akademi), ed. Bhisham Sahni; V.P. Ranga Rao for 'Kamalini', from *Classic Telugu Short Stories* (Penguin), ed. Ranga Rao; Anees Basheer and Orient Longman Ltd. for 'Poovan Banana', from *Poovan Banana and Other Stories* (Orient Longman), ed. V. Abdulla; Amin Kamil and the Sahitya Akademi for 'The Cock-fight', from *Contemporary Kashmiri Short Stories* (Sahitya Akademi); Gangadhar Gadgil for 'The Big Silver Rupee', from *The Throttled Street and Other Stories* (Popular Prakashan); Prabhavati P. Bhave and K. Natwar Singh for 'The Mystery', from *Stories from India* (B.I. Publishers), ed. K. Natwar Singh; K. Natwar Singh for 'The Shroud', from *Stories from India*; Kamala Bandyopadhyay and Thema for 'Prehistoric', from *Manik Bandyopadhyay: Selected Stories* (Thema), ed. Malini Bhattacharya; Kamalakshya Amma and Roli Books for 'In the Flood', from *The Best of Thakazhi Sivasankara Pillai* (Roli Books), ed. K.M. George; the Bharatiya Vidya Bhavan and K. Natwar Singh for 'Ardhanari', from *Stories from India*; Nighat Patel, Nuzhat Arshad, Nusrat Jalan and Mala Dayal for 'Exchange of Lunatics', from *Land of Five Rivers*; M.S. Indiramma, the MVJK Trust and the Sahitya Akademi for 'The Curds-seller', from *Contemporary Indian Short Stories*; Kirit Doodhat and the Sahitya Akademi for 'Womenfolk', from *Indian Literature*; Dinakari Chokalingam and the Sahitya Akademi for 'Redemption', from *Modern Indian Literature*; Chaganti Tulasi and V.P. Ranga Rao for 'Must Visit Eluru', from *Classic Telugu Short Stories*; Kanaklata Das, Harish C. Pradhan and the Indian Council for Cultural Relations for 'Death of a Banana Boat', from *Modern Indian Short Stories* (ICCR), ed. Kishori Charan Das.

While every effort has been made to trace the copyright holders and obtain permission, this has not been possible in all cases; any omissions brought to our attention will be remedied in future editions.

Acknowledgements

While every effort has been made to trace the copyright holders of material in this book, this has not proved possible in all cases; any omissions brought to our attention will be remedied in future editions.

Introduction

The second volume of *Best Loved Indian Stories of the Century* is, like the first, a compilation of short stories culled from the rich and diverse traditions of fiction writing in India. While the first volume comprised stories written originally in English by Indian authors, this volume is a collection of stories translated from various Indian languages.

Since there is a wealth of material to choose from in the regional languages, we were faced with some difficulties in coming up with a representative selection. Eventually, we decided to go by the criterion that is key to this collection—the fact that the stories are 'best loved'. The stories included here are some of the most popular pieces written in their respective languages. Generations of readers have read them in the original, as part of school or college syllabi or anthologies, and they have become part of the essential core of their identified culture. In bringing these stories together, we hope to offer the English-speaking reader an overview of some of the best writing that has come out of India in the past hundred years.

The short story in its present form is a fairly recent phenomenon in Indian literature, dating from the end of the nineteenth century. In the hands of early masters like Rabindranath Tagore and Fakir Mohan Senapati, it soon achieved great sophistication. While traditions of ritual storytelling and folk tales were probably the precursors of the short story in Indian languages, the influence of western writers can also be discerned especially in the earlier stories. The subjects dealt with in the stories have, however, from the start, had to do with quintessentially Indian situations relating to caste, family, class oppression, gender inequality and so on.

Putting together an anthology of 'best loved stories' is a very challenging task. We are deeply indebted to the academicians, writers, Sahitya Academy officials and others who have helped us with suggestions and advice. The constraints of space and the need to be representative have necessarily restricted our choices to one or two stories from the major languages. Most of the stories are by first generation short story writers in each language. For the interested reader, these stories will provide the essential context against which to read more contemporary writing in the Indian languages.

Translation from one language to another is always a risky business. In a multilingual country like India, however, perhaps the only way to acquaint the educated reader with the vast treasure trove of writing in the various Indian languages is to make translations available in English. It is extremely difficult to retain the flavour and complexity of the original in translation. On the other hand, it is better to have at least a rough sense of the original in translation, than to have no sense of it at all. We have looked at many translations while we were preparing this volume and our yardstick for selection was undoubtly connected to the sensitivity with which nuances of the original were reproduced by the translator.

Despite the geographical and occasionally chronological distances which separate the authors, the twenty-three stories in this collection share many compelling themes and motifs. Many of these stories display a common concern with the human spirit, especially with human suffering and the stoicism with which this is borne. The character of Çoachman Ali, who waits patiently to hear from his beloved daughter in 'The Letter', is a deceptively simple but poignant depiction of the enduring and eternally patient nature of paternal love. 'Tabara's Story'—which was made into an award winning film, *Tabarana Kathe*—is another tale of patience, this time concerning a retired civil servant's wait for his provident fund money which he desperately needs to treat his ailing wife. Caught in the tangled web of an indifferent bureaucracy, Tabara suffers a plight which is all too familiar.

Another tale of patient fortitude, albeit this time happier since it is narrated by an appreciative nephew, is 'Tai Eesree'. Tai is the incarnation of the spirit of cheerful self-sacrifice traditionally associated with Indian women. Yet another form of stoicism and optimism is displayed by the protagonist of 'Maguni's Bullock Cart' who is a victim of the inexorable changes brought about by technology which permanently transformed the face of rural India. The Kabuliwala too patiently serves his barren years in prison, longing for his little daughter living in distant Afghanistan—the bond of fatherly love cementing his unlikely friendship with the intellectual Bengali babu who narrates his story with affection and sympathy. The stoicism and forbearance of an older generation is also movingly depicted in 'The Bull Beneath the Earth'—a reminder of the tragedy of war. In 'Rebati' and 'The Encircling Clouds', the inexorable decrees of fate are all too prominent but the central characters rise above their obstacles to face death with fortitude and dignity.

But challenges need not only be faced with fortitude—laughter is another powerful weapon to combat life's problems. Kamalini, in the eponymous story, deals with an erring husband with such delightfully impish humour that one feels his reform will be permanent. In 'Poovan Banana', the roles are reversed and the loving husband tames the shrew. The narrator's charming style transforms a delicate and potentially offensive (to women readers at least) episode into a delightful vignette. A more robust kind of humour permeates 'The Cock-fight'. The wide-eyed wonder of the narrator in 'The Big Silver Rupee' is a picturesque rendition of a child's intense excitement when given the enormous sum of a whole rupee to spend. 'The Mystery' is an amusing though sympathetic look at another stage of life—a youth's awakening to an awareness of romance and the possibilities of matrimony.

But there are problems which cannot be combated with humour and five of the stories in this collection deal with such issues with great sensitivity. In 'The Shroud' and 'Prehistoric', the stark realism with which extreme poverty and the despair which it breeds is depicted suggests that the dividing line between man and beast is indeed tenuous. This idea is reinforced in 'In the Flood', where the detailed insight provided into the mind of the dog brilliantly encapsulates the politics of our responses to times of intense trouble. 'Ardhanari' deals with another form of human crisis—the taboos of caste and the ways of dealing with a problem that can tear individuals apart. The trauma of Partition—another man-made crisis—is vividly captured in 'Exchange of Lunatics', which questions our definitions of sanity.

Women in India have traditionally been perceived as a class apart and the ways in which they deal with their own and the opposite sex are often exceedingly complex. 'The Curds-seller' describes how women resolve their conflicts through Machiavellian diplomacy while 'Womenfolk' is a haunting tale of how women are insidiously oppressed despite their solidarity. 'Redemption' celebrates the indomitable spirit of a woman—a poor widow who has to walk home alone through a dark and dangerous forest.

'Must Visit Eluru' and 'Death of a Banana Boat' explore relationships between men and women. Maṇikyamma in the former story refuses to be constricted by social taboos yet contrives to project her actions in a manner acceptable to society. In the latter, Rupeyee's life is wholly decided by those who occupy positions of power in the hierarchy, leaving her with no voice in deciding her own destiny.

All these stories thus deal with issues that, in one way or the other, have touched our lives. Their gripping portrayal of the human psyche and the range of emotions that they depict render them universally relevant. Yet they simultaneously capture the distinctive character of the regions where they were written—for example, the robust virility of Punjab is evident in every line of 'The

Bull Beneath the Earth' and the magic of Durga Puja in Bengal is captured in a few brilliant sentences in Tagore's story. Some of these stories will be familiar, but we hope that the interesting juxtapositionings that this anthology provides will inspire new interpretations and fresh insights into life and the business of living. After all, these are the stories that have provided the foundation for an ever-growing corpus of literature that is as rich in texture and variegated in colour as our country itself.

We hope you will enjoy reading each of these stories and find the experience as rewarding as we did when we sorted through a wealth of material in order to be able to bring this collection to you.

November 1999

INDIRA SRINIVASAN
CHETNA BHATT

The Letter

DHUMAKETU

In the grey sky of early dawn stars still glowed, as happy memories light up a life that is nearing its close. An old man was walking through the town, now and again drawing his tattered cloak tighter to shield his body from the cold and biting wind. From some houses came the sound of grinding mills and the sweet voices of women singing at their work, and these sounds helped him along his lonely way. Except for the occasional bark of a dog, the distant steps of a workman going early to work, or the screech of a bird disturbed before its time, the whole town was wrapped in deathly silence. Most of its inhabitants were still in the arms of sleep, a sleep which grew more and more profound on account of the intense winter cold; for the cold used sleep to extend its sway over all things even as a false friend lulls his chosen victim with caressing smiles. The old man, shivering at times but fixed of purpose, plodded on till he came out of the town-gate on to a straight road. Along this he now went at a somewhat slower pace, supporting himself on his old staff.

On one side of the road was a row of trees, on the other the town's public garden. The sky was darker now and the cold more intense, for the wind was blowing straight along the road, on which there fell, like frozen snow, only the faint light of the morning star. At the end of the garden stood a handsome building of the newest style, and light gleamed through the crevices of its closed doors and windows.

Beholding the wooden arch of this building, the old man was filled with the joy that the pilgrim feels when he first sees the goal of his journey. On the arch hung an old board with the newly-painted letters: POST OFFICE. The old man went in quietly and squatted on the veranda. The voices of two or three people busy at their routine work could be heard faintly through the wall.

'Police Superintendent,' a voice inside called sharply. The old man started at the sound, but composed himself again to wait. But for the faith and love that warmed him, he could not have borne the bitter cold.

Name after name rang out from within as the clerk read out the English addresses on the letters and flung them to the waiting postmen. From long practice he had acquired great speed in reading out the titles—Commissioner, Superintendent, Diwan Sahib, Librarian—and in flinging the letters out.

In the midst of this procedure a jesting voice from inside called, 'Coachman Ali!'

The old man got up, raised his eyes to heaven in gratitude and, stepping forward, put his hand on the door.

'Gokul Bhai!'

'Yes. Who's there?'

'You called out Coachman Ali's name, didn't you? Here I am. I have come for my letter.'

'It is a madman, sir, who worries us by calling every day for letters that never come,' said the clerk to the postmaster.

The old man went back slowly to the bench on which he had been accustomed to sit for five long years.

Ali had once been a clever shikari. As his skill increased so did his love for the hunt, till at last it was as impossible for him to pass a day without hunting as it is for the opium-eater to forgo his daily portion. When Ali sighted the earth-brown patridge, almost invisible to other eyes, the poor bird, they said, was as good as in his bag. His sharp eyes saw the hare crouching. When even the dogs failed to see the creature cunningly hidden in the yellow-brown scrub, Ali's eagle eyes would catch sight of its ears; and in another moment it was dead. Besides this, he would often go out with his friends, the fishermen.

But when the evening of his life was drawing in, he left his old ways and suddenly took a new turn. His only child, Miriam, married and left him. She went off with a soldier to his regiment in the Punjab, and for the last five years he had had no news of this daughter for whose sake along he dragged on a cheerless existence. Now he understood the meaning of love and separation. He could no longer enjoy the sportsman's pleasure and laughter at the bewildered terror of the young partridges bereft of their parents.

Although the hunter's instinct was in his very blood and bones, such loneliness had come into his life since the day Miriam had gone away, that now, forgetting his sport, he would become lost in admiration of the green cornfields. He reflected deeply, and came to the conclusion that the whole universe is built up through love and that the grief of separation is inescapable. And seeing this, he sat down under a tree and wept bitterly. From that day he had risen each morning at four o'clock to walk to the post office. In his whole life he had never received a letter, but with a devout serenity born of hope and faith he persevered and was always the first to arrive.

The post office, one of the most uninteresting buildings in the world, became his place of pilgrimage. He always occupied a particular seat in a particular corner of the building, and when people got to know his habit they laughed at him. The postmen began to make game of him. Even though there was no letter for him, they would call out his name for the fun of seeing him jump up and come to the door. But with boundless faith and infinite patience, he came every day, and went away empty-handed.

While Ali waited, peons would come for their firms' letters, and he would hear them discussing their masters' scandals. These smart young peons in their spotless turbans and creaking shoes were always eager to express themselves. Meanwhile, the door would be thrown open and the postmaster, a man with a face as sad and inexpressive as a pumpkin, would be seen sitting on his chair inside. There was no glimmer of animation in his features; such men usually prove to be village schoolmasters, office clerks, or postmasters.

One day, he was there as usual and did not move from his seat when the door was opened.

'Police Commissioner!' the clerk called out, and a

young fellow stepped forward briskly for the letters.

'Superintendent!' Another peon came; and so the clerk, like a worshipper of Vishnu, repeated his customary thousand names.

At last they had all gone. Ali too got up and, saluting the post office as though it housed some precious relic, went off, a pitiable figure, a century behind his time.

'That fellow,' asked the postmaster, 'is he mad?'

'Who, sir? Oh, yes,' answered the clerk. 'No matter what the weather is, he has been here every day for the last five years. But he doesn't get many letters.'

'I can well understand that! Who does he think will have time to write a letter every day?'

'But he's a bit touched, sir. In the old days he committed many sins; and maybe he shed blood within some sacred precincts and is paying for it now,' the postman added in support of his statement.

'Madmen are strange people,' the postmaster said.

'Yes. Once I saw a madman in Ahmedabad who did absolutely nothing but make little heaps of dust. And another had a habit of going to the river bed in order to pour water on a certain stone every day!'

'Oh, that's nothing,' chimed in another. 'I knew one madman who paced up and down all day long, another who never ceased declaiming poetry, and a third who would slap himself on the cheek and then begin to cry because he was being beaten.'

And everyone in the post office began talking of lunacy. All working-class people have the habit of taking periodic rests by joining in general discussion for a few minutes. After listening for a while, the postmaster got up and said: 'It seems as though the mad live in a world of their own making. To them, perhaps, we too appear mad. The madman's world is rather like the poet's, I should think!'

He laughed as he spoke the last words, looking at one of the clerks who wrote indifferent verse. Then he went out and the office became still again.

For several days Ali had not come to the post office. There was no one with enough sympathy or understanding to guess the reason, but all were curious to know what had stopped the old man. At last he came again; but it was a struggle for him to breathe, and on his face were clear signs of his approaching end. That day he could not contain his impatience.

'Master Sahib,' he begged the postmaster, 'have you a letter from my Miriam?'

The postmaster wanted to get out to the country, and was in a hurry.

'What a pest you are, brother!' he exclaimed.

'My name is Ali,' answered Ali absent-mindedly.

'I know! I know! But do you think we've got your Miriam's name registered?'

'Then please note it down, brother. It will be useful if a letter should come when I am not here.' For how should the villager who had spent three-quarters of his life hunting know that Miriam's name was not worth a pice to anyone but her father?

The postmaster was beginning to lose his temper. 'Have you no sense?' he cried. 'Get away! Do you think we're going to eat your letter when it comes?' And he walked off hastily. Ali came out very slowly, turning after every few steps to gaze at the post office. His eyes were filled with tears of helplessness, for his patience was exhausted, even though he still had faith. Yet how could he still hope to hear from Miriam?

Ali heard one of the clerks coming up behind him, and turned to him.

'Brother!' he said.

The clerk was surprised, but being a decent fellow he said, 'Well!'

'Here, look at this!' and Ali produced an old tin box and emptied five golden guineas into the surprised clerk's hands. 'Do not look so startled,' he continued. 'They will be useful to you, and they can never be to me. But will you do one thing?'

'What?'

'What do you see up there?' said Ali, pointing to the sky.

'Heaven.'

'Allah is there, and in His presence I am giving you this money. When it comes, you must forward my Miriam's letter to me.'

'But where—where am I to send it?' asked the utterly bewildered clerk.

'To my grave.'

'What?'

'Yes. It is true. Today is my last day: my very last, alas! And I have not seen Miriam, I have had no letter from her.' There were tears in Ali's eyes as the clerk slowly left him and went on his way with the five golden guineas in his pocket.

Ali was never seen again, and no one troubled to inquire after him.

One day, however, trouble came to the postmaster. His daughter lay ill in another town, and he was anxiously waiting for news of her. The post was brought in, and the letters piled on the table. Seeing an envelope of the colour and shape he expected, the postmaster eagerly snatched it up. It was addressed to Coachman Ali, and he dropped it as though it had given him an electric shock. The haughty temper of the official had quite left him in his sorrow and anxiety, and had laid bare his human heart. He knew at once that this was the letter the old man had been waiting for: it must be from his daughter Miriam.

'Lakshmi Das!' called the postmaster, for such was the name of the clerk to whom Ali had given his money.

'Yes, sir?'

'This is for your old coachman, Ali. Where is he now?'

'I will find out, sir.'

The postmaster did not receive his own letter all that day. He worried all night, and getting up at three, went to sit in the office. 'When Ali comes at four o'clock,' he mused, 'I will give him the letter myself.'

For now the postmaster understood Ali's heart and his very soul. After spending but a single night in suspense, anxiously waiting for news of his daughter, his heart was brimming with sympathy for the poor old man who had spent his nights in the same suspense for the last five years. At the stroke of five he heard a soft knock on the door: he felt sure it was Ali. He rose quickly from his chair, his suffering father's heart recognizing another, and flung the door wide open.

'Come in, brother Ali,' he cried, handing the letter to the meek old man, bent double with age, who was standing outside. Ali was leaning on a stick, and the tears were wet on his face as they had been when the clerk left him. But his features had been hard then, and now they were softened by lines of kindliness. He lifted his eyes and in them was a light so unearthly that the postmaster shrank back in fear and astonishment.

Lakshmi Das had heard the postmaster's words as he came towards the office from another quarter. 'Who was that, sir? Old Ali?' he asked. But the postmaster took no notice of him. He was staring with wide-open eyes at the doorway from which Ali had disappeared. Where could he have gone? At last he turned to Lakshmi Das. 'Yes, I was speaking to Ali,' he said.

'Old Ali is dead, sir. But give me his letter.'

'What! But when? Are you sure, Lakshmi Das?'

'Yes, that is so,' broke in a postman who had just arrived. 'Ali died three months ago.'

The postmaster was bewildered. Miriam's letter was still lying near the door, Ali's image was still before his eyes. He listened to Lakshmi Das's recital of the last interview, but he could still not doubt the reality of the knock on the door and the tears in Ali's eyes. He was perplexed. Had he really seen Ali? Had his imagination deceived him? Or had it perhaps been Lakshmi Das?

The daily routine began. The clerk read out the addresses—Police Commissioner, Superintendent, Librarian—and flung the letters deftly.

But the postmaster now watched them as eagerly as though each contained a warm, beating heart. He no longer thought of them in terms of envelopes and postcards. He saw the essential human worth of a letter.

That evening you could have seen Lakshmi Das and the postmaster walking with slow steps to Ali's grave. They laid the letter on it and turned back.

'Lakshmi Das, were you indeed the first to come to the office this morning?'

'Yes, sir, I was the first.'

'Then how . . . No. I don't understand . . .'

'What, sir?'

'Oh, never mind,' the postmaster said shortly. At the office he parted from Lakshmi Das and went in. The newly-wakened father's heart in him was reproaching him for having failed to understand Ali's anxiety, for now he himself had to spend another night of restless anxiety. Tortured by doubt and remorse, he sat down in the glow of the charcoal sigri to wait.

Translated from the Gujarati by the author

Tabara's Story

K.P. POORNACHANDRA TEJASVI

Tabara Setty has gone mad, said the people of Padugere. He was the most recent among the twenty-five-odd lunatics living in the town at the time. For it was not as if those lunatics went mad one day suddenly without any warning. Rather, they would go mad little by little, almost predictably. One watched them go mad, pitied them when they had gone completely mad, and just accepted the fact as though that was how things happened in this world. Yet it seems that there is a story behind every lunatic.

Tabara Setty had been a familiar figure in the town for years. He had joined the government service years ago when the British were still ruling the country. Of the two persons in Padugere who always remembered the British and talked admiringly of their discipline and rigour, one was Dr Silva; Tabara Setty was the other. Often, when reminiscing to people about the old days, each would refer to the other for affirmation of what he was talking about.

When, during the days of British rule, Tabara was put in charge of collecting the excise revenue at the customs house, he walked on air. Not only was he important in the eyes of people, but those who brought vegetables, fish and such other items for selling at Padugere, gave him gifts in kind, in addition to paying the toll.

It was around that time that an agitation of sorts broke out in the country. It was the independence movement. Just as the excitement over World War II was cooling down, this new agitation was heating up the country. Tabara Setty had been newly married to a girl called Appi or Appamma from the Mangalore region. The couple sat at the toll-gate and often talked about the independence movement. They had frequently heard the name of Gandhi, who was leading the struggle against the British. But the precise nature of that struggle was not clear to them except that it was to drive the British out of the country. Though not a patriot, Tabara began to wonder why the British did not stay happily in their own land, among their own people, instead of grotesquely gadding about here in India among the dark natives. He could see that there was some truth too in what Gandhi was saying. But when the satyagraha agitation turned into such activities as the no-tax campaign and cutting telegraph wires, Tabara found himself in a quandary. He could not just excuse himself from taking sides on the pretext that he had no views on the subject, nor could he watch silently when people went about defiantly without paying the tax. Tabara became worried. 'Devil take this Gandhi!' he grumbled. He managed to escape the customs house job by somehow getting himself a caretaker's job at the Padugere Circuit House. There, as a result of serving and waiting on the white sahibs at close quarters, Tabara came to realize that though they looked different they too were human beings like him.

Meanwhile, the satyagraha agitation was spreading like wildfire. There was even news of the children of the rich and the famous leaving home to join Gandhi's struggle. Beatings and shootings by the police and the Non-Cooperation and satyagraha agitations were going on all around. Tabara had no definite views on any of those matters. When he heard that people were cutting telegraph wires, he would get angry with Gandhi; and when he heard of the police shooting people, he would be angry with the British.

The fervour of the freedom movement kept increasing and it spread even to the countryside. Tabara, too, began to have qualms about serving his white masters devotedly. Besides, the Anglo-Indian butlers who accompanied the visiting British officials always treated him with contempt and suspicion. Seeing how humiliated he felt by this, Appi suggested that he get a transfer, this time to the taluk office.

By the time Tabara became an attendant in the taluk office, India had gained independence. One by one, the white faces were disappearing and the government was now in the hands of his own countrymen. In addition to the taluk office it already had, there were now new offices in Padugere like the Taluk Development Board, the Coffee Board, and the Excise Department.

At first, there was a dispute as to which department Tabara belonged to and what his present job-title and salary should be. After shunting him from one department to another, at last it was decided that he was to be an employee of the town municipality. A few more years lapsed, however, before he was given the livery that would firmly identify him as an employee of the Padugere Municipality. By then Tabara had neared retirement age. Sometimes, he would feel the pressure of work; and there would be moments of anxiety and confusion. But this was due largely to the style of functioning of the Padugere administration rather than to any unsoundness of mind on his part. In other words, there was hardly any sign of his impending insanity.

Twenty-five years had gone by since the country got independence. Gandhi was little more than a memory in people's minds.

A few days before he was to retire, Tabara was put in charge of collecting the excise tax on coffee at the Coffee Depot. On the very first day he presented himself in the midst of a dispute between the manager there and the town municipality. The manager contended that because coffee was considered an 'export' item, it was exempt from the excise tax which the municipality wanted to levy. Meanwhile, Ramanna, a coffee merchant in the town, protested that he was being taxed twice—once at the time of buying the coffee from the coffee-growers, and again at the Coffee Depot. The coffee-growers themselves refused to pay the tax. All this was confusing to Tabara. It seemed that though Gandhi had been long dead, his style of agitation still lingered on. While the dispute was still unresolved, Tabara issued a couple of receipts to some coffee-growers who refused to pay the tax.

The president of the municipality blamed Tabara for issuing the receipts without actually having collected the tax and ordered him to pay a fine of three hundred and sixty rupees, the amount for which he had issued the receipts. Tabara had to pay the fine from his monthly salary of sixty rupees. Tabara cursed his hand which had got him into trouble.

Appi's health had been steadily deteriorating all this while. Tabara had often said to his neighbours that the poor woman had taken it to heart that she was childless. 'What can we do?' he had said to them. 'God didn't will it. He kept me too busy to give children to my wife.'

To make matters worse, someone put a suspicion in Tabara's head that his wife had been poisoned by somebody who bore a grudge against them. Tabara subjected her to all kinds of tests like dipping tamarind seeds in her urine and smearing her hand with *nugge* extract, but to no avail. In the end, he gave whatever money he had to one Jubeda Bibi who claimed that she had an antidote to the poison. The medicine induced vomiting and Jubeda Bibi pointed out a substance in the vomit as the poison. Then she gave him some powder saying, 'Let your wife eat this, and in just four days you'll see the colour return to her cheeks.' Appi finished taking the powder. But the only colour she got was when she blushed at what the medicine-woman said.

Tabara had noticed in the course of these tests that ants were gathering around her urine and he suspected that her ailment had something to do with it.

It made him wonder that he loved her so much as to fret over her like this. The thought had never occurred to him before she became an invalid.

When at last he took her to Dr Silva, he at once suspected diabetes and the tests confirmed it.

'Do you know this is the disease of the wealthy?' Dr Silva joked. 'In my time, I've seen only one or two white men who had it. I wonder how your wife got it? Probably it means you are about to become rich.' He gave a prescription for some tablets and told him that if she didn't improve, she would have to take injections. Tabara said to his wife, 'Did you hear? It seems that what you've got is a royal illness. We should be glad that if not the white sahibs' prestige, at least you got their illness.'

From the white sahibs' disease to the subject of the British rule, Dr Silva and Tabara chattered on for a long time. Appi didn't follow much of what they were talking about.

On the way home Tabara began to worry that far from bringing them wealth, the illness would cost them every paisa they had and reduce them almost to begging.

The Padugere Municipality Board had been dissolved, its term having come to an end; it was time for fresh elections. The tahsildar had assumed charge of interim affairs.

Tabara received a notice from the taluk office which stated that he had failed to pay the money for the two or three tax-receipts he had signed, and that if he didn't pay immediately, his salary would be withheld. Tabara went running up to the taluk office and explained what had happened. The tahsildar told him that though at present the charge against him was one of misappropriation of funds, he would write the amount as arrears still to be collected by Tabara. This meant that no matter how he looked at it, there was no way out for him but to pay the three hundred and sixty rupees out of his own pocket.

Never in his life had Tabara felt so humiliated. He

was an honourable man, he protested, he had served under the British rulers and under many important officers; government servants weren't falsely accused like this in those days. He went on to praise the discipline and uprightness of British bosses. 'If you don't believe this old man,' he pleaded, 'ask Dr Silva.'

The tahsildar was so preoccupied with his own professional world of appeals, litigations, notices and signatures that the old man's tales about the past had no interest for him. Besides, by praising British rule, Tabara had unwittingly denigrated the present rule.

In any case, Tabara didn't get his salary that month. There was no money even for his wife's medicine. He had to scrape up some money from here and there so he could feed his wife with some rice-gruel.

At that point, someone suggested that he might be eligible for his pension money. Tabara once again went running to the tahsildar's office. 'Give me a petition in writing. I will send it up to the higher authorities,' said the tahsildar and buried his head among the files.

With the municipal elections just a few days away, there were many candidates bustling about on the lookout for causes to endorse. One of these candidates, Bantappa, saw Tabara as his opportunity to serve society. 'Come, let us find out why you are not getting your pension money,' he told Tabara. 'We'll take the government to court if necessary.'

When the two met the tahsildar, the latter told them that it was not clear whether Tabara belonged to the provident fund scheme or the pension scheme and that he was going to write to the higher authorities to get the matter clarified.

Bantappa made a swift calculation and told Tabara that if he belonged to the provident fund scheme, he had about six to seven thousand rupees coming to him. Tabara was overjoyed. 'My wife's illness must be a royal one after all, if it should bring us all that money,' he thought, and hoped that the money would come soon so that he could buy the medicines needed for his wife.

Buoyed by anticipation of his pension money, Tabara began to run up small debts with all and sundry. He made the rounds of the tahsildar's office routinely. All the while his wife's condition was deteriorating. At first Tabara ignored it. 'All she was losing in her urine was a little sugar, so what?' he thought. But before long it got to a stage when she had to be confined to bed.

Some time before, Appi had hurt her big toe while doing household chores. She applied some herb juice on it and went about her work limping. Tabara hardly noticed it, as he had received some good news that day. A clerk at the taluk office had informed him that there was a reply from the higher authorities and that he was likely to get approximately seventeen thousand rupees as his provident fund. The tahsildar had asked him to collect proof of employment from all the departments in which he had worked. Not realizing the enormity of the task before him, Tabara gloated over the prospect of getting seventeen thousand rupees.

'Dr Silva tells me that there is some injection which would cure your illness in no time,' he told his wife apprising her of their imminent prosperity. 'Let us see what fortune holds for you.'

Tabara began making the rounds of all the departments he had served previously and everywhere it was the same litany he sang. 'Sir, my wife is ill. My money is with the government. To get it, I need your certificate.' Wherever he went, he would invariably reminisce about the old days and praise the ways of the white sahibs. Most listened to him sympathetically, often joining him in his nostalgia for the past. With each certificate he acquired, his file grew fatter.

Bantappa, the candidate in the municipal election, told Tabara that if there was any delay in getting his money, he would take him to Bangalore to the minister to expedite the sanctioning of the money and even offered to bear Tabara's expenses himself. Tabara was worried that if he went to Bangalore, there would be no one to feed the rice-gruel to his wife, especially since the leg-wound had deteriorated to the extent that she could not even walk around. When he took her to the government hospital, he was told that she had gangrene and her leg would have to be amputated.

Tabara got scared. 'The devil take these doctors,' he thought. 'The wound is in one toe and they want to cut off the whole leg. Next they will chop off a man's head just because he has a headache.' He brought Appi back thinking that maybe he could find some native doctor who could come up with a cure for her.

By now, his file was close to completion. The clerks and the attendants at the taluk office who had watched his frenzied running around and his obsession with the case concluded that he was losing his mind and that he was surely possessed by the devil to have turned so patently greedy.

Tabara went to Subbu Setti, the loan-shark of Padugere, and asked him for a loan on the strength of his expected pension but was greeted with derisive laughter. 'You expect money from the government? You might as well expect the dead body to come back from the grave,' said Subbu Setti prophetically. 'You should consider yourself lucky if you get your money before your own death, let alone your wife's.' Still, on seeing his sad face, Subbu Setti offered him four rupees. But Tabara was not so greedy as to belittle himself for a paltry four rupees.

'Sir, I swear to God,' he said before he walked away, 'I didn't come here to beg money for beedis. Of what use are four rupees to me? If you find it in your heart to lend me a bigger sum, you will do me a big favour.' He left with a heavy heart, but he began to see the truth of Subbu Setti's words. It looked as though his slow-moving file was in a race against his wife's rapidly worsening leg-wound. Appi was whimpering in pain as the infection had now spread all over her foot.

The tahsildar told him that his file had been forwarded to the higher authorities for approval. However Tabara was back in his office the very next day to enquire after the file's progress. The tahsildar flew into a rage. 'Do you think your file was sent to the backyard that it should be returned in a day?' he shouted. 'It has to go up to Bangalore before it can come back to us.'

Bantappa renewed his offer to take him to Bangalore, all expenses paid. In return, all he needed to do was to canvass for Bantappa among his neighbours. But since Tabara wouldn't leave his wife uncared-for even for a day, they decided that before making the trip to Bangalore they would visit the Deputy Commissioner's office at Chikkamagalur to check on the file's progress. When they went there enquiring after the file, the clerk fumed at them. 'How dare you come here poking around? Don't you know that everything has to come through the proper channel?' They were asked to leave the office.

As they were leaving, the head clerk called back Tabara and cautioned him about associating with politicians like Bantappa especially where money was involved. He also told him that there might be a delay in clearing the file, as they were all busy with the preparations for the silver jubilee of Independence.

When Tabara returned home in the evening, his wife was howling in pain. She told him that she wanted to kill herself by taking poison. A harried Tabara tried to comfort her by saying that his pension money was due any day now, and as soon as it came he would take her to Bangalore and spare no expense to get her the best treatment.

The following day, with the help of Bantappa, Tabara took Appi to the hospital. The doctor took one look at her leg and told that if she was not taken right then to the Sakaleshpur hospital for amputation, she would not live. Tabara, stunned, was taking her back home when the attendant from the tahsildar's office met him and said that the tahsildar had sent for him. His file had arrived.

With a flickering hope that he might still be able to save Appi's life, he went to the tahsildar's office. It turned out that the file had been sent back from Chikkamagalur with a remark from the concerned clerk that certificates of residence from the shanbhog and patel were required.

Back home, Appi was screaming in agony. 'I can't bear this pain any longer. I don't want medicine or anything. Just get me four annas' worth of poison.' The irony was that Tabara didn't have even four annas with him that day!

How good things were in the days of the white sahibs, thought Tabara. People could get their requests approved then and there, instantly. And the pleased client would reward you. Those days were much better. These stupid sons of bitches! What did they know about the administration except to demand useless records and certificates? Tabara went on cursing the administration of free India.

More days went by as the file kept moving back and forth. How true were Subbi Setti's words, Tabara thought. He had now lost all hope either of saving his wife or getting his pension money from the government.

A few days later, the tahsildar sent for him again. His face contorted in pain, his voice choking in anguish, he went and stood before the tahsildar.

'There is a police report against you,' growled the stern-faced tahsildar. 'It appears that you have been hobnobbing with that Naxalite communist, Bantappa, and making trouble at the Chikkamagalur District Collector's office.' Then softening a little, he said, 'Look, I feel sorry for you. You don't seem to have learnt anything from all the trouble God has given you. Anyhow, I'll write a favourable report on you today. But I would like you to contribute something to our fund to celebrate the silver jubilee of our nation's Independence.'

A strange smile spread across Tabara's face. 'You can take all of it,' he said. 'All of my pension money as my contribution to your fund.' The tahsildar thought that there was something odd about Tabara's behaviour.

Slowly, Tabara began to perceive all around him a

pitiless and meaningless system that ensnared human beings and transformed them into policemen, officers, shanbhog-patels, attendants and so on, a system that enshrined at its heart a heap of files with nonsense written in them. It seemed as though the devil had spread this snare to entrap humanity in order to chew it up and spew forth the pitiful remnants. The tahsildar, like a fiend stuffing his victims into the folds of the file like so many dried fish, was making grotesque, meaningless gestures. Hopping from desk to desk, the battered human souls entered the files that closed themselves on them. As Tabara looked at this infernal machine at work, tears rolled down his cheeks. He felt sorrow for the sake of his wife, for fellow human beings, the tahsildar, for the attendant Javara.

The attendant led him by the hand out of the office. Outside, for quite some time, he stood dazed, just the way the attendant had left him.

Later, he somehow managed to take his wife to the hospital at Sakaleshpur. There he was asked to produce a certificate attesting that he was a former employee of the government, along with some documents clarifying whether an employee of the municipality could in fact be considered a government employee.

When Tabara brought his wife back, she was on the verge of fainting from excruciating pain. She was frothing at the mouth. He went to Yusuf, the butcher, and asked him whether he could chop off his wife's leg, knee down. In the shop, dangling from the ceiling, four or five chopped heads of sheep were staring at the sky with blank looks.

'Planning to cook a stew out of your wife's leg?' laughed Yusuf teasingly. A few onlookers there joined him in the laughter.

A dog that had grown fat on raw meat was chewing on a bone. The carcasses of the sheep hung from the ceiling were dripping red drops. Next to the butcher's shop sat a skinny girl trying to sell the pods inside a cut-open jackfruit, all the while swinging her thin arms mechanically to chase the flies away.

Tabara began to suspect that he had been dead for some time and had been wandering among the ghosts of the dead.

They say that when his wife died, Tabara was laughing hysterically. The people of Padugere were anxious to conclude that Tabara had gone mad. For once he was known as mad, his problems could be dismissed as belonging to another world. Only a very few could see in him the appalling reflection of our own system. It shook them with an unknown terror.

It was just coincidence that Tabara went mad at the time of the twenty-fifth anniversary of our nation's Independence. When all the speakers were lavishing praise on free India, Tabara was babbling about the greatness of the British rule. Everyone laughed at his craziness.

The only man worried by the news of Tabara's madness was the tahsildar. There was still the question of collecting three hundred rupees from Tabara. The tahsildar was hoping to deduct the money from Tabara's provident fund. Besides, he had already sent up a report on Tabara vouching that he was of a sound and dependable character and putting the blame for the arrears he owed on the vagaries of our administration.

And now this, thought the tahsildar! It was enough to make him go mad.

Translated from the Kannada by Narayan Hegde

Tai Eesree

KRISHAN CHANDAR

I was in my final year at the Grant Medical College in Calcutta, and had come to Lahore for a few days to attend my elder brother's wedding which was to take place in our ancestral home in Kucha Thakar Das close to Shahi Mohalla. It was there that I first met Tai Eesree.

Tai Eesree was not really my aunt; but she was the sort of person who made everyone want to call her tai or elder aunt. When her tonga came into our locality and someone shouted, 'There's Tai Eesree!' a crowd of people, both old and young, men as well as women, ran up to receive her. Some helped her alight from her tonga.

Tai Eesree was asthmatic and the slightest movement, speech or even the sight of people left her out of breath. Some relatives produced money from their pockets to pay the tongawala, but Tai Eesree gave a wheezing cackle and told them that she had already paid. The way she spoke, struggling for breath, and her asthmatic laughter, was most attractive to me. The relatives looked crestfallen. They put their money back in their pockets and complained, 'Why did you do that? You don't give us an opportunity to do anything for you.' Tai did not answer. She took a fan from the hand of a young girl standing beside her and came along smiling and fanning herself.

Tai Eesree could not have been a day under sixty. Most of her hair had gone grey, making a pleasing frame for her brown, oval face. Everyone liked to hear her simple words, spoken with her asthmatic wheeze, but what fascinated me were her eyes. There was something about them which made me think of Mother Earth—of vast stretches of farmland and of deep flowing rivers—and at the same time they were full of boundless love and compassion, of fathomless innocence, and of sorrow which could not be assuaged. To this day I have not met a woman with such eyes. They had that quality of timelessness which makes the biggest and the most difficult human problem appear insignificant.

Tai Eesree wore a *gharara* of taffeta with a gold border; her shirt was of saffron silk embroidered with flowers. And her head was covered with a muslin dupatta. She wore gold bracelets on her arms. As she came into the courtyard there was a great commotion. Young brides and aunts, brothers' wives and their sisters-in-law, mothers' sisters and fathers' brothers' wives all ran up to touch her feet. A woman fetched a multicoloured *peerhi;* Tai Eesree smiled and sat down on it. She embraced all the women in turn, put her hand on their heads and blessed them.

And beside them a young girl, Savitri, began to wave a hand-fan with great enthusiasm. Tai Eesree had brought a coloured wicker basket with her, it lay beside her feet by the *peerhi*. As she blessed each person she took out a four-anna piece from the basket and gave one to everybody in turn. She must have given away over a hundred four-anna pieces in twenty minutes. When all the men and the women, boys, girls and infants, had touched her feet and received their four-anna piece, Tai Eesree raised her chin and turned back to look at the girl fanning her. 'Which one are you?' she asked.

'I am Savitri,' replied the girl shyly.

'Ai hai, you are Jai Kishen's daughter! I had completely forgotten you. Come and embrace me . . .'

Tai Eesree took the girl in her arms and kissed her face. By the time she had opened the basket and given the girl a four-anna piece, all the women were in fits of laughter. Aunt Kartaro flashed her sapphire ring and explained, 'Tai, this Savitri is not Jai Kishen's daughter; she is the daughter of the untouchable Heero.'

'Hai, I am ruined!' wailed Tai Eesree. She could hardly breathe. 'Hai, I will have to wash myself thoroughly. I even kissed her on the face. What am I to do?'

Tai Eesree turned her bewildered eyes on the untouchable Savitri. The girl began to sob. This made Tai relent at once. She took the girl in her arms again. 'No, child, you mustn't cry! You are quite innocent; you are as pure as a goddess, a virgin goddess. God Himself lives in your undefiled little body. You should not cry. I have to wash because my religion says I must. No more tears. Here's another four annas for you . . .'

Tai Eesree gave the girl a second four-anna piece, and the untouchable Savitri wiped her tears and began to smile. Tai Eesree then raised her arm to beckon, 'Heeroo! I want water for my bath. You too will get four annas.'

The crowd in the courtyard was convulsed with laughter.

Many people called Tai Eesree the four-anna aunty; others called her the sponsor aunty. It was well-known that from the day elder uncle Bodh Raj had married Tai Eesree to the present time, their marriage had not been consummated. Scandal-mongers even said that before his marriage, young Bodh Raj had so many affairs with beautiful sophisticated women that when he found himself wedded to a simple peasant girl he took an instant dislike to her and left her strictly alone. He did not maltreat her in any way; he sent her seventy-five rupees every month; and she lived with her in-laws in the village and served everyone who came to visit. Uncle Bodh Raj had an ironmonger's business in Jalandhar and often it was years before he went to his village. Eesree's parents tried several times to persuade her to come home, but she refused. Her parents even wanted to arrange another marriage for her, but Tai would not hear of it. She looked after her husband's parents so well that they began to cherish her more than they could have loved their own daughter. Uncle Bodh Raj's father, Malik Chand, handed over all the keys of the house to Tai Eesree. Her mother-in-law became so fond of her that she gave away all her gold ornaments to Tai Eesree.

With many women one wonders how they cope with the problems of their youth, but no one had any doubts about Tai Eesree. One feels sure that even on the day she was born, she must have raised her hand to bless her own mother and spoken to her in her sweet compassionate voice—'You have had to suffer much for my sake; here's a four-anna bit for you!'

It was probably her temperament which made her

relationship with her husband so peaceful. As far as their relatives were concerned, Uncle Bodh Raj was a good-for-nothing bon viveur, drunkard and fornicator. What if he had made good in his iron business? He had no right to ruin the life of Tai Eesree the way he had. But Tai Eesree herself had no regret whatsoever at having wasted her life; from the way she spoke and behaved it did not seem she was even aware of the fact that someone had ruined her life. She was always chatting merrily, laughing, joining people in their fun; always sharing people's joys and sorrows, and always ready to lend a hand. It was inevitable that if there was a celebration in the neighbourhood, Tai Eesree would be there. And if someone was bereaved, Tai Eesree was there too, to share their grief.

Tai Eesree's husband had money, but not Tai Eesree. The seventy-five rupees she received every month she invariably spent on other people. In those days money went a long way. The seventy-five rupees helped a lot of people in distress. But it wasn't Tai Eesree's generosity that drew people to her. There were times when Tai Eesree did not have a pice in her pocket and yet people flocked to her. On the contrary one often heard it said that merely to touch Tai Eesree's feet, gave one peace of mind.

Uncle Bodh Raj was as satanic a man as Tai Eesree was saintly. For thirty years he left Tai Eesree to live with his parents in the village. When they died and the other members of the family had grown up, married and set up homes of their own, the house in the village was empty. Bodh Raj had no choice but to take Tai Eesree to Jalandhar. But Tai Eesree was not able to stay there for more than a few days, because Bodh Raj attempted a liaison with the daughter of a respectable Pathan family from Pacca Bagh. The Pathans told Tai Eesree that it was out of regard for her that they had spared the life of Bodh Raj and it would be best if she took her husband elsewhere. A few days later Tai Eesree accompanied her husband to Lahore and rented a small house in Mohalla Varyaran. As luck would have it, even in Lahore Uncle Bodh Raj's business flourished. And at the same time he began to visit a prostitute Lachmi, who carried on her trade in Shahi Mohalla. The affair developed and finally Uncle Bodh Raj began to live with the whore, and seldom set foot in Mohalla Varyaran. But there was no trace of resentment in Tai Eesree's face.

It was at this time, when there was much talk of Uncle Bodh Raj's affair with the prostitute, that my elder brother's wedding took place. Bodh Raj did not come to the wedding but Tai Eesree spent all her days and nights looking after the comforts of the guests. Her amiable ways smoothed the most uneven of tempers; scowls on people's faces turned to smiles.

I never heard Tai Eesree criticize anyone, complain against fate, or seem out of her depth. Only once did I see in her a temporary disquiet.

This was during the wedding festivities. My elder brother was occupied all night with the wedding ceremonies. Early morning after the ceremony was over, the bride's people spread out the dowry for display. Those were old times when people gave coloured *peerhies*, rather than the now-fashionable sofa sets; and beds with gaudily painted legs. Those were times when drawing rooms were known by their native names, such as baithaks or diwan khanas. But my elder brother's father-in-law was an executive officer in a military cantonment; and the first Indian to have attained this rank. Consequently he gave his daughter a handsome dowry—all of it in the very latest style. Amongst our relatives this was the first time that anyone had given a sofa set in a dowry.

The sofa set was the main topic of conversation amongst our kinsmen. Women from distant localities came to the house to see the 'English *peerhoo*'. This was also the first time that Tai Eesree saw a sofa set. She examined it with great care; then she felt it with her hands and kept mumbling to herself. Unable to contain herself she turned to me for an explanation.

'Son, why is this thing called a sofa set?'

How could I answer a question like that? I just shook my head—'I have no idea, aunty.'

'Why are the two chairs small and the third one long?'

Again I did not know the answer and again shook my head to convey my ignorance.

Tai pondered over the matter for quite some time, clearly perplexed. Suddenly her face lit up with a childish radiance as if she had found the answer. 'Shall I tell you?'

'Yes, aunty.'

She explained to us as if we were a bunch of little children. 'Listen! I think the long sofa is meant for the time when the husband and wife are at peace with each other; then they can both sit on it. And whenever they have a quarrel, they can sit separately on the two smaller ones. The English are a very wise race. No wonder they rule over us.'

Tai's reasoning aroused a roar of laughter. But I noticed that Tai herself was suddenly silent. Was she reminded of the lifelong misunderstanding between her own husband and herself? I could not say for certain. But when I looked up at her, I caught a strange light in her eyes, as if somewhere a door in her mind, always kept firmly locked, had opened for an instant.

After taking my medical degree from Calcutta, I married a Bengali girl and set up a practice in Dharamtola. I tried hard for several years but could not build up a good practice. Eventually my elder brother persuaded me to move to Lahore. He set me up in a shop in Kucha Thakar Das and I started my practice amongst my own kinsmen and neighbours. At Calcutta I had been a young novice without any experience; at Lahore I started with almost ten years' know-how in the art of trapping patients. Consequently I did quite well. I was kept busy at all hours of the day and night.

I had my own family by now, so life went on in a whirl, with no time to go anywhere.

I did not see Tai Eesree for many years. But I had heard that she still lived in the same house in Mohalla Varyaran and that Uncle Bodh Raj lived in Shahi Mohalla with his prostitute mistress, Lachmi. And that once in a while he dropped in to find out how his wife was faring.

One morning when I was making out prescriptions for the crowd of patients in my clinic, a man from Mohalla Varyaran came along and said—'Doctor sahib, Tai Eesree is dying. Come along at once.'

I left my patients and went with the man. Tai's house was at the extreme end of Mohalla Varyaran. Climbing up the flight of stairs, I entered a dimly-lit room. Tai was reclining on her large pillows, breathing heavily. She was clutching her bosom with her right hand as if to keep her heart in its place. When she saw me, she smiled with relief. 'Son, now that you've come, I will be saved.'

'What's the trouble, Aunty?'

'A call from the angel of death! I have had high fever for two days and then suddenly my body went cold,' Tai's eyelids fluttered as she spoke. 'First, life went out of my legs; when I touched them they were icy cold; if I pinched them, I felt nothing. Then slowly life went out of my belly. And when it was about to depart from the rest of my body, I clutched at my kidney,' Tai emphasized this by clutching her heart with greater vigour. 'So I grabbed at my kidney and yelled "Is anyone there? Go and fetch Jai Kishen's son Radha Kishen. He's the only one who can cure me!"—Now you are here—now I know I will live,' she said with absolute conviction.

I stretched out my hand towards Tai's right arm. 'Give me your arm; I will feel your pulse.'

She brushed away my hand with her left hand—'Hai, what kind of doctor are you?' she exclaimed. 'You don't even know that I am holding my life with this hand. How can I let you feel the pulse in this arm?'

In a few weeks Tai was on her feet again. She had high blood pressure. When the pressure went down, she was able to walk about and resume her interest in the joys and sorrows of friends and strangers. Some months after she had got well, Uncle Bodh Raj passed away. He died of heart-failure in the house of his mistress.

Tai did not allow his body to be brought to her house. His bier was taken from Shahi Mohalla. She would not accompany the cortege nor go to the cremation ground. Not a tear came to her eye. Without saying a word she broke up her marriage bangles, changed from her coloured garments into a plain white dhoti, rubbed away the vermilion powder in the parting of her hair and smeared a little ash on her forehead. That was all she did to conform to religious tradition.

The plain white suited her grey hair and she looked comelier than before. There was some gossip amongst the relatives about the strange behaviour of Tai Eesree. Everyone was a little surprised; some were even pained. But so great was their respect for Tai Eesree that no one could dare to say anything to her.

The years went by. My practice now extended beyond Mohalla Thakur Das to Kucha Karmal inside Shahalmi Gate up to the main square in Wachhowali. In the mornings, I was at Mohalla Thakur Das, and the evenings, in Wachhowali. The days were spent in work and at times I was not able to see Tai Eesree for a year or more. Nevertheless I got all her news from the women of the family. Uncle Bodh Raj had left all he had in the bank to Lachmi, but had willed a house and a shop in Jalandhar to Tai Eesree. This gave Tai Eesree a rent of a hundred and fifty rupees every month. She continued to live in Mohalla Varyaran, as busy as before in her rituals and charities.

One day after seeing a patient I happened to be passing through Shahi Mohalla. I suddenly thought of Uncle Bodh Raj and then of Lachmi who lived in Shahi Mohalla, and from Lachmi my thoughts travelled to Tai Eesree. I had a pang of conscience as I had not been to see her for over twelve or fifteen months. I resolved to call on her at the first opportunity in the next day or two.

I was still sunk in thought when I saw Tai Eesree come out of a lane in the Mohalla. Instead of her usual *gharara* she was wearing a black one without any hem or ruffles. Even her kameez was a plain white one and she had a white muslin dupatta which she had wrapped around her head and chin, making her look exactly like an early madonna.

She saw me almost as soon as I saw her. And she suddenly seemed very embarrassed and turned back into the lane from which she was coming. I called out to her. My voice had a note of alarm in it. What was Tai Eesree doing in the prostitutes' quarter?

'Tai Eesree!' I cried, 'Tai Eesree!'

She heard me and turned, facing me, head down, like a criminal acknowledging his guilt.

'Tai Eesree, what are you doing here?' I asked in surprise and anger.

She could not meet my eyes. 'Son,' she said in a faltering tone, 'what can I say? Except that . . . that . . . I heard that that Lachmi woman was not well . . . very sick . . . so I thought perhaps I should go and see her . . .'

'You came here to see Lachmi!' I screamed at her. 'Lachmi, that sluttish whore, the bitch that . . .'

Tai Eesree raised her hand, and silenced me—'Na, na, son,' she said gently. 'Don't say anything against her.' She raised her eyes and breathed a long sigh. 'She was the only thing left by which I could remember my late husband. Today even that remembrance is gone.'

When the riots flared up in 1947, we left Lahore and came to Jalandhar because Tai Eesree had a house there. She kept the top floor for herself. Every day she went to the refugee camp and gave whatever help she could. Sometimes she would return home with an orphan or two. In four or five months, she had four boys and three girls living with her whose parents could not be traced. She also let refugees use her courtyard and the yard at the back of the house.

In a short while her house began to look like a caravan-serai. Nevertheless, not once did an angry frown darken Tai Eesree's brow. She entered her own house as if she was a stranger and had been allowed in by the refugees to whom it belonged. Women have an obsession for personal possession. But I have never met a man—far less a woman—who had as little use for possessions. Perhaps nature had left a vacuum in that part of the head which longs for property. Whatever she owned was in trust for other people. When she came to Jalandhar, she began to eat only one meal a day, but she never complained.

I was tense and easily irritated in those days and Tai Eesree's simple acceptance often annoyed me. I had lost a lucrative practice in Lahore and my house in Model Town had to be left behind. And now I did not have a roof over my head—no clothes, no money, not even enough for a square meal. We ate what we were given, when it was given, and if it wasn't given, we went hungry. And during these days I was stricken with dysentery. Being a doctor myself, I tried all the medicines I knew. But with an affliction like this one, one needs to be very careful about one's diet. How could I manage that? My health deteriorated rapidly. For some time I was able to conceal this from Tai, but then she found out about it. She came to my room and spoke most anxiously,

'Son, you take my advice, this is dysentery. Doctors know nothing about it. What you must do—and I'll give you the fare—is to go straight to Gujranwala. In the goldsmiths' lane lives Uncle Karim Bux, the barber. He has a wonderful medicine which can cure the worst type of dysentery. Your uncle had the same trouble about twenty years ago; it was Uncle Karim Bux who cured him of it. He spent ten days in Gujranwala and came back to Jalandhar absolutely fit and healthy.'

I flared up. 'For heaven's sake, Tai, don't you know I cannot go to Gujranwala?'

'Why not? I'll give you money for the fare.'

'Money is not the problem. Gujranwala is in Pakistan.'

'So what? Can't we go there to get medicine? Our uncle Karim Bux . . .'

'Tai, you know nothing,' said I, interrupting her irritably. 'You go on making the most naïve suggestions. The Muslims have now made a separate country for themselves; it is called Pakistan. Our country is known as Hindustan. No Hindustanis can go to Pakistan now, nor Pakistanis come to Hindustan. They have to have passports.'

Tai's forehead wrinkled in consternation. 'Passcourt? Do you have to go to court for it?'

'Yes, of course,' I replied in exasperation to end the argument. It was too much trouble to explain the details to the old crone.

'No son, it's not nice to go to court. Sons of respectable families never go to the courts. But our uncle Karim Bux . . .'

'Karim Bux be damned!' I yelled at the top of my voice. 'You talk of twenty years ago. You don't even know if your uncle Karim Bux is alive or dead, but you go on repeating his name like a parrot.'

Tai turned away with tears in her eyes. After she had gone I felt stricken with remorse for my quick temper. Why had I hurt the simple, guileless woman? If Tai was unable to grasp the complications of present day life, what fault was it of hers?

It was a time of frayed nerves and tempers. At college I had always talked of revolution. Later, when I prospered in life and my practice flourished, the ardour for revolution was somewhat cooled; in due course the word itself vanished from my vocabulary. The difficult days at Jalandhar revived my zeal for the revolution. I sought the company of like-minded people who too had nothing more to lose; we would foregather and discuss the revolution with great enthusiasm. The meetings were usually in my room, on the second floor of Tai Eesree's house. We would have many rounds of tea and discuss the problems of the world. I, working myself into a frenzy, would wave a clenched fist and shout, 'We are not being treated fairly. We should not expect any justice from these people. I am convinced there will be another *inqilab* in this country and it must come soon.'

Tai Eesree overheard us one day. She came in, extremely worried, and asked, 'Son, are the Muslims coming?'

'No, Aunty! Who told you so?'

'Who is this *inqilab* you said was on his way here?'

Poor Tai, she believed *inqilab* was the name of some Muslim. When we grasped what she was thinking, we went into fits of laughter.

'How simple you are, Tai! Dear Aunty, we are talking

about an *inqilab* which is neither Hindu or Muslim. It belongs to all; we want to bring it here.'

It was too much for Tai; she shook her head and gave up. 'All right, you boys go on with your discussion. I will bring you some tea.'

To help me out of my predicament, Tai sold her gold bracelet. With the money I was able to take my family to Delhi, as Jalandhar was still very unsettled and had a depressing atmosphere. I set up my practice anew in Delhi and, in a few years, I was on my feet again. My clinic was in Karol Bagh where a large number of refugees from Lahore had settled. Many knew me. Slowly but surely, I got them to come to me and began to make a handsome income. In ten years I was able to build a house for myself and buy a car. I became the leading citizen of Karol Bagh. Once again I gave up the talk of revolution. The dysentery left me. So did the irritability. I became as amiable as a good doctor should be.

After thirteen years, I had occasion to return to Jalandhar last March to attend the wedding of a relative. In these thirteen years I had all but forgotten the existence of Tai Eesree. One can make time for relations only when one has no patients. However, as soon as I got to Jalandhar, my thoughts returned to her and all she had done for me; particularly the gold bangle which had helped me to resume my practice. I had never paid back the money. From Jalandhar railway station, I went straight to Tai Eesree's house.

It was dusk. The air was laden with dust and smoke and the smell of oil. The voice of children returning to their homes filled the evening as I entered Tai Eesree's house.

There was no one in the house besides Tai Eesree, her head bowed in prayer. She had lit an oil lamp and was offering flowers to her god. At the sound of my footsteps she stepped back and called, 'Who is it?'

'It is I,' I answered, entering and smiling at her.

Tai came up another two paces but was unable to recognize me. Thirteen years is a long time! She had become somewhat deaf and her eyes were weak. He face looked thinner than before and she walked very slowly.

'I am Radha Kishen,' I said softly.

'Jai Kishen's little boy?' Tai's voice was full of emotion. Fearing she might hasten her step and lose her balance, I went up to her quickly and held her. She clung to me and began to cry. She blessed me a hundred times, kissed my face, patted me on the head, murmuring, 'Son, where were you all these days? Where have you been? It's been so long!'

I felt thoroughly ashamed of myself and lowered my head. I tried to speak but the words would not come. Tai understood my embarrassment and changed the subject, asking, with her old asthmatic wheeze, 'Is Saroj well and happy?'

'Yes, Tai.'

'And the elder boy?'

'He is studying medicine.'

'And the younger?'

'He is in college.'

'And Shanno and Batto?'

'Both the girls are in college. I got Kamla married.'

'Good, good!' she nodded her head in satisfaction. 'I also got Savitri married off,' she said. 'Pooran is at Roorki. Nimmi and Bunny found their parents. They took them away after six years of separation! Wasn't that wonderful? I still hear from them from time to time. Only Gopi is left with me now. Next year he too will leave me, to work as an apprentice at the railway workshop.'

This was an account of the orphans that Tai had adopted during the riots.

I scratched my chin sheepishly and said 'Tai, I haven't yet paid the debt I owe you. I am thoroughly ashamed of myself for not having sent the money. I will send it to you as soon as I get back to Delhi.'

'What kind of debt?' asked Tai, very surprised.

'You remember, the bracelet?'

'Oh that!' It came back to her and she smiled very softly. She stroked my head and said, 'That was in payment of the debt I owed you.'

'You did not owe me anything, Tai!' I exclaimed.

'Son, life itself is a debt we owe other people,' said Tai in a grave voice. 'One should always keep repaying parts of it. Did you come into this world on your own? No, your parents gave you life. Don't you then owe the debt of your life to someone else? If we did not repay this debt, how would the world progress? The day of reckoning will come . . . Son, that is why I say I paid the debt I owed you. You must pay the debt you owe to someone else. Always redeem your debt—that should be the law of life.' So long a sermon left Tai completely out of breath.

What could I say to her? What can the shadow say to the light? I heard what she had to say and kept my silence. She too was silent for a while and then she spoke again, 'Neither my hands nor my feet are any good now; otherwise I'd have cooked a meal for you. When Gopi comes back, he will make something for you. You mustn't leave before I have given you something to eat . . . yes?'

I said humbly, 'Tai, please don't bother about it now. Everything we eat today is because of you.' I spoke slowly, 'I came to attend Tej Pal's wedding. From the railway station I came straight to your house, but I must now join the wedding party.'

'Ah yes,' she said. 'I too was invited. But I have been feeling out of sorts for the last two days and have decided not to go. I have sent them a present. You pat Tej Pal on the head on my behalf and give him my blessings.'

'Most certainly, Aunty,' I said, bending down to touch her feet. She clasped me to her bosom. With her hand on my head, she blessed me a hundred times. 'Son,' she said suddenly as I turned to go, 'can you do something for me?'

'You only have to say it.'

'Please come and see me tomorrow morning?'

'Why, Aunty,' I laughed, 'What's the matter? I've only just see you now!'

Tai spoke haltingly. 'My eyesight is very bad; at night I cannot see at all. If you were to come some time in the daytime I could have a good look at you. I haven't seen you for thirteen years, son.'

My eyes filled with tears. I replied—'I will certainly come, Aunty.'

Next morning, more wedding guests were due to arrive and a few of us went to the railway station to receive them. On our way back, I recalled my promise, asked my companions to excuse me and went towards Tai Eesree's house. Around the corner of the lane on which she lived, there were little groups of people standing with their heads lowered. I ignored them and quickened my pace. On the ground floor of her house, many others were gathered, all of them in tears. Tai Eesree had died that morning while I was at the railway station.

They had laid her on the floor of her room wrapped in a white sheet. Her face was uncovered. There was an odour of burning camphor and incense. A pandit was chanting Vedic mantras.

Tai Eesree's eyes were shut, her childlike face already grey. It had something of an eternal loneliness in it, a peace, a dissolution in fathomless dreams which made it look not like the face of the Tai Eesree that I had known, but of the vast earth itself—the earth in whose eyes ran the rivers of the world, in whose lap were a hundred thousand valleys where human habitations were sheltered by smiling mountains; mountains, from which rose the fragrance of selfless love and the radiance of innocence.

I was standing at her feet gazing on her face when someone put a hand on my shoulder. I turned around and saw a young man. His eyes were swollen with weeping.

'I am Gopi Nath,' he said softly.

I realized who he was but made no comment. I did not know what to say.

'I went to look for you in Tej Pal's house; you had left for the railway station.'

I remained silent.

'Tai asked for you several times this morning. She knew you would come to see her. She waited for you till her last breath. When she knew she could wait no longer, she said to me—"When my son Radha Kishen comes, give him this." '

Gopi Nath stretched out his hand and placed a four-anna piece in the flat of my palm.

I broke down and cried.

I do not know where Tai Eesree is today, but if she is in heaven I am certain that even now she is sitting on her coloured *peerhi,* with her open wicker basket at her feet, patting the heads of the gods and giving them each a four-anna piece.

Translated from the Urdu by Khushwant Singh

Maguni's Bullock Cart

Godavarish Mohapatra

Birth and death. The two inevitable phenomena that happened every day among the two-hundred-thousand-odd people of Khalikote town. Such news, however, never travelled beyond the confines of families and neighbourhoods. But when Maguni died, the news spread through the town, and even beyond, and not only that, whoever heard it reacted, after moments of stupefied silence, with 'So the poor fellow's gone! How sad!'

Who was this Maguni? The ruler of Khalikote? The king of a neighbouring state? A major figure in the administration? A big taxpayer, a rich moneylender? A Congress leader spearheading the satyagraha movement for independence, someone used to delivering stirring speeches to delirious crowds? A patriot born to be profusely decorated? Or a prominent native of the town who was always chosen to receive visiting dignitaries? Who was he? Why did just about everyone in the town as well as in the far-flung villages on the forest's edge know who he was?

Not an important man, all Maguni did was drive a bullock cart. That was how he eked out a living. All his life he had struggled—not for any exalted goals of his country or countrymen, but simply for himself, for his own little stomach. He and a pair of bullocks—the three of them had forged a bond that had cast an indelible impression on people's minds.

As regular as the sun that rose and set over the fort town, Maguni made his daily trip to the railway station. He was as punctual as a clock, people said. Even in the rainy months, when the sun often remained hidden behind the clouds, his passage announced the time of day. The seasons were at times irregular, the monsoons could be late, or the summer not hot enough, but never did a day go by without Maguni's cart rumbling along the road to the railway station. Even on mornings in the dead of winter, when it was so bitterly cold that people, wrapped in blankets, remained glued to their verandas, Maguni drove his cart along the serpentine road beneath the hills with a song on his lips.

So what if the king of Khalikote had two motor cars, Maguni sometimes joked. Did the king have a driver like him? His bullock cart was far better than any motor car. He just had to gently pat Kalia and Kasara on their rumps to rev the engine and belt out snatches of the popular ballad 'Rama and Laeekhana followed the trail of the magic deer . . .' to make the bullocks fly. The hills echoed with his songs and the half-asleep forest fowl and pheasants replied to them, awakening the stray village dogs and making them howl. And, inexorably, his cart rumbled on.

As he carted people across the length and breadth of

the town and beyond, he kept them enthralled with his stories, which flowed from his mouth like an endless stream. The stories of his life. Raised with love and care by doting parents, he had had a wonderful childhood: a comfortable bed, large meals, not having to do a day's work. Life continued to treat him well even after both his parents died and he grew into manhood. He married a beautiful girl, whose words were as sweet as her lips. Her breath was fragrance itself and flowers bloomed where she walked. Life was a dream, a glorious riot of joy and happiness. Only this didn't last long. His young wife departed for the other world, where he hoped to join her when his day was done.

The poignant stories of his life brought tears not only to the eyes of the listeners, but to his own too. Discreetly wiping away his tears, he would change track and launch into something else. The journey would come to an end, but not his stories. With the solitary exception of the king of Khalikote, everyone, from the dewan to the managers, from lawyers and moneylenders to the followers of Mahatma Gandhi, had been in his cart at one time or another. And his cart had been witness to many scenes: young widows on their heart-breaking journeys from their in-laws' back to their parents; merry brides on their joyous rides from their parents' homes to their husbands'; people like Gada Raul of Mandal village, who went to jail for failure to pay his taxes, and whose worldly possessions, down to his last broom, were transported to the king's court in Maguni's cart; or like Madhu Rath of Bendalia, who was sent to prison for committing a murder; prosecution lawyers; handcuffed peasant leaders who courted arrest with smiles. It had seen sorrow, it had seen joy. Torrents of tears had drenched its straw seats just as bursts of laughter had rattled its bamboo ribcage. So when Maguni spoke, a legend spoke, the living voice of Khalikote's history spoke. He brought so much gusto and excitement to his stories that even the bullocks at times slowed down and stopped. 'Look how these animals love to listen to the stories,' he would chuckle. He could never prod them with the goad.

Came the day when Maguni heard that people would no longer ride his cart. The wealthy Singhs were planning to put a bus on the road. He broke into uproarious laughter. A bus to beat his well-nourished Kalia-Kasara team? Would people ever desert his cart for a godforsaken bus?

Everyone laughed at him, but he was unfazed.

A few days later a monster of a motorbus rolled into town.

Poor Maguni's done for, people remarked. Now his business will fold. How can a bullock cart ever match a bus that can carry twenty people at a time and cover forty miles in an hour?

Maguni's heart sank and panic seized him. True, he did not break down and cry, but he came close to tears. He remembered the public meeting at Kodola he had once driven past. A speaker there had asserted that machines were no match for human hands. If so, then wasn't his bullock cart better than the motorbus? He'd go to all those people who had gone to the meeting and listened to the speech. Would they turn a deaf ear to him? If they did, then he'd go to their leader, Mahatma Gandhi. Everyone said he was a great friend of the poor and of the wretched of the earth. Would he turn Maguni away?

Would he say, let Maguni perish and the Singhs prosper?

The bus plied the same route as Maguni's cart. Day after day after day, the bus went full, the cart empty.

Maguni rose at midnight to go and park his cart in front of the railway station before daybreak, but the passengers chose to wait for the bus, which arrived late in the morning.

Maguni changed the old upholstery of his straw seats with new jute sackings, but people still thronged the bus.

Maguni tried to take the passengers by the hand and cajole them into his cart, but they all headed for the bus.

Some days passed, and then some more.

Maguni stuck it out. He cut his meals down from two to one a day.

A few days passed.

Maguni switched from hot, freshly cooked rice to watered-rice.

More days passed.

From one helping of watered-rice a day Maguni made it once in two days.

Still more days passed.

He did not light his hearth for days on end. There was nothing to cook.

Kalia and Kasara became dreadfully thin. Their ribs jutted out. Often Maguni put his arms around their necks and the three of them wept silent tears.

Gone off his hinges, people commented, crazy from hunger and grief.

More days passed.

Then came the morning when people had to break down the door of Maguni's house to get to his body. He lay on a tattered mattress, his goad beneath it.

A pyre was lit for him. Thick black smoke billowed into the sky, and countless birds, flapping their wings in anguish, flew by. The news swept the town, and nearly two hundred thousand people lamented, 'So poor Maguni's gone! What a pity!'

Translated from the Oriya by K.K. Mohapatra, Leelawati Mohapatra and Sudhansu Mohanty

Kabuliwala

RABINDRANATH TAGORE

My five-year-old daughter Mini can't stop talking for a minute. After coming into the world, it only took her a year to learn to speak and ever since she has not wasted a minute of her waking hours by keeping silent. Her mother often scolds her and makes her shut up, but I can't do that. When Mini is quiet, it is so unnatural that I cannot bear it. So her conversation with me proceed with great gusto.

One morning, as I was starting the seventeenth chapter of my novel, Mini came up to me and said, 'Father, Ramdoyal the gatekeeper calls a crow a *kauya* instead of a *kak*. He doesn't know anything, does he?'

Before I had a chance to enlighten her about the multiplicity of languages in the world, she brought up another subject. 'Guess what, Father, Bhola says it rains when an elephant in the sky squirts water through its trunk. What nonsense he talks! On and on, all day.'

Without waiting for my opinion on this matter either, she suddenly asked, 'Father, what relation is Mother to you?'

'Good question,' I said to myself, but to Mini I said, 'Run off and play with Bhola. I've got work to do.'

But she then sat down near my feet beside my writing-table, and, slapping her knees, began to recite *'agdum bagdum'* at top speed. Meanwhile, in my seventeenth chapter, Pratap Singh was leaping under cover of night from his high prison-window into the river below with Kanchanmala in his arms.

My study looks out on to the road. Mini suddenly abandoned the *agdum bagdum* game, ran over to the window and shouted, 'Kabuliwala, Kabuliwala!'

Dressed in dirty baggy clothes, pugree on his head, bag hanging from his shoulder, and with three or four boxes of grapes in his hands, a tall Kabuliwala was ambling along the road. It was hard to say exactly what thoughts the sight of him had put into my beloved daughter's mind, but she began to shout and shriek at him. That swinging bag spells trouble, I thought, my seventeenth chapter won't get finished today. But just as the Kabuliwala, attracted by Mini's yells, looked towards us with a smile and started to approach our house, Mini gasped and ran into the inner rooms, disappearing from view. She had a blind conviction that if one looked inside that swinging bag, one would find three or four live children like her in it.

Meanwhile the Kabuliwala came up to the window and smilingly salaamed. I decided that although the plight of Pratap Singh and Kanchanmala was extremely critical, it would be churlish not to invite the fellow inside and buy something from him.

I bought something and chatted with him for a bit. We talked about Abdur Rahman's efforts to preserve the integrity of Afghanistan against the Russians and the British. When he got up to leave, he asked, 'Babu, where did your little girl go?'

To dispel her groundless fears, I called Mini to come out. She clung to me and looked suspiciously at the Kabuliwala and his bag. The Kabuliwala took some raisins and apricots out and offered them to her, but she would not take them, and clung to my knees with doubled suspicion. Thus passed her first meeting with the Kabuliwala.

A few days later when for some reason I was on my way out of the house one morning, I saw my daughter sitting on a bench in front of the door, chattering unrestrainedly; and the Kabuliwala was sitting at her feet listening—grinning broadly, and from time to time making comments in his hybrid sort of Bengali. In all her five years of life, Mini had never found so patient a listener, apart from her father. I also saw that the folded train of her little sari was crammed with raisins and nuts. I said to the Kabuliwala, 'Why have you given all these? Don't give her any more.' I then took a half-rupee out of my pocket and gave it to him. He unhesitatingly took the coin and put it in his bag.

When I returned home, I found that this half-rupee had caused a full-scale row. Mini's mother was holding up a round shining object and saying crossly to Mini, 'Where did you get this half-rupee from?'

'The Kabuliwala gave it to me,' said Mini.

'Why did you take it from the Kabuliwala?' said her mother.

'I didn't ask for it,' said Mini tearfully. 'He gave it to me himself.'

I rescued Mini from her mother's wrath, and took her outside. I learnt that this was not just the second time that Mini and the Kabuliwala had met: he had been coming nearly every day and, by bribing her greedy little heart with pistachio-nuts, had quite won her over. I found that they now had certain fixed jokes and routines: for example as soon as Mini saw Rahamat, she giggled and asked, 'Kabuliwala, O Kabuliwala, what have you got in your bag?' Rahamat would laugh back and say—giving the word a peculiar nasal twang—'An elephant.' The notion of an elephant in his bag was the source of immense hilarity; it might not have been a very subtle joke, but they both seemed to find it very funny, and it gave me pleasure to see, on an autumn morning, a young child and a grown man laughing so heartily.

They had a couple of other jokes. Rahamat would say to Mini, 'Little one, don't ever go off to your in-laws' house.' Most Bengali girls grow up hearing frequent references to their in-laws', but my wife and I are rather progressive people and we don't keep talking to our young daughter about her future marriage. She therefore couldn't clearly understand what Rahamat meant. Yet to remain silent and give no reply was wholly against her nature, so she would turn the idea round and say, 'Are *you* going to your in-laws'?' Shaking his huge fist at an imaginary father-in-law, Rahamat would say, 'I'll settle him!' Mini laughed merrily as she imagined the fate awaiting this unknown creature called a father-in-law.

It was perfect autumn weather. In ancient times, kings used to set out on their world-conquests in autumn. I have never been away from Calcutta; precisely because of that, my mind roves all over the world. I seem to be condemned to my house, but I constantly yearn for the world outside. If I hear the name of a foreign land, at once my heart races towards it; and if I see a foreigner, at once an image of a cottage on some far bank or wooded mountainside forms in my mind, and I think of the free and pleasant life I would lead there. At the same time, I am such a rooted sort of individual that whenever I have to think of leaving my familiar spot, I am unnerved. So a morning spent sitting at my table in my little study, chatting with this Kabuliwala, served in lieu of wandering for me. High, scorched, blood-coloured, forbidding mountains on either side of a narrow desert path; laden camels passing; turbaned merchants and wayfarers, some on camels, some walking, some with spears in their hands, some with old-fashioned flintlock guns: my friend would talk of his native land in his booming, broken Bengali, and a mental picture of it would pass before my eyes.

Mini's mother is very easily alarmed. The slightest noise in the street makes her think that all the world's drunkards are charging straight at our house. She cannot dispel from her mind—despite her experience of life (which isn't great)—the apprehension that the world is overrun with thieves, bandits, drunkards, snakes, tigers, malaria, caterpillars, cockroaches and white-skinned marauders. She was not too happy about Rahamat the Kabuliwala. She repeatedly told me to keep a close eye on him. If I tried to laugh off her suspicions, she would launch into a succession of questions: 'So do people's children never go missing? And is there no slavery in Afghanistan? Is it completely impossible for a huge Afghan to kidnap a little child?' I had to admit that it was not impossible, but I found it hard to believe. People are suggestible to varying degrees; this was why my wife remained so edgy. But I still saw nothing wrong in letting Rahamat come to our house.

Every year, about the middle of the month of Magh, Rahamat went home. He was always very busy before he left, collecting money owed to him. He had to go from house to house; but he still made time to visit Mini. To see them together, one might well suppose that they were plotting something. If he couldn't come in the morning he would come in the evening; to see his big figure in a corner of the darkened house, with his baggy pyjamas and various hanging sacks around him, was indeed a little frightening. But my heart would light up as Mini ran to meet him, smiling and calling, 'O Kabuliwala, Kabuliwala,' and the usual innocent jokes passed between the two friends, unequal in age though they were.

One morning I was sitting in my little study correcting proofs. The last days of winter had been very cold, shiveringly so. The morning sun was shining through the window on to my feet below my table, and this touch of warmth was very pleasant. It must have been about eight o'clock—early morning walkers, swathed in scarves, had mostly finished their dawn stroll and had returned to their homes. It was then that there was a sudden commotion in the street.

I looked out and saw our Rahamat in handcuffs being marched along by two policemen, and behind him a crowd of curious boys. Rahamat's clothes were blood-stained, and one of the policemen was holding a blood-soaked knife. I went outside, stopped him and asked what was up. Partly from him and partly from Rahamat himself, I heard that a neighbour of ours had owed Rahamat something for a Rampuri chadar; he had tried to lie his way out of the debt, and in the ensuing brawl Rahamat had stabbed him.

Rahamat was mouthing various unrepeatable curses against the lying debtor, when Mini ran out of the house calling, 'Kabuliwala, O Kabuliwala.' For a moment Rahamat's face lit up with pleasure. He had no bag over his shoulder today, so they couldn't have their usual discussion about it. Mini came straight out with her 'Are *you* going to your in-laws' house?'

'Yes, I'm going there now,' said Rahamat with a smile. But when he saw that his reply had failed to amuse Mini, he brandished his handcuffed fists and said, 'I would have killed my father-in-law, but how can I with these on?'

Rahamat was convicted of assault, and sent to prison for several years. He virtually faded from our minds. Living at home, carrying on day by day with our routine tasks, we gave no thought to how a free-spirited mountain-dweller was passing his years behind prison-walls. As for the fickle Mini, even her father would have to admit that her behaviour was not very praiseworthy. She swiftly forgot her old friend. At first Nabi the groom replaced him in her affections; later, as she grew up, girls rather than little boys became her favourite companions. She even stopped coming to her father's study. And I, in a sense, dropped her.

Several years went by. It was autumn again. Mini's marriage had been decided, and the wedding was fixed for the puja-holiday. Our pride and joy would soon, like Durga going to Mount Kailas, darken her parents' house by moving to her husband's.

It was a most beautiful morning. Sunlight, washed clean by the rains, seemed to shine with the purity of smelted gold. Its radiance lent an extraordinary grace to Calcutta's back-streets, with their tumbledown cheek-by-jowl dwellings. The shehnai started to play in our house when night was scarcely over. Its wailing vibrations seemed to rise from deep within my ribcage. Its sad Bhairavi raga joined forces with the autumn sunshine, in spreading across the world the grief of my imminent separation. Today my Mini would be married.

From dawn on there was uproar, endless coming and going. A canopy was being erected in the yard of the house by binding bamboo-poles together; chandeliers tinkled as they were hung in the rooms and verandas; there was constant loud talk.

I was sitting in my study doing accounts, when Rahamat suddenly appeared and salaamed before me. At first I didn't recognize him. He had no bag; he had lost his long hair; his former vigour had gone. But when he smiled, I recognized him.

'How are you, Rahamat?' I said. 'When did you come back?'

'I was let out of prison yesterday evening,' he replied.

His words startled me. I had never confronted a would-be murderer before; I shrank back at the sight of him. I began to feel that on this auspicious morning it would be better to have the man out of the way. 'We've got something on in our house today,' I said. 'I'm rather busy. Please go now.'

He was ready to go at once, but just as he reached the door he hesitated a little and said, 'Can't I see your little girl for a moment?'

It seemed he thought that Mini was still just as she was when he had known her: that she would come running as before, calling 'Kabuliwala, O Kabuliwala!'; that their old merry banter would resume. He had even—remembering their old friendship—brought a box of grapes and a few nuts and raisins wrapped in paper—extracted, no doubt, from some Afghan friend of his, as he had no bag of his own now.

'I told you there's something on in the house today,' I said. 'You can't see anyone.'

He looked rather crestfallen. He stood silently for a moment longer, casting a solemn glance at me; then, saying 'Babu, salaam', he walked towards the door. I felt a sudden pang. I thought of calling him back, but then I saw that he himself was returning.

'I brought this box of grapes and these nuts and raisins for the little one,' he said. 'Please give them to her.' Taking them from him, I was about to pay him for them when he suddenly clasped my arm and said, 'Please, don't give me any money—I shall always be grateful, Babu. Just as you have a daughter, so do I have one, in my own country. It is with her in mind that I came with a few raisins for your daughter: I didn't come to trade with you.'

Then he put a hand inside his big loose shirt and took out from somewhere close to his heart a crumpled piece of paper. Unfolding it very carefully, he spread it out on my table. There was a small handprint on the paper: not a photograph, not a painting—the hand had been rubbed with some soot and pressed down on to the paper. Every year Rahamat carried this memento of his daughter in his breast-pocket when he came to sell raisins in Calcutta's streets: as if the touch of that soft, small, childish hand brought solace to his huge, homesick breast. My eyes swam at the sight of it. I forgot then that he was an Afghan raisin-seller and I was a Bengali babu. I understood then that he was as I am, just a father. The handprint of his little mountain-dwelling Parvati reminded me of my own Mini.

At once I sent for her from the inner part of the house. Objections came back: I refused to listen to them. Mini, dressed as a bride—sandal-paste pattern on her brow, red silk sari—came timidly into the room and stood close by me.

The Kabuliwala was confused at first when he saw her: he couldn't bring himself to utter his old greeting. But at last he smiled and said, 'Little one, are you going to your in-laws'?'

Mini now knew the meaning of in-laws'; she couldn't reply as before—she blushed at Rahamat's question and looked away. I recalled the day when Mini and the Kabuliwala had first met. My heart ached.

Mini left the room, and Rahamat, sighing deeply, sat down on the floor. He suddenly understood clearly that his own daughter would have grown up too since he last saw her, and with her too he would have to become re-acquainted: he would not find her exactly as she was before. Who knew what had happened to her in these eight years? In the cool autumn morning sunshine the shehnai went on playing, and Rahamat sat in a Calcutta lane and pictured to himself the barren mountains of Afghanistan.

I took out a banknote and gave it to him. 'Rahamat,' I said, 'go back to your homeland and your daughter; by your blessed reunion, Mini will be blessed.'

By giving him this money, I had to trim certain items from the wedding-festivities. I wasn't able to afford the electric illuminations I had planned, nor did the trumpet-and-drum band come. The womenfolk were very displeased at this; but for me, the ceremony was lit by a kinder, more gracious light.

Translated from the Bengali by William Radice

The Bull Beneath the Earth

KULWANT SINGH VIRK

Thathi Khara was not far from Amritsar and it was one of the most conveniently situated villages, smack on the metalled road. And the happy impulse which had inspired Man Singh's journey would make any distance seem joyfully short. Although the shades of evening were fast spreading and the tired tonga-pony's steps fell ever more laboriously on the road, Man Singh was carrying a feeling of buoyant eagerness in his heart.

Man Singh—a young soldier on leave from his regiment—was going to his friend Karam Singh's village. Nowhere do men form deeper and firmer friendships than in the army. Man Singh and Karam Singh had been in the same regimental centre and were now serving together in a battalion on the NEFA front. Karam Singh had enlisted earlier and was a havildar; Man Singh had just been promoted to the rank of naik.

Many people in Karam Singh's village kept asking his father about his next spell of leave. A hearty and genial character, Karam Singh had many friends in the village.

And he had such a way with everyone; people loved to sit by his side and listen to his tales of war and adventure in far-off lands. He was not the only youth from that village serving in the army. There were others as well, but when they came home they were at a loss for subjects to talk about with the village folk. With most of them they did not go beyond formal words of greeting. It was different with Karam Singh. When he came home on leave, there were always many more people at the well in the morning for a bathe and they always stayed longer than usual. In winter, people sat by the dying fire of the gram parcher's oven till midnight listening to Karam Singh's unbroken lively flow of colloquy.

In his regiment, Karam Singh was famous as a crack shot. In rifle-shooting competitions, his bullet tore the middle of the target with such precision that it seemed to have been needled through by hand. In battle, many a Chinese soldier had fallen to his uncannily ravaging shot. Thus he paid off the scores for his comrades who had died by Chinese bullets and partially assuaged his regiment's lacerated feeling. Where a whole machine gun magazine could be spent without gaining its object, Karam Singh's one bullet sufficed. Although his limbs had now lost the suppleness of early youth, his feats in the gymnasium were still the envy of many a soldier.

Now, in the time of national emergency, gymnastics and many other things had, of course, been suspended. There were no parades in stiff uniform led by a band. There was no bazaar in the vicinity where one could go in mufti. One never ran into anyone from one's own village or town. So when it was Man Singh's turn to go on leave, Karam Singh was overtaken by a feeling of nostalgia. He wished he could also get his leave at the same time so that they could go home together.

As Man Singh was getting into the military lorry, Karam Singh gave him a parting message.

'You must go to my village and see my people before you return. They will be very happy to see you. You can give them my news. They will feel as if I have met them. And, then, when I see you coming from them and get their news from your lips, it would be so much like meeting them myself.'

Then, to arouse Man Singh's interest in the geography of his village, he said, 'Have you been that side before?'

'No,' he answered, 'I have passed through Amritsar, but never gone beyond.'

'Oh! There are a number of gurdwaras scattered all over the countryside—Taran Taran, Khadur Sahib and Goindwal. You can visit all these and also see my people. I shall write to them . . .' Karam Singh went on in his enthusiastic self-engrossed manner.

And now it was for this very reason that Man Singh going in the tonga to Karam Singh's village at the end of his holiday.

'It is Man Singh, Bapuji . . . from Ambala,' Man Singh joined his hands in reverence as he greeted the old man sitting in the porch of Karam Singh's house.

'Come, take your seat. Welcome to you,' said the old man in a rather preoccupied tone.

Man Singh walked in and sat on a small string-bed. The old man, his face thin and drawn, seemed lost in his reverie. His eyes gradually wandered away from his guest's face and he gazed fixedly down at the ground.

Man Singh was by no means of an impatient disposition, but he had not expected this kind of reception at his friend's house. For a moment he thought the old man was not Karam Singh's father.

'You are Karam Singh's father?' Man Singh, at last, asked demanding, as it were, a little more attention.

'Yes, it is Karam Singh's house.'

'Did he write to you about me?'

'Yes, he did. He wrote that you would come and see us.' The old man got up as he uttered these words and walked away to the courtyard. He unfastened a buffalo calf from one trough and tied it to another. He started caressing the animal with his fingers and gave it his hand to lick. Then he went inside to announce Man Singh's arrival and ask for tea to he sent to him. He paused in the courtyard, as if he feared coming back to the porch, this time near the mare. He turned up the chaff in front of her and put in some more gram.

Then he returned to the porch where Man Singh was sitting.

'Where is Jaswant Singh?' asked Man Singh to break the awkward silence. He knew that Karam Singh had a younger brother.

'He will be here presently with the cart.'

Karam Singh's mother brought in tea.

'Satsriakal, Ma'nji!' There was a note of affection and reverence in Man Singh's words.

The old woman's lips quivered and she seemed to be about to say something. But she did not. Man Singh took the tea-pot and cup from her, and she went back inside.

'These Majhails are strange people,' said Man Singh to himself. 'Well, I shall stay for the night—I have to, in any case—and then leave early in the morning.' Man Singh was cursing himself for having come to Thathi Khara.

At night when Jaswant Singh returned home, Man Singh regained his spirits somewhat.

'Karam Singh's shots are very famous in this NEFA war. Let him pull up the trigger and down comes a Cheena—from where we do not know. We never know how he spots them . . .' Here Man Singh paused, hoping for some curious queries to be made about Karam Singh, the Chinese and the war in general. He was full of news—he wanted to talk the weight off his chest. But here nobody seemed to listen to him; nobody seemed to be interested.

'When do we get our canal water next, Jaswant?' asked the father after a rather prolonged dull interval.

'The day after tomorrow—at three o'clock in the morning.'

This gave Man Singh another opportunity to resume the thread of his monologue. 'Yes, while in the army, Karam Singh is at least spared this bother of rising so early. He loves his morning sleep and is always last among us there to get up.' Man Singh could talk of his friend ceaselessly. But even this last remark of his failed to arouse any visible interest among his audience.

Then food arrived. All the special ingredients of village hospitality were there—*shakkar-ghee* and all. Jaswant Singh kept waving a hand-fan over him as the guest ate. Man Singh was getting over the feeling that he had not been given sufficient attention.

As he was finishing the meal, Karam Singh's little son slowly walked up to where he sat. If he could not talk of

Karam Singh to anyone else in the family, he could talk at least to the child, he thought. Lifting him up to his lap, he said, 'Would you go to see your father? Come with me if you would like to. It snows a great deal there and you would have plenty of snowballs to play with.'

'Take the child away,' said the old man impatiently. 'He would not let him eat in peace.' The mother came and took the child inside.

Man Singh's food stuck in his throat. He felt deeply injured. The only topic he could now think of was his return journey next morning.

How far is Taran Taran from here?' he asked.

'Nearly four miles,' answered the old man.

'Will I get a tonga early in the morning?'

'Don't worry about that. We'll send Jaswant with you and then you two could visit all those gurdwaras in the morning. In the evening you could go back to Amritsar.'

This rather pleased Man Singh, for he thought Jaswant Singh would be a change from the old man's taciturnity.

But when he was out with Man Singh in the morning, Jaswant Singh seemed to have sealed his lips as well. When he met a friend or acquaintance, he would mutter a distant greeting and walk on. Man Singh wanted to stop and talk to people, for he was not sure when he would be able to visit that part of the country again, but he did not have the chance.

'Karam Singh has won himself such a name in the army. Why didn't you also join?' Man Singh tried to draw Jaswant Singh out into conversation.

Jaswant Singh was startled. He recollected himself, and said, 'Isn't one enough in the army?' And then he changed the subject. 'Look, how high this sugar cane has grown,' he remarked, as they were passing through a farm.

'Yes, it stands taller than a man and is thicker than my wrist. One does not see this kind of sugar cane in our district.'

Returning from his pilgrimage to the gurdwaras, Man Singh planned his journey back home. He was to catch the night train at Amritsar.

Although everyone had done his best to make him comfortable, he had enjoyed the visit much less than he had expected to. Even now when tea was being prepared for him inside, he sat in the porch all by himself.

He was looking out into the street and saw the postman walk up with the bag slung across his shoulder. He seemed to be on the point of passing by, but suddenly walked up to the porch, took his seat on the charpoy beside Man Singh and took a thick envelope from his bag.

'What have you brought?'

'Oh, alas, what can it be? It must be the papers concerning brave Karam Singh's pension.'

'Karam Singh's pension . . .? What do you mean . . .? Karam Singh's papers?'

'Don't you know? Even the trees and birds of this village are in mourning for its heroic son. And you sitting in his own house ask me! Karam Singh has been killed in battle. My own ugly hands delivered the cruel letter.'

Man Singh felt choked, his body seemed to have suddenly frozen. Then came the thaw and floods of water rushed to his eyes.

The father, seeing the postman from inside, knew that

they had failed to keep the news from Karam Singh's friend. The control he had maintained for nearly twenty-four hours cracked at last. For a long while, they sat together mixing their tears in an ever-widening pool in front of them.

'Why didn't you tell me, Bapuji?' asked Man Singh in a helpless pathetic tone.

'We just thought the boy is on leave. Why spoil your holiday? You would have to know when you went back to your regiment. I guess you love your holiday as much as Karam Singh did. Perhaps more. People in towns are used to a more comfortable way of life . . . But we were utterly unsuccessful in keeping it from you. We are so sorry. . .'

On his way back, Man Singh's eyes dolefully lingered over the villages and their surroundings which could produce men like Karam Singh and his father. He went past tombs and monuments which enshrined many a brave story of battle against foreign invaders of India. This tradition of heroism was the secret of the old man's strength, his capacity for absorbing shocks. How manfully he had kept his poignant burden unto himself to spare another person a pang of distress!

Man Singh had heard that there was a bull which bore upon its head the burden of the whole earth. Karam Singh's father appeared to him just another similar benevolent spirit which, bent low under its own oppressive load, was yet willing to take on more for the sake of others.

Translated from the Punjabi by Harbans Singh

Rebati

FAKIR MOHAN SENAPATI

But off some shining April morn
Is darkened in an hour,
And blackest grief o'er joyous home,
Alas! unseen may lower.

Rev. J.H. Gurney

'Rebati! Rebi! You fire, you ashes!'

Patpur—a sleepy little village in Hariharpur pargana in the district of Cuttack. At one end of the village stood Shyambandhu Mohanty's house: two rows of rooms, front and back, an inner courtyard with a well in the middle, a lean-to rice-husking shed, a vegetable patch in the backyard and a garden in the front yard. It was in one of the outer rooms that the visitors and farmers keen to pay their taxes congregated and made themselves comfortable. Shyambandhu Mohanty, the zamindar's accountant, was responsible for collecting rents. His salary was two rupees a month. He could make a little more by correcting rent receipts and land records;

all told, he made nothing less than four rupees a month. With this, he could make both ends meet. And not just barely; no, to speak the truth, he was quite comfortable. His family never complained of lacking this or that. They had everything they needed: two drumstick trees in the backyard as well as a perennial patch of spinach and other vegetables and two cows which never went dry simultaneously, so that a little curd and milk could always be found in the pails. Mohanty's old mother made fuel cakes from cow dung and husks, so they rarely had to buy any firewood. The zamindar had given him three-and-a-half acres of rent-free land to cultivate; and it produced just about enough to meet their needs.

Shyambandhu was a straightforward person, and the tenants respected, even liked him. He went from door to door to cajole and coax them to pay up their rent; he never demanded a paisa extra from anyone. On his own, he would stick the four-finger-wide palm leaf receipts in the underside of the thatch of their houses although they did not ask for any. He never let the zamindar's muscleman cast his shadow on the village; he'd pump the fellow's palm, fondle his chin and tuck two paise into the folds of his dhoti at the waist for buying a plug of tobacco, and would see him off.

In his own home, Shyambandhu had four stomachs to fill—his own, his wife's, his old mother's and his ten-year-old daughter's. The daughter's name was Rebati. In the evenings Shyambandhu would sit on his veranda and sing *krupasindhu badan* and many other prayer songs; at times he would light an oil lamp, put it on a wooden stand and read aloud passages from the *Bhagavat*. Rebati always sat next to him and listened with rapt attention;

she had soon learnt a few by heart. Her melodious voice lent the songs more appeal. People stopped by to listen to her. There was one hymn which gave Shyambandhu the greatest joy; every evening he would unfailingly ask Rebati to sing it.

Whither shall I take my prayers, Lord,
If thou turnest a blind eye?
Surely shall I be finished.
Be it salvation or damnation,
To thee, this life a dedication,
To thee, this soul laden.
Empty, empty, all the three worlds
When I am without thee
True refreshment when I thirst
Only thy love can be.

Two years ago, in the course of his visit to the countryside, the deputy inspector of schools had happened to spend a night at Patpur. At the request of the village elders, he had written to the inspector of schools of Orissa Division, and an upper primary school had subsequently been established in the village. The government paid the teacher's salary, which was four rupees a month. That apart, each student had to pay him an anna every month.

The teacher Basudev, a young man of twenty, had passed the teachers' training course at the Cuttack Normal School. Urbane and polite, he never raised his head to look directly at anyone. An orphan from an early age, he had been brought up by his uncle. Basudev—true to his name in every sense—was a fine human being. He was charming and handsome, the indelible mark of a bottle's mouth on his forehead applied by his mother for treatment of diphtheria during childhood enhanced rather than marred his looks. He looked as if he were chiselled out of a single block.

From the time he arrived in the village, Shyambandhu had taken a fancy to him: they both belonged to the same caste.

Occasionally, on a full moon day or a Thursday, when cakes and savouries were made at home, Shyambandhu would call at the school. 'Son Basu, do come to our place in the evening; your aunt has invited you.' A bond of affection naturally developed between them after these visits. Even Rebati, filled with concern, would sometimes exclaim, 'Ah, the poor little orphan! What does he eat, who looks after his meals?' As the visits grew regular, with Basu dropping in practically every evening, she would wait at the door to announce his arrival. As soon as she spotted him from a distance, she would call out to her father, 'Here comes Basubhai, here he comes!' She would then sit down beside him and sing the whole string of prayer songs she knew. To Basu's ears, the songs were fresh and ever-new.

One day, as they chatted of this and that, Shyambandhu learnt from Basu that there was a school at Cuttack where girls could study and learn crafts; instantly the desire to give Rebati an education welled up in his heart. When he confided this to Basu, the young teacher, who had begun to look upon him as a father, said, 'I was about to suggest that myself.'

Rebati, who had been listening to this conversation, rushed inside. 'I'm going to study,' she announced excitedly to her mother and grandmother. 'I'm going to learn to read books.'

Her mother smiled and said, 'Go ahead.' But her grandmother's reaction was sharp: 'What good will it do? How does book-learning help a girl? It's enough if you learn how to cook, bake, churn butter and paint walls with rice-paste.'

That night, when Shyambandhu sat down to dinner on a low mango-wood stool with Rebati beside him, the old lady sat in front of him restive and itching to speak her mind. 'Serve him a little more rice, daughter-in-law, give him a second helping of dal and a pinch of salt,' and so on. Then she brought up the real topic. 'Shyam, is Rebi going to study? Why study, son? What good is it for a girl?'

'Never mind, Ma,' said Shyambandhu. 'Let her study if she wants to. Haven't you heard that Jhankar Pattanaik's daughters can read the *Bhagavat* and *Vaidehisha Vilas*?'

Rebati was furious with her grandmother. 'You silly old hag!' she snorted. And turning to her father she begged, 'Father, I want to study.'

'And you will,' said Shyambandhu.

The matter was left there.

Next afternoon Basu brought Rebati a copy of Sitanathbabu's *First Lessons*. She was so overjoyed that she leafed through the book from cover to cover. The pictures of elephants, houses and cows thrilled her immensely. Kings could be happy to own elephants and horses, others perhaps derived joy from riding them, but for Rebati it was enough merely to gaze at their pictures. She could hardly wait to show these to her mother and grandmother.

The grandmother did not hide her irritation. 'Take that silly thing away from me,' she shouted.

'Silly you!' the girl retorted.

The auspicious day of Sri Panchami dawned. Rebati took a bath early in the morning, put on new clothes and flitted in and out of the house, waiting impatiently for Basu. The usual pomp associated with this ceremony for commencing learning was played down out of fear of the grandmother. Six hours into the morning Basu arrived and taught her the alphabet: *a, aa, e, ee, u, oo . . .*

The lessons went on. Basu never missed an evening. Over the next two years, Rebati studied a great deal. All the rhymes of Madhu Rao were at the tip of her tongue and she could reel them off without faltering.

At dinner one night, Shyambandhu said to his mother, as if to round off a discussion they had been having, 'Well, Ma, what do you think?'

'Nothing could be better,' said the old lady. 'But have you found out his caste for sure?'

'What else was I trying to find out? He may be poor but he comes from a good family. And a pukka karan to boot.'

'Good. Caste comes before wealth. But will he agree to live with us?'

'Why not? After all, the only relatives he has are his uncle and aunt. He may not like to go back to them.'

What Rebati made of the talk only she knew, but a change certainly came over her. She became coy with Basu. In the evening she would hang around the front door as though waiting for someone—which riled her grandmother—but when Basu came, she would hide herself inside the house. It took Basu quite an effort to make her come out for her lessons. Blushing and smiling for no apparent reason, she would refuse to read her lessons aloud and would answer him in monosyllables. As soon as the day's task was over she would rush inside, struggling to muffle her giggles.

Sri Panchamis followed one after another, and two more years went by. The designs of Providence are strange and inscrutable; no two days pass alike. One fine Phalgun day, like a bolt from the blue, the cholera epidemic struck.

Early in the morning the news of Shyambandhu coming down with cholera spread through the village. As always, the immediate response was to bolt all doors and windows and keep out of the path of that demonic deity, as though the evil old hag was out with her basket and broom to sweep heads.

Shyambandhu's wife and mother were almost out of their minds with worry and anxiety. Rebati ran in and out of the house, crying for help. When the news reached Basu, he hurried from the school and, without fear for his own life, sat at the bedside, massaging Shyambandhu's hands and legs and forcing drops of water between his parched lips.

Three hours passed.

Suddenly, Shyambandhu stared at Basu and stammered, 'Take care of my family, I leave them to you . . .'

Basu could not control his tears.

Shyambandhu passed away in the evening.

The women wailed, Rebati cast herself down on the floor.

What arrangements for cremation could the

grief-stricken women and a greenhorn like Basu make? But Bana Sethi, the village washerman, a veteran of fifty or sixty cremations, saved the day for them. He turned up with a towel wrapped around his waist and an axe hanging from his shoulders. Bana was rather philosophical about it: cholera or no cholera, if your time's up, you've got to go either today or tomorrow, but why miss a set of new clothes when there was a chance? Shyambandhu's was the only karan family in the village; help was neither expected nor forthcoming. The two women and Basudev had to carry the dead body to the cremation ground and perform the last rites.

The morning star was shining in the eastern sky by the time they had finished with the cremation. No sooner had they got home than Rebati's mother came down with cholera. By midday the news of her death was all over the village.

Providence has its own mysterious ways—while one man is blessed with a regal umbrella atop his palanquin, another receives lashes on his already fettered hands. Within three months of Shyambandhu's demise, the zamindar expropriated Shyambandhu's cows because he had apparently not deposited the last rent collection. But that was hard to believe. Shyambandhu had always regarded his duties as sacred and did not rest in peace until he had deposited every paisa of the collection in the zamindar's treasury. The truth was that for a long time the zamindar had his eyes on the cows. He also withdrew the three-and-half acres of land he had given to Shyambandhu. The farmhand, with no work left for him, had left on the full moon day of Dola festival. The team of bullocks had already been sold off for seventeen and a half rupees; with what remained of the sum after meeting the funeral expenses, the grandmother and Rebati had hung on for a month. In the month following, they had begun to pawn household items: a brass bowl one day, a plate next.

Basu visited them every evening and stayed with them until bedtime. He offered them money, but they would not touch it. Once or twice he pressed some on them, but the coins lay idle on the shelf. He was given no choice but to accept the couple of paise the old woman produced every eight or ten days to buy them provisions. The house was falling apart, the straw roof had worn thin, but try as he might Basu couldn't get it re-thatched; the bales of hay he had bought with two rupees of his own money rotted in the backyard.

The grandmother no longer cried day and night, she now confined her wailing to the evenings. But she exhausted herself so much that she could only lie slumped on the floor for the rest of the night. Rebati, convulsed with sobs, would lie down next to her. The grandmother's vision had dimmed and she had a wild look about her. She had cut down on crying and taken to reviling Rebati with curses and abuses. The girl was at the root of all her misery and misfortune; her education had caused it all—first her son died, then the daughter-in-law; the bullocks were sold; the farmhand had left; the cows were taken away by the zamindar; and now her own eyes were bad. Rebati was the evil eye, the hell-devil, the ill omen.

The moment the curses started flying thick and fast, Rebati would shrink away from her grandmother and hide in a corner of the house or backyard, tears streaming down her cheeks.

The grandmother held Basu equally to blame. Were it

not for his eagerness to teach the girl, the girl could not possibly have gone and taught herself. But she could not take Basu to task because she couldn't do without him. The zamindar kept seeking flimsy clarifications, and almost every second day a messenger came asking for this account or that; Basu alone could fish them out from the clutter of papers Shyambandhu had left behind. Yet behind Basu's back, the old woman sometimes gave vent to her feelings.

Rebati was no longer the light of the house. Gone were the days when she mourned loudly. Nobody heard her voice, nobody saw her out of doors. Her large brooding eyes, awash with silent tears, looked like blue lilies in water. Her heart and mind were broken, and day and night were alike to her. The sun brought her no light, the night no darkness. The world was an aching void. The memory of her parents overwhelmed her, their images hung before her glazed eyes. She could not bring herself to believe that they were truly dead and gone. Hunger no longer stirred her stomach, nor did slumber soothe her eyes. She went through the pretence of eating only out of fear of the grandmother. She was now thin and emaciated, her skin hung loose on her bones, and she could barely raise herself off the floor on which she lay day and night. The only time she revived a little was when Basu visited them. She would sit up and fasten her gaze on him, and lower her eyes with a sigh only when their glances met. But the next moment she'd feverishly stare at him again. For those brief hours of the day when he was around, Basu completely possessed her eyes, mind and heart.

About five months had passed. One Saturday, on a hot Jaistha afternoon, Basu knocked on their door. Never before had he ever called at such an ungodly hour. The grandmother was full of foreboding as she opened the door.

'Grandma,' said Basu, 'The deputy inspector of schools will camp in the Hariharpur police station and take an oral test of the students. All the schools have been informed. I received the order today. I'll have to leave tomorrow morning. I may be away for five days.'

Listening to the conversation from behind the door, Rebati felt her legs give way. She could barely hold on to the door to stop herself from falling.

Basu bought them enough rice, oil, salt and vegetables for five days, and bade them goodbye.

'Son,' said the grandmother, with a sigh, 'Don't walk about in the sun for long. Take care of yourself. Eat your meals on time.'

Rebati could not take her eyes off him. Usually, she would drop her glance when their eyes met, but today she stared unblinkingly, unabashedly into his eyes. A change had come over Basu too. All this time he had contented himself with stolen glances, but today he did not avert his eyes. They looked deep into each other's.

Evening came. Darkness filled the house and covered the earth. Rebati remained rooted to the spot, until her grandmother's piercing screams jolted her to her senses. Basu had left a long time ago.

Rebati counted the days.

On the sixth morning she even rushed a couple of times to the front door, a place she had shunned since her parents' death. Six hours had passed that morning when the schoolboys arrived back from Hariharpur. They carried the news of Basu's death. The teacher had succumbed to cholera under the big banyan tree on the outskirts of Gopalpur on his return journey. The village folk mourned; the women and children shed copious tears. 'What a handsome fellow!' said one. 'So polite!' said another. 'Never hurt a fly,' remarked yet another.

The grandmother cried so much that she choked. 'Poor boy!' she repeated between sobs. 'You only brought it on yourself!' The implication was that but for his foolhardiness in teaching Rebati he would not have perished in his prime.

Rebati sank to the floor and lay there without a whine or whimper as the day wore on.

The grandmother woke up the following morning without Rebati beside her and shouted in anger, 'Hey, Rebati! Rebi! You fire, you ashes!' She worked herself into a rage, and the passers-by heard these terrible words repeated throughout the morning.

Half-blind and angry, she groped her way through the entire house. When she finally found the girl, a shock awaited her. Rebati, burning with fever, was unconscious. Worry and fear gnawed at the old woman's heart. She couldn't decide what to do, who to turn to for help. Exasperated, out of breath, and without hope, she observed tartly, 'What medicine can there be for an illness of one's own making?' Rebati had brought the fever on herself by her own folly in daring to study.

One, two, three, four, five days passed. Rebati remained glued to the ground, her eyes and lips shut. On the sixth morning she let out a whimper or two. The old woman ran her hand over Rebati's body. It was cold to the touch;

perhaps the fever had left. She called out to Rebati, and the girl mumbled a reply, then asked for water, stared wildly around and broke into an incoherent babble. One simple look and even a country doctor could have quoted from his text: 'Thirst, fever, delirium; of imminent collapse these are the symptoms.' But the poor grandmother was overcome with a sense of relief. The fever had left, the girl was able to speak two words, open her eyes and ask for water. A little gruel was all she needed to rally her strength and get back on her feet.

'Don't get up,' the grandmother said. 'Stay where you are. I'm going to cook you a bit of food.' She went out of the room and rummaged in vain among the earthen pots and pans for a handful of rice. Her head clouded with despair and she sat down with a sigh. If only she had eyes to see, she would have realized how the provisions meant for five days had already lasted for ten.

But there was a flicker of hope in her yet. She picked up the only object of value left in the house—an old brass bowl with a hole in the bottom—and set out for Hari Sa's store. The so-called store in Hari's residence was in the middle of the village, and he kept a paltry stock of rice, salt, cereals and oil to sell to travellers passing by.

Hari saw the old woman with the bowl. He understood immediately, but let her plead first. He then took the bowl and examined it minutely, turning it from side to side. 'There's no rice,' he said, handing it back. 'Who's going to give you anything for a bowl like this?' Of course he had both the rice and the inclination to sell it, but getting the brass bowl for a song was his main concern. The grandmother staggered at his words, as though lightning had hit her. What would she do if she didn't get any rice, what would she cook for Rebati, how would the girl fight her weakness? She sat there for hours, depressed and silent, still as a log, casting imploring glances at the shopkeeper.

The day wore on. She had left the sick girl alone for a long time, and fear stirred her old heart. 'Time I got back home,' she mumbled to herself, picking up the bowl. 'God knows how that girl of mine is doing.'

'Never mind,' said Hari grudgingly. 'Give me the bowl. Let me see if I can scrape a little something up for you.' He gave her four measures of rice, half a measure of cereals and a handful of salt. The old woman hobbled back home, resting every four paces or so to catch her breath. She hadn't even washed her face since morning, and her mind was filled with panic.

She reached home hoping that Rebati was better. She would ask the girl to draw water from the well. The rice wouldn't take long to cook. She called out to Rebati once, twice, three times, but got no response. Then she yelled at the top of her voice, 'Rebati! Rebi! You fire, you ashes!'

By now Rebati was fast sinking. Her body, already feeble with spasms of excruciating pain, had turned ice-cold. Her thirst was so terrible that she felt as if her tongue was being sucked back into her throat. She found the room unbearably hot and crawled out to the inner courtyard. Even that brought her no relief. She rolled out to the veranda at the back and propped herself against the wall.

Dusk had fallen and a gentle breeze was blowing. A bunch of bananas hung from the tree which her father had planted before his death. The guava tree her mother had planted two years ago had grown to a goodly height and was covered with blossoms. Rebati remembered how she had drawn water from the well with a small jug and tended the sapling. It brought back a rush of memories of her mother. Her head was in a whirl, her thoughts jumbled, but the image of her mother clung to her vision.

Night slowly descended. Darkness stole out from behind the boughs of the trees and shrouded the garden. Rebati tilted her head back and watched the sky. The lone evening star was gleaming brightly. She could not take her eyes off it, and it grew and grew and grew, bigger and brighter; it possessed the whole sky, and behold! Her loving mother sat in the heart of it, her face glowing with love and kindness, her arms extended towards Rebati in invitation. Rebati was overwhelmed. Two shafts of starlight pierced her eyes and moved down to her heart. Her breathing, heavy and laboured, rose and fell, breaking the stillness of the night. She wheezed, choked and cried out to her mother twice. Then there was silence.

The grandmother crawled around the house, from the living room to the courtyard to the rice-husking shed, but Rebati was nowhere to be found. Then it occurred to the old woman that with the fever abating, the girl might be taking a stroll in the garden at the back. 'Rebati!' she screamed. 'Rebi! You fire, you ashes!'

She crawled out to the narrow veranda, which was only an arm's length in breadth and two in height, and bumped smack into the girl. 'Death to you!' she cried. 'Sitting here, are you?' She wanted to shake her up, but she could sense something was amiss with the girl.

The old woman ran her hand over the length of the girl's body and then held a finger close to her nostrils. The silence of the night was momentarily broken by her eerie wail. Two bodies fell off the veranda and thudded onto the ground. That was the end of the line for Shyambandhu Mohanty.

And the last words which emanated from his house were, 'Rebati! Rebi! You fire, you ashes!'

Translated from the Oriya by K.K. Mohapatra, Leelawati Mohapatra and Paul St-Pierre

The Encircling Clouds

KRISHNA SOBTI

Lying in the small cottage at Bhowali Sanatorium, I look at the hills stretching away in front of me. I look at the encircling clouds, swollen with rain, and at the barren ones, wisp-like and shrivelled. I look at the mist groping in vain, and at my own body, bare as a tree that has shed its leaves. In front of me, the path to Ramgarh is etched into the dry vegetation of the sloping mountain, like the thick veins standing cut on my arm. The breeze, wayward like my own breath, now caresses and now pummels at the window. My body tucked inside the blanket gradually disintegrates like a thin layer of lime slowly dissolving in water, and I live in constant dread that my life, woven with the warp and woff of years, will suddenly stop pulsating.

The curtains at the door and the windows hang listlessly, silent like me, day and night, morning and evening. Nobody lifts them with firm hands and stands at the threshold to greet me with a smile. Night, morning, evening, gather turn by turn around my bed. I lie in the iron bed and look with dimmed eyes not at darkness and light, but at myself, at my wasting body from which life is ebbing away. I am helpless. Nothing else remains.

I look at my thin arms sticking out of my shoulders and am reminded of those plump arms, that perfumed hair, and those soft lips which gave me life. I had everything. Living together, sleeping together, walking together. Early in the morning someone would bend over my bed and say, 'Won't you get up? It's morning.'

With closed eyes, I would put my arms around that alluring body, draw it to me to smell those moments of the night and mumble, 'What's the hurry?'

A laugh and the arms would relax, eyes open, and domesticity dawn.

Breakfast in the garden. The mistress of the house, chic and debonair, confident of her authority, would turn the dream of the night into tangible reality. I would look at her fingers while she poured milk into the cup, those fingers which had caressed my hair in the night, and at the end of her sari jealously hiding her gently heaving breasts. For a fleeting moment I would wonder if what I felt deep down in my being was merely the outer trappings and the reality lay somewhere still deeper in those transient moments where two beings become one . . .

But the night here at the sanatorium is tubercular and dark. Lying under the blanket, I look at the phials of medicine, read their labels over and over again, and realize that when the sap of life dries up, bones and flesh become wood, not earth, because from the earth life sprouts once. I am yet to turn to earth.

In the vacuity of this dreary existence I try to resurrect that memorable night when on receiving a message I hurried to her room. Under the blue light of the lamp, two tired eyelids fluttered and after gazing at an infant, sleeping in the crook of an arm, two eyes came to rest on my face. They seemed to say, 'I have given form to your embrace and made it live.' I got up, touched her cold brow with my lips and marvelled how love, that is born in the body, grows of the body, can also take a form and come into the world.

But there is another form of love which never comes to fruition, like the mountain clouds which promise rain but never break into a shower.

It was years ago. I had gone to the hills one summer. One bright morning we had just got up from the breakfast table when my aunt introduced me to her. I still remember those beautiful eyes. 'Ravi, meet Manno. She's here just for two days.' My aunt's introduction lacked warmth, a sigh escaped her lips. There was something hollow about the way my aunt said that she was here for two days. I didn't like it.

She acknowledged my greeting with a nod and I perceived a faint smile on her face. Thin but lively, her face wore a far-off expression. I could not take my eyes off her face with its tightly swept back hair. I was left feeling as if I must atone for someone else's reproach.

When we came out, my aunt's children became playful. They tugged at Manno's sari and clung to her arms and cried, 'Mannojiji! Mannojiji!' My aunt, who was about to go in, turned round on hearing the shrill laughter of the children. I still remember her face as she tried to hide her stern expression. With a firm hand she pulled away the children. Looking coldly at Manno, she said in a limp voice, 'Manno, better go for a stroll. These children will not let you alone.' Seeing the reproach in their mother's eyes, the children ran off.

My aunt's arms fell to her sides, Manno looked at her steadily.

But before my aunt could get over her discomfiture, Manno was out of the gate.

'Tell me, Aunt,' I asked, 'what's this mystery?'

My question had apparently irritated her. 'She is ill, Ravi,' she said shortly. She paused and added, 'For two years she has been staying at the sanatorium. Now her father has bought her a cottage there, and an old family servant looks after her. When she gets fed up with the place she comes to the city for a brief spell.'

I was too shocked to believe her words.

'Ravi, when I see her on her rare visits, I lose my appetite.'

'But you shouldn't have sent the children away so abruptly,' I said trying to probe further. 'Didn't you see she felt hurt?'

My aunt looked hard at me, as if she thought it futile to explain things to me, and went inside. The children were busy playing. I stood there puffing at a cigarette, trying to blow away my vague apprehension with the curling smoke. I walked out of the gate and, climbing down the ridge, took the road running along the bank of the lake. In the sunlight, little waves shimmered and broke against the bank. I stopped in front of the Naini Temple, and leaned on the railing to watch the boats. In one boat two young men, rowing strongly, sped past towards Tallital, leaving behind an old man dozing in another boat. Then followed a few European women in the club's boat.

Suddenly I see that pale face in the water, those big eyes, those thin arms. I repeat the name, Manno, Manno, Manno . . . I stand on the high bank and Manno flows towards me on the water. Pulled-back curly hair, unblinking lashes . . . But my aunt says Manno is ill, Manno is ill.

Turning away from the railing, I looked in the direction of my aunt's house. The Cheena Peak stood firm in its exalted glory, looking down at me . . . I stood on the road bewildered. Everything was the same as on other days, but for two eyes, their image imprinted deep in the caverns of my mind, and the illness behind those eyes, inaccessible and beyond release.

My aunt had gone out with the children. I went into the drawing room, and having nothing better to do, looked at the decor and admired my aunt's taste. On the cabinet stood a family photograph, in a heavy frame. What was so attractive about my aunt's husband that she spends days and nights, months and years, bound to him? But no, it was unbecoming of me to harbour such thoughts in my aunt's own house.

I climbed the stairs to my room. Lighting a cigarette, I gazed out of the window. Bright red tin roofs dotted the hills and grey hill tracks meandered over the hillside. Aunt would be back soon . . . and Manno. I kept turning the pages of an old magazine.

'May I lay the table sahib?'

'When will Aunt be back?'

'She said she won't have lunch.'

'And the guest?'

'She will lunch alone. Upstairs.'

I crushed the cigarette underfoot, relieved that I should

not be tortured by her presence—or was it at my helplessness that I could not keep her company? I do not remember what else passed through my mind. All that I remember is that I toyed with my food absent-mindedly and kept looking out.

I was finishing the last course when I heard hoofbeats.

'Will you be able to get there in two hours?' The voice was low but firm.

'Yes, hazoor.'

I heard her going upstairs. Lunch was over, but I did not go up. After helping myself to another cup of coffee, I kept sitting at the table. It struck me that to be disturbed by such a brief encounter was a sign of terrible weakness. Why should a casual introduction make me so restless?

After an hour I found myself climbing the stairs. A curtain hung across the open door. I knocked.

'Please come in.' Manno was standing by her suitcase, holding a cashmere shawl. She did not lose her composure on seeing me. 'Please sit down,' she said, removing clothes from the sofa.

This was the brightest room in Aunt's house. New furniture, costly curtains, and Manno was wearing light yellow clothes. It cheered me.

'You've had your lunch, of course?' I asked just for the sake of saying something.

'Yes.' She gazed at me.

'Is Aunt out?'

Manno nodded. She folded the shawl and put it in the suitcase saying, 'I'll be gone before the evening. Please tell Aunt I came for a day only.'

'But she'll be back soon.'

She said nothing, nor did she indicate anything by her expression.

'Won't you stay for another day?' I asked.

Silently, she bent over her suitcase, putting things into it. After a pause she said, laughing, 'What's the use? This small city holds no attraction for me after a big village like Bhowali.' After so many years, her laughter still rings in my ears and the pallor of her face is still vivid in my mind.

We came down together, I carrying her coat on my arm. The servant and the gardener bowed and were given tips . . . The syce patted the horse.

'Will you ride?'

She cast a fleeting glance at the coat. 'No, I would rather walk. Lead the horse.'

I wanted her to ride, but could not force the words out of my mouth.

At the gate she turned her head as if she was taking a last look at the house. She quickly collected herself and started off briskly down the slope. We walked in silence.

Her things were put in the taxi. The driver sensed the tense situation.

'Shall we start?' he asked.

With a blank look she stretched out her hand for the coat. As she sat down in the car, the attendant took a rug and with professional dexterity spread it over her knees.

She looked tired. I could see the fish-faced golden bangles on her wrists. But what was in her eyes? I could not make out for the life of me. She gazed steadily at her hands lying inert on her knees.

The car started and I looked back. No arms were raised. No lips moved in farewell. Till the car disappeared round the bend I kept looking at the ribbon tied in a simple knot round her hair falling at her nape and hearing that painful thank you—'No, no, that's all, thanks.'

Even today when I conjure up those moments, something happens to me. After the road had swallowed up the speeding car, I turned back and trudged along the bank of the lake. In vain I tried to blot out her face; it kept bobbing up before my eyes, again and again. It was a slow ascent to the house, halting and weary. The thought of it tires me even today. The coolies were shifting the furniture on the veranda. Something clutched at my heart. So it was all a game, a make-believe! Manno's room had been furnished with hired furniture. I saw aunt in a new light; the favourable impression I had formed of her was suddenly reversed. My aunt was standing at the door. 'Ravi, go and wash,' she said in a strained voice. 'Tea will be ready in a minute. Don't be late.'

We sat down to tea. The children were not about. Only my aunt. She poured tea and pushed the cup towards me.

'Aunt!'

She pretended she had not heard me.

'Aunt,' I said again. 'Why did our visitor leave so abruptly?—She had come for two days, right?'

My aunt kept stirring her tea. Her silence made me more cruel.

'She asked me to tell you that a day's stay was enough for her.' Why do I think of all this now? Why these futile thoughts?

My aunt seemed unable to hear any more. Sighing deeply, she looked at me and said, 'Say no more, Ravi,' and left the room, leaving her tea untouched.

That night Uncle was to return from his tour but the servant told me a telegram had arrived to say he would be two days late. I wanted to go to my aunt's room but felt shy. Finally I found myself on the stairs in front of Manno's room. I went in and put on the light—all empty, no curtains, no furniture, no Manno. I looked at the wood piled in the fireplace and thought, had she been here tonight she'd have sat up late into the night and perhaps I would have come here like this to her and . . . Why am I thinking all this! Why . . .

Gripped by a vague nervousness, I hurried down. I switched off the light and tumbled into my bed. Lying awake I thought of that small cottage in Bhowali where Manno would have reached by now.

'Ravi!' It was my aunt.

She came and sat down near me and caressed my hair. For a moment her hand became still and then passed over my brow.

'I'm not fondling you but that unfortunate girl,' she said in a trembling voice. 'This hand will never touch her again.'

My hand trembled in her grasp. I felt I was holding Manno's hand.

'Ravi, stop thinking of her. She will not be in our midst for long.'

I trembled at my aunt's touch. 'Aunt, I may not live long either.'

Today, years later, lying in a cottage in Bhowali, I wonder countless times what made me utter those prophetic words whose horrid truth I feel in my pulsebeat, day after day and night after night. I don't know how Aunt reacted to those words. But I remember her suddenly switching on the light and looking full in my face with reproachful eyes. 'Have you gone crazy?' she said. 'Do you want to compare yourself to a girl who gropes in a blind alley and for whom there is no point of return?'

She sat down in the chair. 'Ravi, you have seen her only for one day. But I've known her for years and my heart has been squeezed dry of all feeling. All the care I have lavished on her has been in vain. There was a time when I eagerly looked forward to her homecoming and now I wait anxiously for her departure and keep my children out of her way.'

She looked at me uncertainly, got up to go but stopped suddenly. 'Ravi, this will lead you nowhere.' Her voice was stern with warning. 'There's no use pining for a derelict for whom all doors are closed.'

That day I did not understand my aunt. I couldn't even if I wanted to.

The next day I roamed about like a lost soul. I raced the horse to Lariakanta, and back to the Band Stand. When I turned homewards, I found that I was bound for elsewhere. I stood at the ridge thinking. In the afternoon, when I descended the slope to Tallital, I was clear in my mind about my destination. I had to go to Bhowali.

I got out of the bus. At the Ramgarh bus stand I saw heaps of luscious red apples and I knew I was not far from Bhowali. In the bus, I had imagined it would be a small congested place. But here the tall pines swayed in the breeze and the place was drenched in sunshine. Bhowali looked beautiful. Passing through the square, I came to the post office, and obtained her address. The way to 'The Pines' lay through a small bazaar. A narrow path at the turning of the main road took me towards a small hill. I looked down from the railing. Between the hills lay a small valley, criss-crossed with small fields—a piece of patchwork. Far off, towards the south a lake shone like a sheet of silver.

After this, my first visit, I came to Bhowali times without number. But not like this. This visit was different, utterly different. I walked on unthinkingly, unaware that I was going to Manno. I just walked on, that's all I was aware of. 'The Pines' was boldly etched into the trunk of a tree. I pushed open the wicket gate. Walking between the two rows of flowerpots, I came to the veranda. Treading softly on the carpet, I knocked gently. A bent man with a shrewd face answered the door.

'Anybody in?'

'Son, are you looking for the child?'

I nodded in reply.

'The child has gone to the lake. She should be back soon.'

I sat down in the open and waited. After a while I turned my back towards the gate. When you decide a person won't come soon, he turns up soon.

The sound of horsehoofs. I forced myself not to look back.

'Baba,' someone called. I felt two eyes on my back. I got up. Of course, I knew it could be none else than Manno. There was no surprise, no eagerness in her eyes. Nor were they sad. They were just two eyes, very much like Manno's, looking at me steadfastly.

'Baba!'

The old servant came towards the horse in swift strides and said in a caressing voice, 'Child, get down. It's already late.' He held out his hand to help her dismount. Manno said, 'Please call Amma. I'm not feeling well.'

'I hope there's nothing wrong, child.'

She gave a little laugh on seeing his anxious look. 'Please tell Amma to prepare my bed.'

The servant pulled up a chair for her. 'Want to lie down?' he asked her anxiously.

'Yes, Baba.'

She avoided the servant's gaze as if she was guilty of some indiscretion.

Then she bent towards me, 'Have I kept you waiting long?'

'Oh, no,' I shook my head. 'Are you unwell?'

In reply, Manno closed her eyes.

The old maidservant came running with a shawl and wrapped it round her shoulders. 'Manno, that old man is put out by trifles. You'll come round in a moment. May I bring tea for the gentleman?'

Manno did not know what to say. 'Amma, ask him yourself. He may not like the idea.'

Her meaning was lost on me. I said, 'No, no, I'm not thirsty.'

Manno didn't seem to have heard. Nor did she look at me.

'How is Aunt?' she asked after a pause. 'Is Uncle still away?'

The maidservant now knew who I was. 'You should have informed us you were coming. I would have asked you to bring a few things for Manno.'

'Amma, please make the bed. I'm tired. I can't sit any longer.'

I sat on, looking like a fool. How thoughtless of me. I should have at least brought some fruit for her.

Manno seemed to have read my mind. 'It wasn't

necessary,' she said as if musing to herself. 'It's not proper to bring anything or take anything from here.'

I cursed myself for my senselessness. I followed her into the cottage. Amma put her to bed, loosening her hair. She pushed a chair towards me and left the room.

'Manno!'

Without speaking, she stretched her thin arm towards me and then suddenly withdrew it. Today when I am myself reduced to Manno's state, I would make a thousand sacrifices to win back that hour. While sitting there why didn't I touch that arm, stroke that hand? As if some mysterious force held back the flood, I sat glued to the chair, motionless.

Why this hesitation? It must have been the same fear which now keeps away my near and dear ones from me. That night when I got up to leave her room, love and fear waged a grim struggle within me. When I reached the dak bungalow I felt a great sense of release from a bond which had held me in its shackles every oppressive moment. I wish Manno were alive today to see the fruits of that liberation.

I couldn't sleep properly all night. Each time I woke up, I felt I was still in Bhowali in that room at 'The Pines' with its large windows. I was lying in Manno's bed and sitting by the bedside. Manno was gazing at me. I stretched out my hand. Manno laughed and shook her head. 'Tuck it under the rug. Who would care to touch it?'

'Manno!'

Manno says nothing, only laughs.

After this phantasmagoric night when I woke up again, I saw my aunt. 'Ravi, it will lead you nowhere.'

That morning I rushed to the bus stop. The thought

came to me, ' "The Pines" . . . no . . . no . . . nothing . . . go back.'

When I got home my aunt looked sharply at me and asked, 'Where were you yesterday?'

'Went to Ranikhet, Aunt.'

'Why didn't you tell me?'

'What was there to tell, Aunt?'

In the afternoon I met Uncle. He had returned the previous day and he wore a grave expression as always. I caught his expression when he raised his eyes from the plate. I had no doubt that Uncle and Manno's father must have been brothers. His eyes had the same tranquillity and steadiness as Manno's.

Getting up from the dining table, Uncle said, 'Ravi, your aunt wants to go to Lucknow. Do you mind going with her?'

'Uncle, I'll accompany her.'

My aunt, her children and I were coming down from Nainital. As the bus took a turn down the broad hill road, I saw Bhowali shrouded in a haze. The same Bhowali I had visited yesterday. And then on to Kathgodam and Lucknow.

After a day's stay at my aunt's place when I went to take leave of her, she insisted on my staying with her for a few days more. She was not prepared to take a no from me, it seemed. But I was adamant. 'But where will you go?' she asked at last.

'I don't know,' I said.

Something seemed to be weighing on my aunt's mind. 'But your uncle wants you to go back to Naini.'

'No, Aunt, I'll go south, to Father.'

'Ravi, you didn't enjoy yourself at Naini this time.'

'No, no, Aunt.'

Parting, I touched my aunt's feet. She is not much older than myself. But I felt I was in need of her blessing.

She was taken by surprise. 'Ravi, you have touched my feet,' she said smiling. 'I'll bless you for it. May you get a beautiful wife.'

She had said this half in jest, and when I stood glum she felt embarrassed.

After buying my ticket, I left the luggage with the coolie and began to stroll on the platform. There was no train in the yard. The straight railway line stretching into the distance seemed to have uncoiled the skein of my tangled thoughts. I kept thinking not about Bhowali, 'The Pines' and Manno but of the blessings of my aunt. A cosy home, a beautiful wife and I . . .

My aunt's prophecy came true. I did set up a house, and marry a beautiful girl. That is a different story though. But the train did not take me to the destination I was bound for.

The train steamed in. The coolie found a seat for me and put in my luggage while I stood watching the rushing crowd—passengers, coolies, women, children, old men.

'Sahib, the train will leave in a minute.'

I looked at my watch and nodded my head. Adjusting his turban, the coolie said, 'Sahib, don't you see? The green light is on.' I looked at the green signal. And then everything swam out of focus . . . The same bright thin figure, the same pallor on the face.

'Coolie, take down my luggage!'

'Sahib!'

'Hurry up, quick . . .'

The coolie was again following me with my luggage.

I returned the ticket and purchased a new one. I bought baskets of fruit, gulped down some tea, and took the train to Bareilly. I would go where I liked. Who was there to stop me—and why?

In the afternoon I sat basking on the front lawn under the winter sun. Mother came from inside and sat down by my side. 'Now that you have come on leave, why are you in a hurry to go? Why be so stubborn?'

I smiled, the wise prodigal son. Contrary to her expectation, I said, 'Mother, any girl who is acceptable to you is acceptable to me.'

'Son, would you like me to see the girl then?'

'Yes, Mother.'

I felt my mother was smiling to herself.

After dinner when I returned from a stroll, the room was quiet.

I no longer had that youthful eagerness, curiosity, desire to see someone. Having lived so long alone, I perhaps had no hope of companionship.

I started dozing while reading in bed. I dreamed I was working my way up a hill. I saw a thick cluster of pines. The sky was empty, a voice resounded in the silliness of the night and then a trembling hand groped towards my neck. The same feeble wrist, the same thin trembling fingers . . . I woke up with a start. My brow was damp with fear. I parted the curtains at the window. The lawn lay covered with light, filtering from my father's room.

I came to myself, sighed, touched my hair, my cold brow. A terrifying desolation, and in the dark that hand . . . that hand.

Why was I reminded of this hand that night, a hand

that I had almost forgotten and had seen for the last time, many years ago, while coming down from 'The Pines'?

I won't say I touched it because to move your hand forward numberless times with the intention of touching is not to touch.

Staying in Naini for a month and returning time and again from Bhowali, there came one final day when I returned from Manno and wished to turn that return into a point of no return. Three times I descended, and three times turned to ascend again.

Manno, a shawl thrown over her shoulders, was reclining in an easy chair. I was standing by her side. 'Tomorrow I will be gone from Naini,' I said, breaking the ice.

Manno slowly gathered the shawl which had slipped from her shoulders. The far-off expression, which I had seen on her face a month ago, had again returned.

I wanted to say something. But what should I say? Should I tell her that I would soon return?

Every passing moment confirmed my resolve to return. But the way she looked at me suggested that I was going away for ever.

'Manno . . .' I said.

'Ravi.'

For a fleeting moment her face became taut and then it was suffused with a faint smile. She joined her hands in farewell, 'Namaskar.'

I stood rooted to the ground speechless, looking at those folded hands, wanting to step forward and bid farewell, but unable to move.

'You are getting late, Ravi.'

I lowered my eyes and without a word of parting

hurried on. Would I return again, or was it the final parting?

I looked back and stopped for a moment. Manno was sitting in the same posture, like a statue.

Perhaps she had a hunch that I would turn back. 'Please sit down, Ravi.' She pointed towards a chair. There was no anguish in her voice nor any sign of surprise. She looked at me questioningly as if she knew I had something on my mind.

'I don't feel like going, Manno,' I said with the simplicity of a child.

I looked at her, tense with expectancy. Oh, how excruciating her silence was.

She wanted to say something, as I could see. But the words seemed to stick in her throat. 'But you'll have to leave sooner or later,' she said at last.

I was overwhelmed. I could have touched, could have kissed the very timbre of her voice. 'Manno.'

I stepped towards her. As if to arrest the outpouring of my heart, she raised her feeble hand. 'Manno.' I wanted my plea to reach her. 'No.' And nothing more.

Then she raised her thin hand in a gesture of farewell. Feeling empty and helpless, I made my way down from 'The Pines'. My eyes had become misty. I looked back, bewildered. I was again standing on the bank of the lake and Manno was drifting by in a boat. She had not seen me. Her bowed head was hidden by her uplifted hand. Perhaps her eyes were closed. Or maybe she was weeping. The thought of that stern wounded pride made me throb.

I heard her sobbing inside. In my heart I cried out, 'Manno, Manno.' A voice seemed to reply, 'Don't wait. Don't stop.'

Then I ran towards the road, increasing the distance between me and the cottage, the inmate of the cottage and those two eyes. But I could not blot out the memory of Manno. Even today the thought of her is fresh in my mind. I vividly recall that afternoon when Manno and I went for a walk along the big lake. The afternoon was drenched in mild sunshine, golden and glorious. I was carried away by the pallor of her face. Her shoulders, covered with a shawl, were duly erect in spite of the tiredness of her gait. I gazed at her curly hair, her shoulders, her feet.

When we came to the end of our promenade, we sighted two small temples under a giant tree. Their tin doors were closed. Manno stood thinking for a moment, and then taking off her shoes, she stepped over the rocks and plucked a lotus from the temple pool. She covered her head with her shawl and placing the lotus in front of the closed door, bowed her head in worship.

When she got up, she looked strangely different, as if she was not Manno but an incarnation of her own helplessness which had bowed its head before the closed door of its destiny.

Anguish rose in me for this melancholy loneliness. 'I'll look around for the priest and have the temple door opened,' I said.

'No, Ravi, no need,' she said shaking her head. 'I've no blessings to ask for. All doors are now closed to me. May those doors remain open for those from whom I have been separated.'

Casting to the wind the fear of catching infection from her disease which stood in my way, I bent over her head. 'Manno . . .'

She gently pushed my hand from her shoulders. 'Ravi, don't stretch out your hand for that which you can't endure.'

There was no reproach in her voice, no irony, no bitterness. She simply said what had to be said. That day I could not answer her. Not even though I went to her again and again, not even in those moments of farewell when I left Manno weeping. The weakness that made me a coward has me in its grip today. Today I curse that cowardice, on my own behalf, on Manno's behalf.

The house was full of gaiety. Mother had got a bride after her own heart and I a life companion. When I looked at Meera's innocent face, I completely lost my head. A throng of relatives and friends—it gladdened my heart to see the house filled with laughter. We went on a month's honeymoon to the seaside, and then to my place of posting where we set up a new home together. My life had found equilibrium.

In our newly discovered world, endless and fathomless like the sea, we would roam for hours together, doting on each other. Morning, evening, day and night, we would lose ourselves only to find ourselves again. Lost in ourselves, we saw everything and yet saw nothing.

And thus ten years passed. Oblivious of impending doom, absorbed in each other. Torn away from Meera and the children, lying in the cottage, I recall those halcyon days. I feel as if I still hear somebody breathing by my side. I wish I could peep into someone's eyes and tell her how happy we were then. But now there is no one at hand to listen to me. Because of the children, Meera has become cold towards me.

Last month, while going to Ranikhet, Meera had

dropped in for an hour with the children. Lying in bed I saw the three of them coming up. For a brief moment she had paused at the wicket gate. Then she had gathered the children and led them up.

'Rani, Munna, bow to your father, children!' They raised their hands awkwardly at their mother's bidding and then looked at me with curiosity. Their own father was a stranger to them.

Meera cried all the time. She was too shaken to talk coherently. For fear of infecting them, I dared not touch my own children. I kept gazing at Meera who had come to see me. I tried to search for the wife in this woman, whom I had once called my own.

I was hurt by the heartlessness of Meera looking at her wristwatch with tear-filled eyes.

Abstractedly, I stared at the wicket gate through which my own family would presently pass, leaving me alone to my fate. I was overpowered by a strong urge to hold Meera's hand and say, 'I won't let you go. No, I won't let you go.' But the apathetic look in my children's eyes killed my desire.

I looked up startled. Meera had come up. Bending over me, she lightly brushed my forehead with her lips and then stepped back. Wiping my tearful eyes which had become wet with Meera's tears, I looked around with misty eyes. The dam had burst. The torrent of emotions had carried away everything. There was no Meera by my side, nor the children.

Propped against the pillow, I looked out. They were now at the third turning of the descending path. With her back towards me, Meera stooped slightly as she walked. Holding hands, the children walked on, now looking at their mother, now at the path.

With bated breath I watched them, hoping that they would look back at me. But no heads turned. Only my daughter's ribbon, tied round her head, kept bobbing in the air, as if proclaiming, 'Daddy, we are going, we are going for ever.'

Yes, they were gone—all of them. They left because I was also preparing to depart. In the same way, I too had sped down the path when I sensed that Manno's end was near. Like me, Manno too had wept. Now I know what it means to cover your face and shed tears in sequestered loneliness with no one around to console you.

That time when I parted from Manno, I did not think I would ever see her again. I saw her in sleep, I saw her for years together. The same thin body, the same big eyes and the arms resting over the blanket. I would wake up, greatly agitated, and shifting closer to Meera, cuddle myself against her.

I had come to Lucknow on tour and visited my aunt. We sat chatting when my aunt's tone suddenly changed. 'Ravi, do you know, Manno is no more in this world.'

I was stunned. But hiding my feelings, I put on a grave expression befitting the role of a newly-made father.

'Yes, she passed away in her sleep,' my aunt looked at me as though I was still the Ravi of those bygone years. 'The maidservant was on leave. When Khayali, the old servant, came in the morning there was no life in her.'

'Aunt . . .' I said in a choked voice, on the verge of asking something.

'Ravi, you should have written to her once, at least,' Aunt said in a strained voice, wiping her tears.

I put my handkerchief to my eyes to wipe my tears.

'And she had left a packet for you,' my aunt added. 'It contained a woollen jersey.'

I called on my aunt again the next day. Touching her feet in a hurry I said, 'Well, Aunt . . .'

'Ravi . . .' Aunt said in the same tone in which she had been speaking to me yesterday.

Shaking my head I said in a defeated voice, 'No, Aunt, no.'

My aunt realized that I didn't have the heart to dwell on the subject. Her heart brimmed over for Manno. 'I wonder why Providence had doled her out a love which could not be requited,' she said.

When I returned from Lucknow, her memory kept haunting me for many days. I saw her sitting in 'The Pines', knitting a jersey for me. The same hands, the same visage.

After lying in bed at home for a year, at last I found myself at Bhowali with its mild sunshine and its cold wind rushing through the pines. Yes, I was here again. But this time I did not have to call at the post office to find someone's address. The first time I moved into the accursed cottage facing 'The Pines', I wept bitterly. The whole night I kept repeating the same name, 'Manno! Manno!' If she had been alive today . . .

Meera, whom I had known for years, now looks remote and alien. The woman whom I had loved ardently, kissed passionately. But when my heart brims over and I pine for someone, it is of Manno I think and not Meera.

Tired of my dreary existence, when I gaze out of the

window, I still see her curly hair and her face dimly outlined in the encircling clouds.

The frequently changing colours of the medicine bottles remind me that my soul will not grope for long in this transient body. One day while looking out of the window I will merge in these clouds . . . in these encircling clouds.

Translated from the Hindi by Jai Ratan

Kamilini

GURZADA APPARAO

'The door! Open the door!'

The door did not open.

The clock in the room struck a startling one o'clock.

'How late I am! That is crassly stupid of me. I shall be careful from tomorrow. My mind was captivated by the nautch-girl's song despite all reformist anti-nautch feelings. It wasn't the song alone; the singer too distracted me. Otherwise, why should I have sat through to the end of the song like a lewd fellow? How can I explain this inclination to get a chance to have a few words with her by whatever means? All right, here and now I slap my cheeks; I swear I shall not go to her singing from tomorrow. (Thou shall not swear, that is another new rule to observe.) Never again shall I go. That's decided. Definitely decided . . . Now, if I raise my voice and call, Kamilini may wake up. If I knock softly on the door and somehow rouse Ravudu, I can quietly join her in bed and pretend to be a gentleman.'

Gopal Rao touched the door and it swung slightly open.

'Arre, what is this?' he thought and quietly opened the door wider. He found that there was no lamp in the passage. He stepped through the doorway and opened the bedroom door. There was no lamp there either. Tiptoeing across the room without making the slightest noise, he approached the bed and tried to find out if Kamilini was awake or asleep, but he couldn't make out in the dark. He groped for the matchbox on the table and lit a match. There was no Kamilini on the bed. He was stunned. The match dropped from his hand. The darkness filled the room and his mind. Crazy doubts and crazier explanations awoke and died in his mind. He became vaguely angry, with himself, his foolish conduct, or perhaps with Kamilini for not being around. He came out of the bedroom and stood in the courtyard of the house. In the starlight he could not find either the manservant or the maidservant.

Returning to his bedroom, he lit a lamp and looked carefully all around the room. Kamilini could not be seen anywhere. He went to the main door and opened it. Right in the middle of the street, smoking a cheroot and looking at the stars was the manservant Ravudu. 'Rama!' Gopal Rao called.

Ravudu was startled; the cheroot slipped from his mouth and fell.

'Come here, you useless fellow!'

Dragging his feet, Ravudu came up.

'Where is your amma?'

'My mother, babu? In our shack.'

'Not your mother, you stupid fellow! I mean my wife, the mistress.'

Ravudu was dumbfounded. He thought furiously for

a while and said, 'Amma garu is sleeping in her room, babu! Where else will she be, babu?'

'She is not anywhere in the house, you idiot! Where did you go, leaving the house?'

Ravudu looked away and said, 'A servant can get a pain in the leg or a pain in the stomach, babu. The big master told you again and again, when handing her over to you, never leave amma garu alone and go at midnight to the dancing girl . . .' Two extra-heavy blows landed on his back.

'Killed me, babu!' Ravudu cried and fell in a heap. Gopal Rao was a kind man. His anger subsided instantly and he felt sorry. He helped Ravudu to his feet and massaged his back.

'In my anger I behaved like a beast,' he said and took Ravudu into his room.

He sat on his chair and said miserably, 'What could have happened, Rama?'

Ravudu looked in all directions and said, 'It is all like magic, babu.'

'Do you think she could have gone to her mother's place?'

'Isn't she capable of doing that, babu? If you lose your temper again, I cannot tell you . . . What happens when women are educated?'

'What do you know of the value of education, Rama?' said Gopal Rao. As he was leaning his elbows on the table thoughtfully and putting his head on his hands, he saw the letter in Kamilini's own pretty hand on the table. He read it aloud:

' "*Ayya*"—not "beloved", it has come down to "sir"!' [illegible] the calf been lost, babu?'

'Keep quiet, you fool . . .'

'Ayya, for the last ten days, I found you are not returning home at night. You said you were attending meetings. You said you were waging campaigns sleeplessly for the amelioration of the world. I have come to know the truth from my women friends. It is only because I am at home that you are compelled to tell lies. If I were at my mother's place, your freedom would not be restricted and there would be no need for untruths. Instead of forcing you to tell lies every day, it is better for me to move away from your path. That is the duty of any wife who desires the welfare of her husband, isn't it? I am going tonight to my mother's place. Be happy. If any kindness for me is still left in you, think well of me.'

Finishing the letter, Gopal Rao muttered, 'I am a beast.'

'What is it babu, why are you uttering such things?'

'I'm a hopeless beast.'

Ravudu could control his laughter only with great difficulty.

'A virtuous lady, an educated lady, rich in modesty. Now she has given me my deserts for my wicked lapse.'

'What has mistress done, babu?'

'Gone to her mother's place. But how did she leave without your knowledge?'

Ravudu skipped two steps backwards and said, 'I must have gone to sleep. If you lose your temper, I cannot tell you, babu . . . If a woman wants to go to her mother's place without informing you, you must give her a few slaps and stop her. Teaching women reading and writing like men . . . won't unnatural things happen, babu?'

'You fool! The most marvellous thing in all God's creation is that precious gem, an educated woman. Lord Siva gave away half his body to create his consort Parvati, you know. The Englishman calls his wife his 'better half', meaning the wife is superior to the husband. Do you understand?'

'Not at all, babu.'

Ravudu was finding it difficult to suppress his laughter.

'Aren't we sending your daughter to school? You will yourself come to appreciate the value of education. Just see how much more civilized than your folks she is already. Let's not talk of it now, but now either you or I should immediately leave for Chandravaram! I can't get any leave to go. You have been a servant in this household for generations. Kamilini likes you. So, it is better that you alone should go. Go and fetch Kamilini.'

'If you order me, how can I not go? I shall go. But if she refuses to come . . .'

'Here's ten rupees. If you can somehow persuade her to return, I shall give you ten more rupees.'

'Yes, master.'

'Then do you know what to say to her?'

'What else could I say, babu? "What a wonderful thing you have done, leaving like that without informing anyone. The master almost broke my back! Please come back, amma." I will tell her this.'

'Please forgive me, forget the blows. Never tell Kamilini about them. You will remember this, won't you?'

'Yes, master.'

'I shall tell you what you are going to tell her. Listen

carefully. Tell her that the master has learned his lesson . . .'

'What is that, babu!'

'Is that any of your business? Just remember well what I tell you and convey it to her. Tell her that Pantulu has learned his lesson, will never go to listen to dancing-girls. He has sworn firmly on it . . . (No, I said that absent-mindedly, don't mention that to her.) Hereafter, never will he stir out of home at night. This is for sure. Understand?'

Ravudu nodded.

'There is more to say. Please tell her I plead with her in all humility, and with great affection and love. Take pity on him, you must say, don't expose Pantulu's weaknesses to anyone. (This is a most important point, have you heard?) Please come back in two or three days. Without you, he looks as if he's gone crazy. Each hour is like a year. (Don't forget this point, mind you.) Now you know what to tell her. Don't forget a single word of it.'

'I have got it, babu.'

'Let's hear what you are going to tell her.'

Ravudu scratched his head.

'What . . . what . . . I don't know all that, babu. I shall tell her, "Amma, take my advice. I have seen long years pass. I have seen young people, I have seen elders, do you hear? Womenfolk should accept every command of the men and behave themselves. Otherwise, like the elder Pantulu, the younger Pantulu also will take to bad ways. Let me tell you a secret. A most attractive, golden doll-like dancing girl has arrived in the town. From the time he first saw her, Pantulu has been totally out of sorts. Take my advice, come back home. Otherwise, I am not responsible." This is what I'll tell her.'

'You scoundrel!' said Gopal and leaped out of his chair angrily. Evading him, Ravudu slipped out of the room like a bead.

At the same time, from under the bedstead was heard a most delicious, merry laugh and the most bewitching music of anklets.

Translated from the Telugu by Ranga Rao

Poovan Banana

VAIKOM MOHAMMED BASHEER

I

I am not writing this story of the poovan banana because I want to do so. I am writing it because Abdul Khader Sahib insisted that I should. He thinks it has a moral. The story is about his wife Jameela Bibi.

Jameela Bibi has a university degree, a BA. As for Abdul Khader Sahib, he has studied only up to the school finals. According to convention, was it proper for such a person to marry a woman with a degree? But Abdul Khader Sahib proudly says he acquired his bride as a conquest of war. In ancient days men would steal women. They would even make running knots on ropes and lasso women into captivity. Men inflicted many indignities on women. They used to to force women into submission. But as Abdul Khader Sahib was a civilized person, he did not resort to such tactics. He was a well-known strongman of the village in addition to being the secretary of the local Beedi Workers' Union and a good football player. Abdul Khader Sahib says he studied from class four till the final year in the same school as Jameela Bibi, and right from the beginning he was in love with her. Jameela Bibi says that this is a lie.

Be that as it may, Jameela Bibi passed her BA. With the money from her father's beedi factory, she could be a very fashionable woman. All the eligible young men of the place were in love with her. The amateur poets of the village wrote verses about her ranging from mere sonnets to epic pieces. An army of young men lined up in military formation laid siege to Jameela Bibi's heart. In other words there was a regular queue for it. Abdul Khader Sahib was not one of the queue. He did not attempt to write verses or love letters. Abdul Khader Sahib says he did not know how to write either. Jameela Bibi says that he composed a ballad about her. Abdul Khader Sahib totally denies this. What he says he did was this: one day he stopped Jameela Bibi as she was walking along the country lane and asked her, 'Your name is Jameela, isn't it?'

Jameela Bibi did not care for the question. Was there any young man in that village who did not know her? She put on the dignified air of a fashionable woman and asked haughtily, 'And if it is?'

Abdul Khader Sahib laughed. It was an attractive laugh. Jameela Bibi had heard him and seen him laugh before. And she had liked it. But that abominable attitude of his! As though he were sizing her up! Jameela Bibi did not care for that.

'What do you want?'

'Oh, nothing very important!' Abdul Khader Sahib said. 'Your father's beedi factory has one hundred and twenty workers. I am the secretary of their trade union.

My name is Abdul Khader!'

'Well, well,' Jameela Bibi replied. 'I have heard that you are the village bully.'

'The beedi workers are thinking of going on strike. We will make you close down your factory.'

Jameela Bibi asked, 'Why do you tell me this? Go and tell my father.'

'I have a reason for telling you this, Jameela Bibi.'

'What is that?'

Abdul Khader Sahib said, 'I love you, Jameela Bibi!'

Jameela felt a thrill of satisfaction. But she felt that he should be put to shame. So Jameela Bibi laughed. A very sarcastic laugh.

'That's fine,' she said. 'What else is new in the village?'

A question like that would have stunned the ordinary young men in the queue. But Abdul Khader Sahib took it as a challenge and replied, 'Jameela, if you don't marry me . . .!'

Jameela Bibi also took it as a challenge. 'What will you do if I don't marry you?'

I'll hang myself! thought Abdul Khader Sahib, but he did not say it. He said instead, 'Jameela, I will break every bone in your body!'

Jameela Bibi said nothing in reply.

Abdul Khader Sahib continued, 'Jameela, don't throw away my life. I love you. I love your dress. I love every inch of you. I love even the roads and lanes you walk on!'

Jameela Bibi was happy in her heart. But could she show her feelings? How could she talk about them? She asked, 'Are you in the habit of stopping all young women passing by and talking like this?'

'No, my Jameela, I have talked to no woman other

than you. I have not even looked at any other woman. You are the very sight of my eyes!'

She asked with an attempt at dignity, 'And what else?'

He replied, 'You and I, we are for each other.'

'Oh, very good,' said Jameela Bibi and walked away.

Then the war started. The two families opposed the connection. People were against their getting together. There was conflict. There was a strike. Why prolong the tale? Finally Abdul Khader Sahib married Jameela Bibi and they lived happily for a while until the incident of the poovan banana.

II

The time was five-thirty in the evening.

It was during the monsoons. Sunshine and rain followed each other without warning. The water rose steadily in the river. Abdul Khader Sahib wanted to have a look at the flood water and also to have a bath. He wound a towel round his waist and was about to step out when Jameela Bibi came near the door and called out to him, 'Listen . . .' Abdul Khader thought to himself, she wants me to put on a shirt before I go out. Jameela Bibi had begun issuing ordinances about deportment and behaviour soon after they were married and began living together.

Abdul Khader Sahib must dress like a gentleman! He could go out only if he was properly dressed. He must be dignified in his behaviour. He should not stop on the way and talk to riff-raff or his former rowdy friends. Beedi workers, poets, porters, politicians, drivers, rickshaw-pullers—these should not be treated as equals.

They needed to have a maid at home. Abdul Khader Sahib must not cook. They must live up to their status. They should get ahead in life. He had to realize that a woman marries to raise her husband's standard of life . . . And so on. Similarly Jameela Bibi believed that it was the inalienable right of the wife to keep her husband on the straight and narrow path, to intervene in all matters, physical and spiritual, relating to her man and generally to create confusion in his life. Every woman believes in this. Abdul Khader Sahib did not comment on these examples of a woman's perverted thinking.

What could he say? After all they had not been married a long time. He asked her in all reasonableness, 'My dear Jameela, I'm going to take a bath. Should I put on a shirt for that?'

'Oh!' Jameela Bibi replied as if her heart was in anguish, 'do you ever listen to me?'

'Have I ever gone against your wishes?' So saying, he ran inside, put on his shirt and came out. But his shirt was not buttoned.

Look at the carelessness of these men! She buttoned his shirt for him; all the three buttons.

Abdul Khader Sahib walked away.

Jameela Bibi again called out to him: 'Listen . . .'

Abdul Khader Sahib turned round. He thought to himself, God in heaven, now will come the problem of a maidservant! What is one to do? Couldn't one live without a cook? One must learn to do things for oneself. Why can't one cook merely because one has a BA degree? Never mind BA, even if one is an MA or a Ph.D, one must know how to cook. If she didn't know, he, Abdul Khader Sahib, could teach her. He had already begun teaching her. He could make anything from tea to biriyani.

'What is it, Jameela?' he asked. 'Is it the problem of the servant?'

'No,' Jameela Bibi pouted as she replied. 'After all, I have passed my BA just to be a cook!'

'My darling,' Abdul Khader Sahib replied. 'My pet need not enter the kitchen. I'll look after everything. All right?'

'Oh . . . you say that every day.'

'My queen, look after the kitchen just one more day. From tomorrow this humble servant of yours . . .'

'Empty words! It's your usual trick.'

'Why did you call me now?' He thought that perhaps she wanted him to wear better clothes, comb his hair or powder himself before going out. But Jameela Bibi said with a great deal of hesitation, coyly and without a trace of annoyance, 'Poovan banana.'

'What poovan banana?' Would these women ever say anything clearly? He asked, 'What are you saying?'

'Poovan bananas! Would you buy me two?'

'Havoo! It's poovan bananas you want, is it? Greedy for them, are you? I'll certainly bring them. They're there in the shop by the riverside. If not, I shall take the ferry boat, cross over and get them from the small bazaar two furlongs away from the other bank. I shall get you a whole bunch of poovan bananas.'

'I only want two,' Jameela Bibi said. 'Don't you go loafing around here and there! Come back soon. Don't wait till it's dark. I am afraid to be all alone. Don't forget anything!'

He said, 'No,' and walked along. Listen to these women! Don't go loafing around! Abdul Khader Sahib laughed to himself. All of a sudden he felt a wave of love come over him. Poovan bananas! It was the first thing Jameela had asked of him. God in heaven, what things other women would have demanded of their husbands! Gold, silk, bangles, cars, aeroplanes; even those were easy to get compared to their sillier demands—two strands of the whiskers of a lioness lying in the forest which had just given birth to cubs! And if these were not brought to them, they would get angry and say, 'After all, I just wanted two strands of hair from the lion. Isn't it after all just a big cat? So that's how much you love me!' And straightaway they would begin crying. What could the husband do? There was another type. All they wanted would be a lump of snow from the one side of the peak of Everest which no one had scaled. And if they did not get it, their eyes would fill and they would sob, 'Just one small lump of snow and you couldn't get me that. Why don't you kill me?' What could the husband do? Had Jameela Bibi ever demanded such impossible things of him? No. She had just asked for poovan bananas! Abdul Khader Sahib thought to himself, I must have a bath, perform my ablutions and then go and buy a bunch of poovan bananas. And so he reached the river bank.

The river looked like a saffron-coloured ocean. What strong currents! The trees on either bank which one usually saw leaning into the water were not to be seen. They were submerged. All kinds of things were floating down. The river looked frightening.

Abdul Khader Sahib had a bath. That is to say, he took just one dip. The water was icy cold. He forgot to perform his ablutions. He hastily wiped his head and body dry and walked to the riverside shop. When he went there, he saw kannan bananas, palankodan bananas, padati bananas, in fact, all varieties of the species except the poovan! What was he to do? He got into the ferry boat.

By the time the boat reached mid-river, a strong wind began to blow. With that it suddenly turned dark and the skies became threatening. Somehow the ferryman got the boat across to the opposite bank. Abdul Khader Sahib got out and ran in the direction of the bazaar. By the time he was halfway there, it began to rain. He ran for shelter to the nearest shop. The rain poured down. Slowly the lights came on in the shops. He waited for the rain to stop. There were strong winds also. He did not realize how time passed. He chatted with old companions and acquaintances taking shelter in the shop veranda. Suddenly he realized it was nearing eight! He felt quite upset. Jameela Bibi was all alone and would get frightened. He left the shop he was in and asked for poovan bananas. They were not available anywhere! What should he do? He was thoroughly disappointed. Finally he bought a dozen oranges. Weren't oranges better than bananas? They were more expensive and contained more vitamins. He had the oranges packed in a paper parcel and set out for home. It was dark and it was drizzling. There were no lights anywhere. It looked as if poovan bananas and the rain were in deep conspiracy. Abdul Khader Sahib reached the ferry. There was no one there. He looked into the darkness and called out for the ferryman. He shouted more than ten times. Who was there to hear him? It was to no avail except that his throat became sore with shouting. He made up his mind—come what may, he would swim across. He took off his shirt. He wrapped up the oranges in the towel and put them on his head. He tied the ends of the towel firmly around his chin. He tied his shirt and dhoti into a bundle and put them on top of the oranges. What would she be doing now? He thought to himself, look, Jameela, if I had not married you I could have slept somewhere else tonight. Look at the way male freedom has gone! I am going to jump into the river and swim. God in heaven, you have to save me. Abdul Khader Sahib walked upstream for a furlong. The river was flowing westward. If he walked a furlong towards the east to swim, there was a chance that the current would take him down one furlong to the other bank. Or would he be taken further down?

Abdul Khader Sahib stepped bravely into the river. Suppose he drowned? But would not even that be for the sake of Jameela Bibi? The water came up to his waist. He could not get a foothold. He began swimming with his head above the water. He moved forward, working his hands and feet. But in the darkness with the swift current, which way was forward and which way was backwards? He could not decide. He moved on, mainly on conjecture. He did not know whether he had reached mid-river or whether he was approaching the other bank. His arms and legs began to feel fatigued. Suddenly he caught hold of something. The current was dragging him on forcefully but he would not let go. He gulped down two or three mouthfuls of water. Finally Abdul Khader Sahib realized that he had caught hold of a bamboo cluster. Avoiding the thorns and the sharp twigs he managed to set foot on the other bank. He sat down on the ground shivering; shivering with cold and with fear at what he had escaped. What was the use of sitting there? Abdul Khader Sahib walked through the thorny bushes and bramble. He was totally nude! He had lost his shirt and dhoti. But he had not lost the towel and the oranges as they had been tied round his head. Abdul Khader Sahib broke off the shoot of a tree with tiny branches and used it as a walking stick. He was passing through a banana grove. There was a flash of lightning. He saw his surroundings for a brief moment. He recognized a house and realized where he was. He was a furlong down the river from his house.

He passed the house he had seen and crossed the canal by a rough coconut-palm bridge, tripping and stumbling on the way. A dog barked. Then another. Soon all the dogs in the neighbourhood took up the refrain. He thought to himself, these dogs are barking as if they are the guardians of morality in the world! What could he do? He walked across many paths large and small, crossed many streams and finally reached home. Good God! There was a light there. His dear Jameela had not gone to sleep. Here was a wife who loved her husband! 'Jameela, open the door.' No, he did not say that. He first draped the towel round his waist. He stepped onto the veranda and looked in through the window. Although he was shivering in the cold Abdul Khader Sahib could not help laughing. What a lovely scene!

A lighted lamp stood on the table. There were two big plates near it, covered with two other plates; four or five smaller plates around them, all covered. They contained rice and various curries. The wife sat there waiting for her husband. She held a murderous-looking hacksaw in her hand. She looked tired as she dozed with her head on the table.

He also noticed other things. The front door was

closed and latched from the inside. Even then suppose some thief pushed open the door by force from the outside? So a big table had been dragged up close to the door to form a barricade. As if that was not protection enough, a small stone had been placed on top of the table! Wasn't all this enough?

Abdul Khader Sahib thought to himself, how wise women can be! He was about to wake up Jameela Bibi when he espied another remarkable thing—light flooded the backyard through the open kitchen door! He went to the back to take a closer look. She had forgotten to close the kitchen door while taking so many other safety precautions! Abdul Khader Sahib realized that all the thieves in the world could march in through the kitchen door. He went in. Noiselessly he closed the kitchen door and latched it from inside. He put the stick which was still in his hand in a corner of the kitchen and went into the dressing room. There were small cuts and scratches all over his body. Blood oozed out of some of them. He said to himself, Jameela, look how much blood I have shed for you! He took the tin of fragrant talcum powder which she used and sprinkled it all over his body. Then he put on some clothes and combed his hair. He left the oranges in the dressing room and was about to wake up Jameela Bibi when he remembered that he had not said his evening prayers, neither Maghrib nor Isha. He decided he would finish saying these. He went into the adjoining bathroom, did the ceremonial ablution, came back and said his prayers. He thanked the Almighty God for having saved his life for the sake of Jameela Bibi. He then put the oranges on two plates and placed them on the table. He called out, 'O, queen!'

Jameela Bibi woke up, startled. She opened her eyes with fear, gripping the hacksaw more firmly.

'Please do not hack down this man before you!' said Abdul Khader Sahib. 'This is no thief. The person standing before you is the humble and foolish Abdul Khader!'

'You have come back after loafing all over, have you?' She looked at the front door. 'How did you come in?'

Abdul Khader Sahib said, 'Before this young man all doors open of their own accord and all hearts—'

'Don't be silly! How did you get in?'

He said, 'Through the kitchen!'

She asked, 'You must have opened the latch from outside with a stick. Suppose some thief had seen you doing it? Now they will also enter that way! How can I live with peace of mind in this house now?'

Abdul Khader Sahib retorted, 'You fool, the door was not closed!'

Jameela Bibi said, 'Talk with better manners. I like that—the door was not closed!'

God in heaven, Abdul Khader Sahib thought to himself, is it possible to make a woman admit that she has made a mistake? He asked her, 'Have you said your prayers?'

'Yes, I have,' she said and got up. Then she saw the oranges. Her face reddened. What a fruit to bring! Who could eat the foul things? Jameela Bibi looked at the oranges with eyes that blazed fire, enough to burn them up. But she made no comment.

Abdul Khader Sahib said, 'There are no poovan bananas anywhere.'

Jameela Bibi did not reply. That awful stuff he had

brought! What could she possibly say?

She brought water and both of them washed their hands. They ate.

'The curry is good,' Abdul Khader Sahib said. Actually all the curries tasted bad. There was no salt in some and some were too spicy. But was it proper to find fault with his newly-wedded wife?

She made a happy announcement, 'I am going to sleep!'

He said, 'Eat the oranges before you go to sleep. I could not get poovan bananas anywhere. I swam through the river to bring these oranges.'

She said, 'Don't tell me lies. I don't like oranges. If you have brought them, you can eat them.'

She stood up with her nose in the air, went to the bed and fell on it.

Abdul Khader Sahib peeled the oranges. He filled a plate with the segments. Then he called: 'Jameela . . .'

'I don't want it!'

'You don't want it?' Abdul Khader Sahib thought to himself, I should have given the woman half-a-dozen blows immediately after the wedding ceremony. 'Jameela! Get up and come here now!'

'I'm feeling sleepy.'

'Is that so?' He got up and went to her and said softly, 'Jameela, I've brought these after going through great danger. Look, suppose I had drowned in the river?'

Jameela Bibi continued to lie on the bed and pressed her face into the pillow.

'Jameela!'

Jameela turned her face slightly. 'What I wanted were poovan bananas!'

'There are no poovan bananas anywhere in the village. Tomorrow I shall bring poovan banana saplings from somewhere.'

'Oh, shall I eat them when they grow and bear fruit?'

'Well, eat these oranges. They are full of vitamins.'

'I don't want them.'

'You have to eat them.'

Jameela Bibi sat up in bed. Imperiously, and in typical ladylike fashion, she asked, 'Do you think you can feed them to me by force?'

Right, Abdul Khader Sahib thought to himself, a good idea! He quietly went into the kitchen, picked up the stick which he had brought from the riverside and cut off a small piece from it. He came into the bedroom with it.

Jameela Bibi saw the stick. She looked on indifferently, as if she wanted to defy the whole world.

He said, 'Get up!'

'I refuse to!'

'You refuse?' He went to get the hacksaw.

Jameela Bibi continued to look on indifferently.

'Come,' he called.

'I refuse,' she answered back.

'Is that so?' He gave her two stinging blows on her thigh with the stick. Then he showed her the hacksaw. 'The next weapon is this. A clean cut.'

She got up, her eyes brimming over.

Those tears . . . Abdul Khader Sahib's heart broke when he saw them. What could he say! He was a mere male. How could he be indifferent to a woman's tears? Anyhow, Abdul Khader Sahib decided to harden his heart into a ball of granite for a short while. He said,

'Jameela . . . don't waste your tears! If you want, weep into a jar and collect the tears in it. I'll take a bath in it afterwards. Understand?'

Jameela Bibi asked with a sob in her throat, 'Are you . . . are you . . . going to kill me?'

'I—ahem!' he said. 'I am going to kill you, cut you into pieces and make biriyani out of you!' He caught her by the hand and dragged her to stand in front of the orange segments. 'Pick them up and eat them,' Abdul Khader Sahib ordered.

Jameela Bibi pretended not to hear him. She looked on as if ready once again to defy the world.

'So you won't listen to your husband?' He lifted the stick and gave her six whacks which fell whistling on her posterior.

She picked up one segment and ate it slowly.

'No, eat more of them!' He spoke in a low roar, pointing at the hacksaw. 'Do you see that? It'll get rid of you for good. Eat!'

She started eating the segments rapidly.

He said, 'Remove the seeds and eat them slowly!'

So Jameela Bibi, tears streaming from her eyes, picked up the segments, removed the seeds and started eating them.

Abdul Khader Sahib decided that other unresolved disputes between them should be settled right then. He asked, 'What's my relationship to you?'

She replied, 'Who knows?'

'Look at this hacksaw! What is my relationship to you?'

'Husband.'

He said, 'Do you see this hacksaw? Will you try to

reform me hereafter? Say "no" quickly. See the knife?'

'No.'

He asked, 'What are you eating?'

'Oranges!'

Whack came a blow on her behind.

'See this knife? Say you are eating poovan bananas.'

'Poovan bananas!'

'Do you want a cook? Say "no". Can you see the knife?'

'No.'

'Are you a fashionable woman? See the knife . . .? You are my woman, aren't you?'

'Yes.'

'Can I talk with motor drivers, poets, politicians, and beedi workers? See the knife? Say "I can" . . . repeat it!'

'You can, you can.'

'What are you eating?'

'Poovan bananas.'

'My darling!'

Abdul Khader Sahib dropped the stick and the knife and caught Jameela Bibi in a close embrace and kissed her. There were marks of the beating on her thighs and backside. His heart broke when he felt them.

He asked, 'Was it very painful, my darling?'

She sighed deeply and said, 'N-no!'

III

And so that night passed. The day came. The floods rose and subsided many times in the river. Jameela Bibi gave birth to nine children. Many changes took place in the world. There were two world wars. New ideas took over. Mankind progressed in many directions. Both Abdul

Khader Sahib and Jameela grew very old. Their hair turned grey and they lost their teeth. They became hunched, decrepit, old people who had many grandchildren. Even then they sometimes thought of the old days. Abdul Khader Sahib would laugh and ask Jameela Bibi, 'O queen, once when you wanted poovan bananas, what did I bring you, swimming the river?'

Jameela Bibi would laugh and reply, 'Poovan bananas!'

He would ask, 'What did they look like?'

She would reply, 'Round, like oranges!'

'Ha—ha—ha,' he would laugh and ask again, 'what did I bring?'

She would say again, 'Poovan bananas!'

Translated from the Malayalam by V. Abdulla

The Cock-fight

AMIN KAMIL

The moment Shahmal spied Ghulam Khan entering the compound with the bird in his hands, she was up on her feet. She even forgot to wash her *pheran* which had been soiled by her six-month-old baby. She felt as if she had found a treasure and cried to her husband instantly, 'So you have brought it! I was apprehensive that you would come empty-handed even today.'

She almost snatched the cock from her husband's hands and began to stroke its feathers and comb. 'Four-and-a-half rupees I paid for it,' Ghulam Khan stressed the word 'rupees', as though to convince Shahmal that the cock was not a poor weakling.

Shahmal did not seem interested in the price he had paid; she had an eye only for the rooster, and joy bubbled within her at the sight of it. She placed it on the ground and cast a glance at the window of the adjacent house, raising and arching her brows. Then she addressed her husband again in a slightly louder tone, 'This is the type of cock I was looking for. Of course the markets are flooded day and night with scavenger cocks, which the whole neighbourhood has bought.'

Ghulam Khan made no comment and walked off indoors.

The cock's legs were tied together with a bit of string and he hopped about with difficulty. He pecked at the string that bound him, throwing glances upwards as if to size up his surroundings.

Shahmal already owned two hens. They were, in the meantime, burrowing for food in the heap of refuse in the compound. When the rooster's crow fell on their ears, they stood stunned and looked at him suspiciously; or were they trying to evaluate the demeanour and nature of this newcomer? One of the hens moved towards him swaying her body gracefully, in a seemingly disinterested manner, as if strolling about just for her own pleasure. The other hen, who was all the while clawing at the heap of refuse, raised a cloud of dust around her and bathed herself in it. 'Ugh! I thought it was someone worthwhile. What is it to me? Let him be, whoever he is!'

Shahmal fetched a handful of rice and sprinkled it before the cock. He fell upon it hungrily and went on stuffing his crop with huge mouthfuls as if he had been starving for days.

When the hens saw this special favour done to the cock, they ran and pecked hastily at the scattered rice grains.

Shahmal cast another glance towards the window of the adjacent house. Seeing no one there, she shouted loudly at the hens, 'Shoo, shoo! A plague on you! The poor hungry fellow! You won't let him feed in peace. One would think you had had nothing to eat for days!'

The hens ran away, clucking loudly. They knew for whom Shahmal's reproof was intended. Why, otherwise, would they have run for their lives? But, at a safe distance, they still pecked nervously at the stray grains of rice scattered around the cock.

'Congratulations!' Jani the Skinny leaned out of her window and called to Shahmal. 'When did this cock come?'

Shahmal had been waiting for this call ever since the rooster was brought, and the instant it came, she struck up an attitude, lifted up her head, smoothed out the imaginary creases in her *pheran* and, flourishing her silver earrings, said, 'My husband has just bought it. Four-and-a-half rupees he paid for it.' Shahmal stressed the word 'rupees' more than her husband had done a short while back.

'Must be from the countryside,' Jani the Skinny expressed her opinion quite innocently. 'Yes, so it seems. A good cock.'

'And just imagine, it is only seven months old,' Shahmal fixed the age of the cock arbitrarily. 'It is of a special breed, not usually brought to the town. And so expensive! Who would buy them?' After a pause she added in contemptuous tone, 'People here would want only those scavenger cockerels!'

This remark set Jani's heart on fire. She knew that she herself was the target of these contemptuous words. Flushing scarlet, she moved away from the window, crying, 'I have something on the frying pan. You feed him as best you can.'

Shahmal chuckled at the empty window and scolded the hens with pursed lips, 'Shoo! Shoo! May a blight fall upon you!' Again she turned towards the rooster with pride and joy.

The truth was that Shahmal had wanted this cock out of spite for Jani the Skinny. While Jani had five hens and one cock, Shahmal had only two hens. She had had three in fact, but one had died of sickness along with her five chicks.

Jani the Skinny's cock would hop up from its compound to the wall which separated the two houses and from there it would hop down to Shahmal's compound. Having no male bird of her own, she welcomed these visits as providential, but disliked them intensely when she left the paddy or corn to dry in the sun. He would cling to her courtyard like a parasite. No amount of chasing could restrain him from coming back to eat and scatter the corn. Shahmal was afraid to leave anything to dry in the sun. When at last her patience was exhausted, her pent-up wrath burst out and she released a volley of abuse on the cock. Jani the Skinny heard her and, leaning out of her window, retorted mockingly, 'You should buy a cock of your own, do you hear? You welcome him on certain occasions, do you not? Yet the loss of a few grains of rice pinches you.'

Shahmal was cut to the quick by this remark. From that very moment, she was after her husband to get a cock. Jani the Skinny also took all possible care not to let her cock reach the other side of the wall.

Ghulam Khan evaded his wife for about a fortnight with one excuse or another; but it was impossible to put her off any longer. He had to buy the cock from a dealer in Maisuma Bazar for three rupees, though he added a rupee and a half to its actual price to impress his wife, so that she might not say in her characteristic tone, 'Ugh, what a stinking cock you have bought! Were there no better ones to be had anywhere?'

Jani the Skinny's cock was red, dotted with black here and there; Shahmal's new one was snowy white and dazzlingly fair. His gait also was more impressive than that of Jani the Skinny's rooster. But the latter looked stronger with his sturdy limbs. This was the only distinction; otherwise they were both of the same breed and almost the same price.

Night fell. Everyone went to bed. Shahmal propped up her elbow on the pillow and resting her cheek on the palm of her hand, the baby at her breast, thought of the new cock. 'How the sight of the cock must have set the Skinny's heart on fire! Can I ever forget her pointed, poisoned words? Let her cock just venture towards this side of the wall. If I don't break his leg, don't call me Shahmal!'

With this decision, she chanced to look at her husband's face. He seemed indescribably handsome and a flush came to her face. She slid her elbow away and was laying her head on the pillow when there was a sudden crowing from the pen. 'Cock-a-doodle-doo . . . !' Shahmal was stunned. She raised her head and listened intently, thinking that perhaps it was her fancy playing tricks on her. But there was another unmistakable crowing: 'Cock-a-doodle-doo . . . !' And Shahmal felt as if her neck had been twisted and broken. She sat up in bed and cried, 'Oh, listen! Do you hear? Do get up and see.'

'Why, what's happened?' Ghulam Khan woke up with a start. 'Did you call me?'

'Didn't you hear? The cock. He is crowing now. At

the fall of the night!' Shahmal's voice was a wail. 'What a creature of ill-omen to bring home!'

'Crowing?' Ghulam Khan puckered up his face. 'What then? Are we to wake up for the Ramadan fast that the timing might delude us?'

'See what nonsense he talks!' Shahmal retorted angrily. 'Get up quickly and kill him. Don't you know that a cock who crows at the fall of the night should be killed immediately? It is a creature of ill-omen.'

'Oh, bother the ill-omen! Go to sleep and forget those old wives' tales,' and Ghulam Khan pulled the quilt over his head and ears. Shahmal persisted for some time but she could not persuade him to utter another word. He fell into a deep, undisturbed sleep and woke up at seven in the morning as usual.

Shahmal was not so worried by the cock's crowing as by the fact that Jani the Skinny had heard it. It would certainly stir her sharp tongue into action. Her sarcastic remarks would bore holes into Shahmal's skin: 'Was this why you were saying that you wanted such an excellent cock? Cocks all over the world announce the arrival of dawn and light, but look at this ill-omened wretch; how Satan enters his nose soon after dusk!'

Shahmal did not go out to the compound after opening the door of the pen for fear of Jani the Skinny. This was very hard on her because she had hoped to answer Jani the Skinny's spiteful words by more spiteful remarks addressed, as it were, to the walls and windows but obliquely meant for the next-door neighbour.

Shahmal was crushed and stayed indoors while the hens frisked about the compound with the cock. She felt her heart turn upside down with aversion at the sight of the cock. And the cock, unaware of all this, stretched his wings and danced round the hens one by one, fanning them politely. But the hens fled away as if saying, 'What's happened to you? Is it proper? You don't seem to look about you.'

Then they looked towards the door of the kitchen wondering, 'Why is she nowhere to be seen today? Wish she would throw us some grains to peck at!' They ran towards the kitchen. The cock read their thoughts and followed them.

Shahmal's glance chanced to fall on his legs. They seemed to her, from the claws to the top, the two ugliest cock legs she had ever seen. Her repugnance deepened. But she dared not shoo the hens away because she did not want Jani the Skinny to show herself at the window at her words. She quickly took out a handful of rice and threw it to the birds from a distance. She would not have thrown any to the cock, but what could she do to the hens? The poor things could not be starved for the whole day.

When Jani the Skinny's cock heard the unfamiliar crowing from the other side of the wall, he stiffened his neck and stretched his chest; his body became tense, all his nerves taut. 'Koota-katak-kootak,' he crowed at the top of his voice as if calling out to the other compound.

'Koota-koot-koot-kootak,' Shahmal's cock also stiffened his neck, as if in answer. 'I am the fair one. I wish you would come here and see for yourself. Why do you show me your fist from the other side?'

Shahmal did not like this noise. She wished the cock would choke and be stricken dumb, so that Jani the Skinny would not hear him and be glued to the window.

Instead of shooing him away, she picked up a lump of earth and threw it angrily at the cock, aiming at his head. It missed him, but he was startled and started crowing loudly and Jani the Skinny leaned out of her window, 'Why are you angry so early in the morning? What has the poor thing done?' she asked.

Shahmal felt like a thief caught in the act of stealing. All her body exuded sweat. The careful steps she had taken to avoid this encounter were of no avail. Jani the Skinny's words confirmed her suspicion that the woman had heard that cock crow at nightfall and her words were disguised mockery. She mustered up courage and said, 'Why should I be angry? He doesn't let the poor hens come near the grain. That's why I scared him away.'

'Newly come he is, that's why. Just wait and see him feeding them himself from tomorrow,' laughed Jani the Skinny.

'Yes, but that would be true only if we had to keep the bird. He has been brought for meat.' Shahmal felt she should not leave Jani a chance to taunt her afterwards. 'We would have killed the bird yesterday itself. But we decided to wait till the morning.'

'But why? Why will you kill him?' Jani perhaps thought that if they kept him, her own cock would be left alone. 'See how handsome he is! And his voice too is impressive.'

Shahmal turned. She has heard it after all, why else would she praise his voice? But she preferred to ignore the jibe in her reply.

'Oh, you think I would care to keep these filthy, stinking cockerels which literally flood the markets? We cannot find the breed we want. But someone has promised to get it for us.'

Jani the Skinny could make nothing of those words. She wondered at Shahmal's new coldness. Hadn't she been praising the rooster to the skies? But then perhaps Shahmal's words were meant for her—that she was keeping a scavenger cock. She was about to make a sharp retort when Shahmal walked off indoors. Jani had to swallow her anger.

Blowing into the samovar Shahmal was still deep in thought about the problem created by the cock. She would make her husband kill him; and if he did not agree, she would have the bird killed by Samad the slaughterer. 'Let me see how he protests when the dish is brought before him at dinner.'

When Ghulam Khan came home from the mosque, Shahmal poured him a cup of tea and spoke sternly. 'Drink up your tea and then get rid of the cock. What will the neighbours say? Don't we have to live amongst them?'

'What have the neighbours got to do with it?' demanded Ghulam Khan, munching a piece of bread. 'It's not the month of Ramadan that confusion would arise about the dawn.'

'Hunh! You only know how to talk and argue!' She added after a while, 'If you don't want to, don't. I myself shall have him killed by Samad, the slaughterer. Do you think that I'll fatten this monster of ill-omen?'

'Do as you like,' Ghulam Khan ended the discussion. 'Only don't ask me to buy a cock again.'

'I won't. As if there were a famine of cocks in town!' Shahmal blew fiercely into the samovar. 'And then, Jani the Skinny's poor cock hangs about the courtyard the whole day; what do we need another cock for?'

Shahmal wanted to be rid of the cock by any means. She was filled with a profound disgust for him. She saw Jani's white teeth grinning at her. The flutter of the cock's wings sounded like Jani's chuckle to her ears. He seemed to her to be the sole cause of all her shame and humiliation.

As soon as Ghulam Khan left for work, Shahmal went to Samad to see whether he was in. He lived two or three houses away; and killing the cocks of the neighbourhood was his speciality. There were others too who knew the craft but his reputation for the expert slaughter of fowl had somehow been established.

Samad was at home. He saw her from his window and, guessing her business, said, 'Go and bring him here. I'll kill him right now. But remember, I'll come to you for dinner. Don't imagine that only the two of you will share the feast!'

'You are welcome,' said Shahmal.

She came back home with a light heart, a smile on her lips. She was happy that she could now hold her head high; no longer would she have to listen to Jani's piercing taunts day in and day out. But a strange sight met her eyes when she stepped into her compound. The hens had retreated to a corner. Jani's cock and her own were struggling desperately with each other, raising clouds of dust around them. Jani the Skinny was enjoying the cock-fight from her window. Shahmal discerned a flush of joy on her face. She was apparently sure of her cock's victory, perhaps because his comb was smaller but thicker, his wattle clung to his throat, and his sturdy limbs made him look a thorough fighter. He had trounced all the other cocks of the neighbourhood in fight.

The colour drained from Shahmal's face and her heart beat violently. The feathers on the cocks' necks stood erect in perfect circles. Their heads trembled and shook with rage. This shaking seemed to have electrified their feathers. Their bodies seemed elongated and the tail-feathers swollen. They glowered at each other and stretching their trembling necks, transmitted messages of fire and rage. Recklessly they attacked each other, pecking and tearing sharply with their beaks.

When Jani the Skinny saw Shahmal entering the courtyard, she sat confidently and conspicuously on her window sill.

'What chance does my weakling of a cock stand against your four-and-a-half-rupee rooster? But who can prevent an ass from running risks? Will he have a sense of shame?' Reducing her sarcasm, she added, 'But let me warn you. He will chase your cock away. As a matter of fact, he has already trounced all the other cocks in the neighbourhood.'

Shahmal's heart sank. But what could she say? She was stunned by the course events had taken. The suspicion rose in her mind that the Skinny had deliberately sent her cock to her compound. She was filled with an overwhelming desire to rise and strangle Jani's cock. But she repressed it and started to defend her position before she could be mocked.

'The foreign cock chasing the native cock away! Don't you know the old saying? Besides, mine is not the one for fights. He is of a different breed, you know. That's why he is so expensive.'

The cocks raised hell, struggling furiously. They plucked each other's feathers till blood streamed forth.

Jani the Skinny gripped the window sill tightly and her head jerked, her face grew flushed with every movement of the cocks.

Shahmal too was taut with suspense. She was also devastated, sunk in misery at what was happening. The sight of Jani's cock inspired such horror in her that she abused him under her breath, 'May your beak fall in pieces! May your legs be stricken with palsy!'

Blood did not show so much on Jani's cock because of his red and black colouring. But Shahmal's spotlessly white cock seemed bathed in blood. Seeing this, she could no longer restrain herself and burst out, 'May all calamities fall on the wretch! May palsy strike his sharp beak!'

'Take care, Shahmal, don't go too far,' said Jani the Skinny, pretending to smile. 'Just watch when one makes the other run for his life. What did you expect?' she added mockingly, 'Stinking cockerels are not as cheap as all that.'

Shahmal was in utter desperation. All sorts of misfortunes had befallen her one after another since this cock arrived. She would have answered Jani back in the same bitter tone, which the latter wouldn't have gulped down, because she was not a whit less talented than Shahmal in her power of sharp retort. This would have led on to a sharp exchange of abuse, a battle of tongues, had not one of the cocks all of a sudden run in flight. It was Jani the Skinny's cock, and Shahmal's cock started chasing it round and round the compound.

Shahmal saw that Jani the Skinny was dripping with sweat and her face was the colour of the sooty side of a pan. But she also saw that Jani pretended that she was not in the least interested in the outcome of the fight.

'Are you going to kill this cock?' said Jani, propping her chin up on her hand. 'Will you listen, and not slaughter him?'

'Did you take my word seriously?' said Shahmal, flourishing her silver earrings with a jerk of the head. 'A cock of mine may have a thousand vices, he may even crow at the fall of the night, these are of no account in my eyes if he has the proper fighting mettle. This was the type of cock I wanted. Otherwise, is not the market flooded with innumerable, stinking, scavenger cocks?'

Translated from the Kashmiri by Neerja Maitra

The Big Silver Rupee

Gangadhar Gadgil

'Here is something for you, son,' said my father. My palm opened automatically when he said that. My father was in a very cheerful mood because one of his clients had given him a thick wad of currency notes.

That something was so heavy that my palm was weighed down. Had I not been alert and clutched it firmly in my hand, that something would have slipped to the floor and rolled away under the table or a chair.

I lifted my palm and opened it. I couldn't believe my eyes when I saw what was in it. Why, it was one whole big shining silver rupee. Rupees are a dime a dozen these days, and they are generously given to kids in tens or even twenties by their doting parents. Things were, however, very different when we were kids. A rupee was pretty hard to come by in those days, when salaries could be as low as twenty-five or thirty rupees a month. Moreover, fathers in those days were not the pliable lumps of clay that they are now. They were stern, unbending and grim. They never made the mistake of pampering their children for fear of spoiling them and as far as possible avoided giving them any money so that they would not get into the bad habit of spending it.

I have only to cite the instance of my friend Sadu who had the temerity to ask for one nickel anna (sixteen annas made a rupee in those days) from Tatya, his father.

Tatya stared at Sadu and cried, 'You are a small boy, no bigger than a man's thumb, and yet you have the temerity to ask for money? What on earth do you want it for? You get food to eat twice a day and you have clothes on your back. What else does a boy need? In any case, if you need anything, ask for it. If it is something that a boy must get, I will bring it for you. But I will certainly not give money in your hands. If boys can lay hands on money, they get into bad habits. They buy halwa and other sweets at will and they are even tempted to place bets on playing cards at street corners. That, my boy, is the beginning of a short and quick journey to penury.'

Sadu pleaded. 'But, please listen to me, Tatya!'

That threw Tatya into a rage. He shouted, 'You are talking back, are you? Do you know what I will do? I will break your leg to teach you to behave yourself.'

Sadu was a sensible boy with considerable experience in dealing with an angry father. The moment he heard the raised voice of his father, he took to his heels and remained out of Tatya's sight for quite some time.

That little episode will tell you what fathers were like in those old days. They were particularly prone to threaten to break the legs of their errant offspring. If no legs were ever actually broken, the credit must go entirely to us clever boys, who could sense danger well in advance and had strong and nimble pairs of heels to get away from it pretty fast.

My father was an exception to this general run of parents. He used to give me a nickel anna every day so that I could buy some snacks and sweets in the midday break at school. Sometimes, when he did not have change, he even gave me a two-anna coin. All the boys in my class envied me for having a father like that. Their parents, however, would shake their heads and mutter about the dire consequences of such misplaced generosity. These feelings of theirs were promptly conveyed to my father by my mother, grandmother and others in our household. But luckily my father just tossed his head, guffawed and continued to give me one anna every day. I must mention, if I am to be truthful, that there were some other fathers too who used to give a copper paisa or two to their sons.

However, even my father had not until then gone so far as to gave me one whole big shining silver rupee. That really would have been much too much. A rupee was a very substantial sum of money in those days. If my mother went shopping with a rupee tucked in the fold of her sari, she could buy a bagful of groceries and sweets and still have a few copper paise left in her hands. Why, the whole family could go to the ferry wharf in a horse-drawn victoria for less than a rupee. We did that every year when we went to our village in Konkan in the summer vacation. No wonder I was taken aback when my father put such a huge amount of money in my palm. In fact, I felt quite certain that he had made an error. I did not want to be blamed for not pointing it out to him. So I said to my father, 'Father, what you have given me is a whole big rupee.'

'Is that so?' said my father with a great show of surprise and laughed loudly. Being a shrewd boy, I immediately made out that my father really meant to give me a rupee. I was so overjoyed that I ran all over the house, leaping around with raised hands. That was not enough to express my jubilation, so I cried, 'Victory to Mahatma Gandhi! Victory to the great king Shivaji!'

You may wonder why on earth Mahatma Gandhi and the great Shivaji came into the picture. Well! Those were the days of Gandhiji's Non-Cooperation movement. People organized big processions and marched through the streets shouting slogans. The most popular slogan was 'Victory to Mahatma Gandhi!' We would walk out of our classes at school and shout 'Victory to Mahatma Gandhi!' whenever a call was given to organize a general strike. We looked forward to such calls because they meant extra holidays. No wonder we had become great patriots and shouted 'Victory to Mahatma Gandhi!' whenever we wanted to express jubilation.

However as I soon learnt it was unwise to run around shouting slogans in the house. Mother immediately came to know that Father had given me a rupee. She expressed her strong disapproval to Father and wanted to confiscate the rupee right away.

She cried, 'Hand over the rupee to me, will you? I will keep it for you safely in the steel almirah.'

I knew from bitter experience that whenever I gave money to my mother for safekeeping, I never saw it again.

So I shook my head and said, 'No! I shall not give my rupee to you. Once you take it, you never give it back to me.'

My mother said, 'Your money is all there sitting safely in my box. It is yours and it will be spent for you.

What I plan to do is to buy a gold ring for you when there is enough money.'

I did want a gold ring to wear on my finger during wedding ceremonies. So I was half-inclined to give the rupee to mother. But alarm bells began to ring in my ears and I pushed away her extended hand. I took as stubborn a stance as I could and said, 'No. I don't want a gold ring.'

'In that case, I will buy you a silver tumbler in which you can drink your milk,' said my mother with sweet persuasiveness.

It is almost routinely impressed on the mind of every Indian boy and girl that the best thing in the world is to own silver and gold. I was no exception. But I had discovered that one had to sacrifice far too many good things one craved in order to get a gold or silver trinket in some distant future. Over the years, I had been convinced that it made no sense to deny one's self so many things. So I took an even more stubborn stance and said, 'I don't want gold and I don't want silver.'

'What then do you propose to do with one whole rupee?' asked Mother.

'Well! I will buy sweets, eat bhelpuri and even buy chocolates which the white sahibs eat!'

'Death be on you, you brat,' shrieked my mother. 'Do you propose to eat one whole rupee's worth of bhelpuri and sweets and such other things? Your stomach will burst if you do anything so foolish.'

I said defiantly, 'Well! If my stomach is going to burst, let it burst. It is my stomach, isn't it? Don't you worry about it. I will stick it together with gum.'

'Never in my life have I seen a boy as perverse and

wrong-headed and nasty as you,' cried my mother in disgust.

'All right! Let good boys give their rupees to their mothers for safe keeping. I prefer to be perverse, wrong-headed and nasty. What do you have to say about that?' I said with a real nasty smirk. In fact I gave my lip a wicked twist and narrowed my eyes in a devilish manner to show my mother how terribly nasty I could get.

Mother got quite mad. I could sense the menace in the air. She advanced towards me and I could see her hands itching to box my ears. I wasn't such a fool as to let her do that. So I ran out of the house and went over to Sadu, my bosom friend who lived in the neighbourhood.

I made sure that his family wasn't around and then beckoned to him in a hushed voice and with loud gestures. I then walked out and stood at the street corner to wait for Sadu. He soon found a suitable opportunity to slip out of the house and join me there.

Sadu looked at me and said, 'Why? You seem to be mighty pleased with yourself.'

'What makes you think that?' I asked trying to look very innocent and surprised.

'Well! You are walking as stiffly and haughtily as a wrestler who has won a bout.'

I looked at Sadu with disdain and said nothing.

'And why on earth are you leaning so much to your left and clutching your pocket on the same side?'

'What else do you expect me to do? Do you know how heavy a whole big silver rupee is? It is not easy to carry a rupee in one's pocket without supporting it with one's hand. Why, the pocket may get torn,' I explained with even greater disdain.

Sadu's eyes became so big that they almost started out of their sockets. He cried, 'Did I hear you right? A whole silver rupee, did you say? I guess your mother needs some medicine very urgently and has sent you to buy it as there is nobody else around.'

'Nonsense!' I cried. 'Do mothers ever give a rupee to any of their children? A copper paisa or two or a nickel anna is the most they are prepared to trust a boy with. Why, if my mother gives me a small four-anna silver coin to buy something for her, she admonishes me umpteen times not to lose it. Would she ever give me a rupee to buy something for her?'

Sadu nodded assent because that was his experience too. He asked, 'Who was it then that gave it to you?'

'My father gave it to me,' I said proudly. 'And I can do what I like with it. I must say I have the nicest father a boy can ever have.'

Sadu stared at me. He felt very sore about the injustice of it all. He protested angrily. 'This is as unfair as unfair can be. I go to the temple of Lord Ganapati every day. I devoutly walk around the idol of Ganapati not less than five times and beseech him to put Tatya in a generous frame of mind. Yet Ganapati does not put a drop of generosity in Tatya's mind, while he pours a bucketful of it in your father's mind. It is not fair.'

Sadu certainly had excellent reason to feel sore. But there was nothing that I could do about it. In any case, I was too eager to talk and make plans about my rupee. So I said, 'Sadu, don't you want to see my rupee? It has Emperor George V on it.'

Sadu asked, 'Did you test it by dropping it on a

stone? The rupees of this emperor are sometimes fake. Tatya had got one such fake rupee, when he went to the market. It was quite some job to pass it on to somebody else. The rupees of Queen Victoria are, however, always genuine.'

My face fell, I had never imagined that a big bearded emperor like George V could be a cheat. It would have been a terrible disappointment and humiliation if my precious rupee had turned out to be fake. I said in a tearful voice to Sadu, 'No, I didn't test it. Shall we do so right away?'

I took the rupee out of my pocket so hastily that it fell out of my hand and dropped on the footpath, which was paved with stone. It rang loud and true, and went rolling straight towards the stormwater drain. If Sadu hadn't been around, that rupee would have fallen into the drain and I wouldn't have seen it ever again. But Sadu pounced on it and grabbed it just on the brink of the drain. He then slapped me on my cheek and said, 'You fool!'

I deserved the slap. I even deserved to be punched on my back with a clenched fist. I wiped the rupee clean with the loose end of my shirt and said to Sadu, 'Well! Now you better do the testing.'

'Idiot!' Sadu cried. 'Didn't you hear it ring true when it dropped on the pavement? There is no need to test it again. In any case rupees are too precious to be tested on the pavements of streets.'

'It did ring true, didn't it? Are you absolutely sure?' I asked anxiously.

'Yes, yes. I am absolutely sure. And you are not supposed to discuss your rupee loudly in the middle of a busy street. What do you think will happen if thieves overhear us? They would certainly steal it from us. Don't you know that thieves always roam around in the streets looking for things to steal?'

That scared me out of my wits. I hastily pushed my hand into my pocket and clutched the rupee firmly in my palm. I then walked on in constant dread of a thief pouncing on me.

No wonder I jumped high in the air with a scream when somebody clutched my shoulder. Luckily it wasn't a strong burly thief who did that. It was one of the residents of our neighbourhood. He eyed me suspiciously and asked, 'Aren't you the son of Gopalrao, the lawyer?'

I smelled what was coming. So I said sheepishly, 'Yes, I am.'

'Why are you playing about with money on the street? Don't you know that good boys aren't supposed to do that? I saw that you were playing around with a silver rupee? How come you have so much money with you?'

In those days all the parents in our neighbourhood had some kind of a secret pact. They kept a sharp eye not only on their own children but all the children in the neighbourhood, and any parent could scold any child found doing anything wrong. The parents of children scolded thus did not protest but warmly thanked those who had scolded their offspring. In fact they were told, 'Do not hesitate to give the boy a stinging slap if you find him doing anything wrong.'

I was therefore quite scared when that man shot all these questions at me. In fact, I feared that he might go so far as to confiscate the rupee and hand it over to my father.

I mustered up all my courage and said, 'My father gave me the rupee. You can ask him if you like.'

'I will certainly do that,' said the man, fixing me with a stare. He added, 'I will also tell your father that it is not advisable to give so much money to small boys.'

I felt relieved when he stopped at that. I knew of course that my mother would soon come to know about me playing with a rupee in the street. What she would do thereafter was unlikely to be pleasant. I sighed and braced myself for the things to come. Yet I was quite happy that the rupee was still there, sitting in my pocket.

Life was pretty hard for us boys in those days of unionized parents. Things, however, have greatly changed since then. Now people say nothing even if they see their neighbour's son smoking cigarettes or drinking liquor.

When the neighbour walked away, Sadu caught hold of my arm and punched me on my head. He cried, 'I haven't yet seen a bigger ass than you. If you carry on like this, soon somebody will go and tell tales about us to Tatya. Thereafter as soon as Tatya sets his eyes on me, he will give me a thrashing.'

I could see that Sadu's Tatya was not only prone to break the legs of young boys but also to thrash them. That scared me quite a bit. At the same time I developed a greater respect for Sadu who could live with a father like that.

I told Sadu, 'You can tell Tatya that it was I who was dropping rupees on the pavement.'

'I certainly would do that. But that would not do me any good. Our Tatya administers a resounding slap to begin with and then asks questions,' said Sadu with admirable calm.

I, however, squirmed with fright and asked, 'In that case what is the way out?'

'Well! In any case I am likely to be thrashed. So I may as well make the best of a bad bargain by joining you in eating all the snacks and sweets that the rupee can buy,' said Sadu with fortitude, resignation and down-to-earth good sense.

I cast an admiring glance at Sadu and said, 'I can see some chewy sweets in the grocer's shop across the street. Let us go and buy some.'

Sadu once again thumped me on the head. He said, 'You are really an ass if ever there was one. We don't know that grocer, do we? Supposing he takes the rupee and does not return the change, what will you do?'

'How dare he do that? If we give him a rupee to buy the sweets, he jolly well has to return the change,' I said in righteous indignation.

'Supposing he says that we never gave him the rupee, what will you do?'

'What do you mean, what I will do? I will scream at the top of my voice and tell all the people around there, that the grocer is a big cheat and a crook.' My righteous indignation had now reached boiling point.

'Well, you can certainly scream as much as you like. But will the people believe that a mere boy had a whole rupee of his own? Or will they believe the grocer?' asked Sadu looking straight into my eyes.

My jaw dropped and stayed dropped for a very, very long time. I was flabbergasted by the enormity of the dirty tricks that people play on simpletons like me. I gazed at Sadu with growing admiration. Here was a boy, I said to myself, who would be able to outsmart all the crafty grocers and cunning thieves in the world. I was glad that he was around to take good care of me and my rupee.

My eyes still glittered with admiration when I said, 'Really Sadu, I do not know what I could have done without you. But for your smart thinking, my rupee was as good as lost! Well, I now know what to do. We shall go to Nana Mehendale's shop and buy sweets there. He is the grocer who supplies your family and mine. He certainly will not cheat us out of our rupee.'

Sadu bent low and bowed to me with feigned reverence. I was not such a fool as not to realize that Sadu was indulging in biting sarcasm. I asked, 'Now what have I done wrong?'

'Well!' he said, 'Nana Mehendale will certainly not cheat us, but he will certainly tell Tatya that he saw me with you and that we were squandering money on sweets.'

'Oh God! I hadn't thought of that. But what then shall we do?' I asked.

As far as I could see, we were in a nice pickle. We couldn't buy sweets from a grocer we did not know, nor could we buy them from a grocer whom we knew quite well. Having a rupee to spend seemed to create far more problems than I could imagine.

But luckily Sadu was with me and he could find a way out of any pickle. He pondered over the problem for a while and said, 'Here is what we will do. We will go to Nana Mehendale's shop and tell him that your mother is suffering from a stomach ache and she asked you to buy for her a copper paisa worth of ginger and another paisa worth of *ova*.'

'Let us go,' I said. But, a little later, I stopped and

asked, 'But wouldn't Nana Mehendale ask my mother how her stomach ache is when he runs into her next? Wouldn't that expose me?'

Sadu was very philosophical about it. He said, 'It doesn't matter a fat lot if you are exposed. After all your father doesn't slap you if he is annoyed with you. Your mother of course would do that. But mothers' slaps and punches don't hurt.'

I couldn't quite see eye to eye with Sadu on that matter. My mother too could administer a stinging slap. Moreover, sometimes when she really lost her temper she came at us children with a big iron ladle or anything else that came to hand in the kitchen. But I was keen to start spending that rupee. I therefore allowed myself to be propelled into Nana Mehendale's shop.

I stood dumb for a while there because I had forgotten what I had to say. But Sadu said, 'Don't you remember what your mother told you?'

At the same time he pinched me without letting anybody see what he was doing. The pinch did the trick and I told the story about my mother's stomach ache.

Nana, the grocer, looked at me suspiciously over the rim of the glasses which as usual had slipped way down his nose. He said, 'Stomach ache? Your mother has it? How come I saw her walking past my shop a few minutes back?'

That rattled me completely. This was something that usually happened to me. In the first place, when it was necessary to lie, I could not think of a good fib. If a fib was suggested to me by a resourceful friend like Sadu, I was immediately found out.

Luckily on this occasion Sadu was with me. He saved

the situation very skillfully. He thumped me on the back and said with a big smile that split his face from ear to ear, 'Silly! It is your grandmother who has a stomach ache, isn't it?'

I looked at Sadu with an utterly vacant expression and exclaimed, 'Grandmother!'

Sadu again pinched me without letting anybody notice it and said, 'Yes, yes. Your grandmother. Don't you remember?'

Once again it was the pinch that did the trick. I nodded my head with great emphasis and said loudly, 'Yes, yes. Of course, my grandmother. She wants a copper paisa worth of ginger and a paisa worth of headache.'

'What?' snapped Nana Mehendale. Sadu gave me a nasty look and then broke out into loud laughter. He explained to Nana, 'His grandmother doesn't certainly want a paisa worth of headache. She wants a paisa worth of *ova*.'

'Yes, yes, of course, a paisa worth of *ova* is what she wants.'

Nana Mehendale eyed me suspiciously while he tied the two things I had asked for into nice bundles. When the bundles were ready, I handed over to him the big silver rupee.

Nana looked at the rupee very suspiciously. He said, 'One whole rupee! In the hands of a boy? To buy two paisa worth of stuff? How on earth did your mother do a thing like that?'

Sadu did not wait for me to answer that question, because he knew that it was beyond me to improvise an answer quickly. He said, 'It was like this, his mother didn't have any small change. So she gave him a rupee and asked me to accompany him to make sure he didn't lose it.'

Nana Mehendale continued to eye us both suspiciously. He said, 'I am wondering whether I should hand over to you this fifteen-and-half annas of small change. I think I will rather hand it over to your father, when he goes past my shop in the evening on his way home.'

My heart sank, because I thought that the game was lost. But Sadu again came to my rescue. He said sweetly, 'But, Nana, his mother has asked us to buy some medicines from a pharmacy down the street. We will therefore need the money.'

Nana eyed us for a while and reluctantly handed over the handful of change to me.

At this juncture Nana's brother interjected, 'It was really not necessary to send any money at all to buy things from our shop. Gopalrao has a running credit account with us.'

This observation could have given rise to further queries and complications. But as soon as the money was handed over to me, I was propelled out of the shop very hurriedly by Sadu. He didn't let me stop until we were quite some distance away from the shop.

I was scared by the way things were turning out. Moreover, the fifteen-and-half annas of change made my pocket bulge conspicuously, and the way the change jingled in my pocket made me even more noticeable. Passers-by looked at me curiously when they heard the jingle of the coins in my pocket.

I said, 'Sadu, all this is more than I can take, I think I will go home, hand over the change to my mother and forget about the rupee.'

Sadu thumped me on my back and said, 'You cry-baby! Is this the time to quit? Why, you have not even chewed a sweet so far.'

That restored my courage. Moreover, I realized that I was getting quite hungry and the very idea of eating an assortment of sweets began to make my mouth water. So I fell in with what Sadu suggested and bought two paise worth of chewy sweets. In fact, I spent one more paisa and bought a handful of another variety of sweets.

We both went to the Ganapati temple, sat on the long cement bench in the yard and ate our sweets with great relish. That whetted my appetite and I said, 'Sadu! Have you ever eaten the chocolates which the white sahibs eat? They are expensive. A small bar of chocolate costs one whole nickel anna. That really is the sort of thing we should buy when we have a rupee to spend.'

Sadu said, 'I have never yet eaten a chocolate in my whole life. What does it look like? What does it taste like?'

I had eaten a chocolate not once but twice. I therefore explained to him as vividly as I could what it looked and tasted like.

Sadu looked all around us with suspicious eyes, he then becokoned me to a far corner of the temple yard and whispered, 'Does that thing called chocolate contain eggs? The trouble with these white sahibs is that they put eggs into everything they eat.'

We both belonged to brahmin households and there would have been hell to pay if we had eaten eggs. I pondered deeply over the matter and whispered back in Sadu's ear, 'I have eaten a chocolate. My father once gave it to me. But I did not find an egg in it. In any case my father wouldn't have given it to me if it had contained eggs.'

When Sadu learnt that my father himself had given me a chocolate to eat, all his fears melted. We looked at each other, nodded in silent agreement and went to an Irani shop to buy a one-anna slab of chocolate.

Sadu looked at it very carefully and removed the silver foil wrapped around it without tearing it. We then carefully broke the slab into two equal parts and ate it slowly so as to relish every bit of it as much as we could.

Sadu seemed to like it immensely. He expressed his deep satisfaction by nodding his head appreciatively several times. He raised both his hands in a gesture of blessing. He said, 'It is awfully tasty. It fills the mouth with its delicious taste and goes into the belly smoothly. These white sahibs may be rotten chaps otherwise, but they certainly know how to make truly delicious sweets.'

I licked the chocolate which had stuck to the corner of my mouth and asked, 'Shouldn't we eat one more?'

Sadu concurred saying, 'You have said exactly what I wanted to say. But is it proper to spend money so recklessly? A slab of chocolate costs no less than one whole nickel anna.'

'I don't care,' I cried, 'I wouldn't be bothered the least bit even it costs two annas a slab. What do you have to say about that?'

Sadu said, 'Well! If it doesn't bother you, why should it bother me? Let us go and get another slab.'

That is exactly what we did. Sadu once again divided the slab into two equal parts. He also carefully saved the silver foil, which he gave me as he had kept the first one for himself. Sadu could be scrupulously fair when he wanted to be.

In the Irani shop I saw in a glass jar tiny cricket bats, which contained little silver pills which were very tasty. That bat costs two whole nickel annas. But I was indeed in a very reckless mood. So I said to Sadu, 'Let us buy this cricket bat. It contains very tasty silver balls.'

'What does it cost?' asked Sadu.

'Two annas.'

Sadu thumped me on my head and pursed his lips in dissapproval. He said, 'Do you mean to say that you propose to spend another two whole annas on this thing? Have you gone crazy? No, I wouldn't let you do that. We shall instead buy lumps of ice bathed in syrup. They cost only one paisa each and one can keep on sucking a lump for a very long time.'

Sadu, it seems, had nothing against being reckless once in a while. But he was stoutly opposed to being recklessly reckless. When I thought over his suggestion, I realized that it was quite sensible. So we purchased two lumps of ice bathed in three syrups of different colours and began to suck them noisily with great gusto and relish.

While we were thus enjoying ourselves, Sadu all of a sudden took to his heels and disappeared into a small lane opening on to that street. I ran after him and caught up with him. I asked him in a whisper, 'What happened? What made you run away like that?'

The brave sagacious Sadu had been transformed into a frightened little boy in tears, 'Tatya, my father, is coming that way. I hope he has not seen me. If he has, I am a goner.'

We both hid behind a big red postbox standing on the pavement. Our hearts were racing pit-a-pat. We stood there for what seemed like hours. At last Sadu's Tatya walked past the lane we were hiding in. We hid behind the postbox until we felt sure that Tatya had gone a long way down that street. Thereafter we emerged from behind the postbox with happy beaming faces. We noticed, however, that a few people around us were eyeing us with suspicion. So we made haste to get out of that lane.

While we were walking in a hurry, Sadu said, 'I think I want no more of this. I had better go home. I get into trouble in the company of boys like you. Left to myself, I would never have polluted myself by eating a chocolate with eggs in it, nor would I have eaten lumps of ice bathed in syrup. It was because of you that I did all these wrong things.'

I was amazed at this complete turnaround. I cried, 'Now, there! It was you, Sadu, who egged me on to do all these naughty things. I, for one, wanted to hand over the rupee to my mother and quit. But you suggested . . .'

'Now there, Gangadhar, I shall not take that from you. Who was it that said that we should buy chocolates?' said Sadu staring right back into my eyes.

'Ha, ha. And who suggested that we buy those two lumps of ice bathed in syrups of three different colours?' I stared back at Sadu and stood my ground.

'And who . . .' said Sadu vehemently.

'But who . . .' I protested indignantly.

So it went on for quite some time until we ran into Mahadu Shinde, one of the boys in our class.

Mahadu was the son of Dagadu, the head peon of our school. He had entered the school rather late and he was about two or three years older than us.

He put his hands on our shoulders. 'What are you gabbing about? You are carrying on so that you don't even notice friends like me when they are passing by.'

I said, 'Tell me Mahadu, how can I take it if Sadu blames me for no reason at all? Why, he says that he is getting spoilt in my company. He says that it is I who make him eat chocolates with eggs in them. He also put the blame on me for making him eat lumps of ice bathed in syrups of three different colours. I must tell you, Mahadu, that it was entirely his idea.'

Mahadu caught hold of the collars of our shirts firmly and cried, 'You two chaps seem to have a lot of money jingling in your pockets. Where did you get it from? Eh? Did you steal it from your mothers' boxes?'

'Nonsense,' I cried. 'We are not thieves. It was my father who gave me one whole big silver rupee. We are having a bit of fun with that money.'

Mahadu gave such a start that he made us jump too. He cried, 'One whole rupee? Oh my mother! If a rupee had come my way, I wouldn't have eaten lumps of ice. I would have gone right away to a big restaurant, and I would have eaten a large dish of spicy minced mutton and bread. I would have washed it down with a glass of bubbly red sweet drink, loaded with ice.'

This talk of eating meat made our stomachs churn quite unpleasantly. Sadu said, 'No Mahadu, we don't eat that kind of stuff.'

'You gutless brahmins,' cried Mahadu. 'All that you eat is rice and insipid stew of potatoes and leaves. Well, it is your rupee. So we won't eat minced mutton. But how about eating a roti or bread dunked in a thick gravy of beans loaded with chillies? Or are you afraid of eating that fiery stuff too?'

I strongly resented this slight. I cried, 'Who is afraid of eating chillies? And who minds spending money in a big restaurant? I am not that kind of a chap, Mahadu. I can spend money like Lord Falkland if it comes to that.'

None of us had any idea who Lord Falkland was. In fact, we were not sure that a such a person existed. But somehow he had come to represent a reckless spender among many other things.

This mention of Lord Falkland greatly cheered up Mahadu. He shouted, 'Well, then what is stopping three Lord Falklands from walking into a restaurant?'

I said, 'I think Sadu is scared of going to a restaurant.'

Sadu protested, 'Who is scared? Not I. It was you who were scared when we were in Nana Mehendale's shop, remember? But for me, you would have returned home like a sissy and hid behind the pallu of your mother's sari. And do you think that I am scared of the beating I will get from Tatya? Let me tell you I have taken not a few of these beatings and I am not scared of taking some more. If it comes to that, I will enter a restaurant with my chest thrust forward even if Tatya sees me. Come on, let us see who is the sissy around here.'

Mahadu clapped his hands and guffawed and entered the restaurant with the air of a Lord Falkland. So did we.

Mahadu then beckoned the waiter with an imperious gesture. 'Wipe the table clean,' he barked, 'and bring three glasses of water with ice.'

He thumped the table to add emphasis to his command.

We were quite taken aback and greatly impressed by the grand style in which Mahadu conducted himself in the restaurant. I wondered whether I would ever be able to emulate him.

Mahadu then asked us with a sweeping gesture. 'What dishes would you like me to order?'

Sadu said hesitantly, 'I will eat a *besan laddu* and *shakkarpare*.'

'What rubbish,' cried Mahadu. 'Nobody shall eat such sweet sissy stuff. Let us eat hot *misal*. It is so hot that it will bring tears to your eyes. Why, you will remember your mother when the first morsel burns your tongue.'

He then placed an order for three special super-hot servings of *misal*. Soon enough three little mountains of *misal* steaming in big plates were placed on our table.

'Oh, my father!' I said. 'Are we to eat these mountains?'

Mahadu broke into a loud guffaw, thumped us on the back and cried, 'You had better finish the plateful if I am to believe all that talk of how brave you brahmins are.'

Confronted with this challenge, both Sadu and I rose to the occasion and fell to digging into that mountain of *misal*. It was certainly hot but not unbearably so. It was also very spicy and tasty. It contained *chivada*, *shev*, *usal*, potatoes, eggplant, groundnuts and onions. On top it had a sprinkling of green *kothmeer* leaves. It was a grand assembly of a dozen things, all tasty in themselves. Our mouths burned, our noses began to run, but we could not resist the *misal*. We finished it all, sipping cold iced water at frequent intervals to quench the fires raging on our tongues.

At last when those mountains of *misal* were fully eaten, our stomachs were about to burst. Sadu burped loudly as one is wont to do at the end of a wedding feast. That made all of us laugh.

Mahadu ordered three rose-coloured drinks, bubbly and sweet. When we had finished eating, they were placed before us in big glasses which had bouquets of white froth at the top. He told us that each of the glasses cost three copper paise. When he said that, I leaned back and smiled recklessly like Lord Falkland.

It was quite an effort to find room for the contents of those big glasses of drinks in our overloaded stomachs. But we bravely managed to do so. I paid the bill under Sadu's knowledgeable supervision and we walked out of the restaurant with our tummies protruding miles ahead of us.

Mahadu said grandly, 'Oh my mother! We must now eat masala paan.'

It was a very appropriate suggestion. It is customary to eat paan enriched with various tasty powders at the end of a feast.

We stopped at the paan stall outside the restaurant and Mahadu straightened the collar of his shirt to place the order for three paans in an appropriately grand manner.

But the order was never placed. For while he was straightening his shirt collar once again, Sadu and I saw Mahadu's father approaching us on the sidewalk. Mahadu did not notice him, but his father certainly noticed Mahadu. Mahadu's father stopped dead in his tracks and stared at us in amazement and disbelief. He then rushed at Mahadu and hit him on the cheek with a big, powerful swipe of his arm. Mahadu was a sturdy boy. But so powerful was the swipe that he collapsed. Even in that predicament, however, he had the presence of mind to understand what had happened and to react swiftly. He rose from the pavement like a ball on rebound and ran. Nothing stopped him. When a victoria stood in his way, he crawled underneath the belly of the horse and went to the other side of the carriage.

Sadu and I stood rooted to the ground. Mahadu's father caught us by our arms and said, 'You boys! You come from good families and yet you misbehave like this. I will report this to the headmaster of the school and ask him to give you such a caning that you will never again even think of such things.'

A crowd had promptly gathered around us, as usually happens in India on such occasions. They all nodded their approval of the scolding being administered to us. Dagadu informed them that we were guilty of squandering money in a restaurant.

You must know that though Dagadu was only a head peon, he had a far more impressive personality than any of our teachers had. The impressiveness was heightened by his uniform, turban and a big moustache. He also carried far more weight and was far more feared in our school than our headmaster. He had been in the school for forty years and had scolded many of our teachers when they were students like us. He was a strict disciplinarian too. We knew therefore that his threat was not an empty one. We quailed at the prospect of going to school the next day.

When Dagadu thought that he had scolded us enough and released our arms, we took to our heels. Sadu ran with such alacrity that he dashed into the ample stomach of a policeman.

The policeman caught us both by our arms and said, 'Now you boys! I have been watching you for sometime. You have been walking around and hiding behind postboxes. What are you up to? I bet it is not anything good. You look like boys from good families. So I will let you go now. But if I ever see you again loitering in the street, I will lock you up at the police station.'

When he let us go, we were shaking all over. When at last I reached home, I heaved a sigh of relief and sank in a quiet corner. No sooner had I done so, than my mother noticed me. She put her hands menacingly on her hips and asked, 'What was it that you told Nana Mehendale when you went to his shop?'

Nana Mehendale had certainly not wasted any time in letting my family know what I had been up to.

I am not too keen to tell you what happened afterwards; I need not tell you why.

All I can say is that we young boys had a pretty hard time in those days. But come to think of it, we also had a lot of fun.

Translated from the Marathi by the author

•

The Mystery

P.B. Bhave

Dinu was very disturbed that day. He was not himself at all. Something in him had risen in a little rebellion against him. The perfume of attars hung thick around him like a cloud. For this had been his main job for the last few days: sprinkling rosewater and scents at the guests and visitors who came for the wedding reception.

'Well, young man,' someone asked, 'your cousin has already done it. How about you?'

'If he managed it at twenty-three, why could you not do it at twenty-one? This is a tropical country, this is India,' another remarked.

And a third one said, 'Well, prince, it is just not enough that this lovely place of yours serves as a wedding pandal for the relatives. It's where your marriage ceremony will eventually take place, we imagine. And what was that you said? "Taking the BA exam this year" . . . no, no, and no. Examination! So what? Even the great men of the past were married, when they were just children in fact. They got through their exams all right, eh!'

M-A-R-R-I-A-G-E . . . Everyone talked to him in the same manner, and gave him the same searching looks. It was as if Vasant, the new bridegroom, had already been bundled out and all were now anxiously waiting for Dinu's turn to face the music. He had attracted a lot of attention from the parents of a number of eligible young girls, when he moved about smartly as man-in-waiting. In fact, the bridegroom himself was of no consequence at all. The visitors had already taken a careful look at the palatial bungalow and the beautiful limousine of the young man's father, and the fact that Dinu was just a young college student reading for his BA exam made hardly any difference. Wrinkled hands were folded before Dinu's father. The high-and-mighty talked in soft and sweet tones, and polite questions were asked: when could the daughter's photograph be sent, when could some precious time be spared, when could the girl be brought along for a meeting? Everyone seemed to be talking about marriage. Not about Vasant, the bridegroom, who was in the wedding pandal, mind you, but about Dinu who was just not ready to think about it for a couple of years or more.

Dinu too felt a certain attraction for the opposite sex, just what a normal young man would ordinarily feel. But he surely had never thought of marriage seriously. For the last three days, however, things had changed. He moved in an atmosphere so surcharged with it, and so many fingers had pointed in the one and only direction, that he gradually became more and more conscious about what was happening. Greatly startled, as if at some mysterious happening, his attention was now focussed in one direction. He began to see there something he had never seen before.

Someone was playing classical music outside on the shehnai, and it had an exquisite charm about it. Luckily, the fellow had not fallen for the temptation to play some cheap film song, and had chosen a real masterpiece. As he lay in his room, Dinu could picture the player. A little cyclonic world of music and emotions was being created, and Dinu was being sucked into the cyclone.

How wonderful were the three days that had gone by! The magic tunes of the shehnai had woven together the delicate world that existed during these three days. The smoke of the incense, the rising flame of the sacred fire, columns of banana trees, the clusters of mango leaves, heaps of flowers, beautiful garments, attractive ornaments, gay faces, precious carpets, and above all the mantras—beautiful and sacred words compact with meaning.

And then there were faces too; of people coming from somewhere and going someplace. Faces that were approaching and vanishing, raised and drooping. But all were smiling and happy. His house had undergone a transformation in the last few days. It was not just a stone-and-mortar building any more, it was turned into a temple of marriage. New hopes were flowering. New expectations and a novel joy were blossoming forth. The whole thing was magical, exceedingly magical. Vasant Patwardhan and Leela Paranjape—where had they come from? They came from far-off places. They had never cast their eyes on each other before in their lives. A couple of months back, they did not even know of each other's existence. And now, the two had come together, for ever, in a lifelong union. They were now going to share each other's lives with their joys and griefs, hopes and disappointments. They had a common future before them, and the lives of these two, who were unknown to each other just a few days back, now merged into a single life. The unknown woman was now to be as near and dear to him as his own parents. Perhaps even more than the parents in a sense. The parents might part company, but not this young girl who was a stranger to him just the day before. Without rhyme or reason, she had become his partner for the rest of his life. By just taking seven steps together in the wedding ceremony, they had become united for seven lives. How wonderful and how mysterious!

The men and women outside laughed loudly. Dinu could imagine what was happening. The ritual bath was going on, and certainly there could be no better occasion for fun and frolic. Vasant was a handsome young man and Leela was a beauty. But the charm that surrounds a couple on the occasion of their wedding has something special about it. Right from the time they entered the pandal, some flame from within had lighted up their bodies, their faces, their whole beings in fact. When they sipped kheer from the same vessel, when he whispered her new name in her ears and wrote it down on the grains of rice with his ring, when they garlanded each other, when she worshipped, and when they took the seven steps together, and then at the time of the ritual bath, his face had brightened up and she too had bloomed. Beautiful was hardly the word for it. It was something ethereal.

The shehnai played some fine melody outside. Occasionally, the music was submerged by loud guffaws, and one could hear the splashing of water. Then the new bride was asked formally to pronounce her husband's name, and when she did, there was an explosion of laughter. The laughing gas was on once again. The thick voices of men, soft voices of women, tinkling sounds of bangles and vessels were in the air. Dinu was trying to snatch some rest after the heavy and strenuous work of attending to the guests. As he lay in his bed in his room, various scenes in the wedding ceremony flashed before his eyes. In that half-awakened and half-asleep state, a number of voices jostled together asking him, 'Well, young man, when does your marriage take place?'

'What's up, eh?' Dinu said and staggered to his feet, looking in the direction of the door for some seconds. Hira was standing there on the doorstep. Hira—the daughter of his father's friend, who had come to attend the wedding festivities. Hira—a young, unmarried girl. She probably had come round to his room for the last two days quite often and intentionally, when he was in there. She had given up participating in the fun that was going on outside, and had come in.

'Will you just get up for a moment, please?' she asked.

'Well, what brings you here?'

'Oh, I'm sorry. My sari is lying there on the bedstand. Would you mind if I just take it away?'

Dinu was up in a flash. Her costly sari, with the border of golden thread, was lying on his bed. The heavy meals and the pressure of ceaseless work had made Dinu pretty drowsy and as soon as the bath-ritual had begun outside he had made his escape into his room. This was what kept happening all these three days. He had come last night to his room, completely fagged out, all ready to go to sleep straightaway, only to find that this girl and another one were already sleeping there on his bed. Perforce, he had had to spend the night outside on a bench and he was lucky that it was not cold out there. Otherwise, he would surely have caught a cold, thanks to these intruders in his room.

He took the sari, and handed it over to her.

'Excuse me please. I never seemed to notice it, you know.'

'Oh, not at all. My mistake in fact.' Her tone was apologetic.

'Well, that's nothing in a crowded place like this,' he said. The delicate damsel then withdrew, her eyes still lingering on the young man.

Dinu looked at her receding figure. He looked at his bed and at the room which appeared to have been completely transformed. It did not look like one belonging to a collegian, but more like a women's dressing room. It was not just the sari that had been lying on the bed. There was a new sari thrown on the back of his chair, and then there was an old one lying on the floor which someone had taken off. There were brassieres, and there were powder tins, combs, hairpins, flowers, and sundry other things. All the essentials for any fashionable young lady. His room had been turned into a godown. Without a word of permission or consent, the girls and women had taken charge of his room. In the bookcase stood Shakespeare and Ruskin, their faces looking small.

Dinu had never been in such close contact with women. And what was that? Women's hair on his table! He was upset, and marching angrily up to the table, he picked them up. They were very soft to the touch. At once, Dinu understood. These were Vimal Joshi's—the golden-haired damsel's. She was one of the bridegroom's party. Though a college student, she was not as bold as the other girl, Hira. She never appeared in his presence on purpose. She was beautiful and modest, her hair long, soft, and golden. And her father, too, had talked with Dinu's father—his hands folded, courtesy incarnate.

Dinu was all excitement. Again the boisterous laughter echoed from outside. His eyes surveyed once again the riot of toilet articles, powder tins, nailpaints and lipsticks, combs, the folded new sari hanging from the back of the chair, the used one that was lying on the floor, and finally they rested on the old lemon-coloured sari with the red border. At the same time, the shehnai unwound a delicate melody outside.

The pandal had become empty and deserted by now. The chairs and carpets had been removed. Dried plantain and betel leaves, petals of flowers, empty cigarette packets lay scattered on the floor. The kids in the house, who had not left yet, were playing with the plantain leaves, from which they made little trumpets. The pandal itself would soon be removed. The drops were being taken out, the strings wound up, and the 'kitson' lamps taken away. The big gathering of people who had assembled for the occasion quickly disappeared. The house that bustled with activity had now regained its original sobriety and calm. But this was unbearable to Dinu now. Ceremony and bustle seemed to him the natural atmosphere of the place.

Hira and her mother, the Joshi couple and their daughter Vimal left that evening by train. Hira's mother talked for quite a while with Dinu's mother in private.

Till the train left, Hira looked searchingly at Dinu. Vimal's father again talked with Dinu's, his hands folded when he did so. Before the train left, Vimal bade goodbye to him, and how much did she blush then? She appeared to have guessed what her father must have talked to Dinu's about.

'Well, goodbye then, and when do you invite us to visit here once again?' Vimal's mother had said, when Dinu had done a namaskar.

'Any time. You are welcome, always,' he replied.

'Well, try and give us the opportunity, young man,' Vimal's father had remarked meaningfully, looking through his glasses.

'The opportunity is there for your asking,' the young man replied.

'Okay then. Don't hesitate afterwards, when the time comes. Your Dad says, everything is up to you to decide,' the Rai Bahadur said, following it up by loud laughter.

'Well, do invite us for your wedding. Won't you?' Hira whispered looking at Vimal.

'And the invitation would be mutual, I suppose,' Dinu replied.

'Oh . . . uh . . .' Hira said coyly. But she actually wanted to add if possible, 'Could it not be so that our wedding parties will be just one? . . .' But there was no time to elaborate on this.

The green signal was on, and the guard whistled with shrill impatience. Back came the long whistle from the engine driver, and the train left. Dinu returned home after listening to the open and veiled hints about his marriage.

The pandal was completely vacant by now, and the

house seemed deserted. Now his room was not occupied by women, nor was any single thing belonging to them left behind. Dinu flung his coat and cap on the bed and reclined in the easy chair. From there, the marriage pedestal with the picture of Lord Ganesha painted on it, the columns of banana trees created for the auspicious occasion, could be seen. He had seen all these things before, but now they seemed to take on a magical appearance. It was a great transformation undoubtedly. Hardly a week before, he was alone. He had moved about alone, lunched and lived all by himself. Now a young woman had appeared from somewhere, and had become part and parcel of his life. One can always understand the love of parents, of brothers and sisters. They are one's blood relations after all, and one has the advantage of living together with them under the same family roof. But how about this love? From where does this fountain of eternal love spring? What magic is this? Vasant was never before acquainted with Leela. His was just a simple marriage in strict, orthodox fashion. There was no question of the couple knowing each other beforehand, nor of friendship before marriage. Even so, Vasant had been greatly distressed when some blighter had stepped on Leela's foot, at the time of the wedding procession. His brow had cleared only when she began to smile. How does this feeling appear? From where does this pure love spring—love that resembles rain falling from a clear blue sky? M-A-R-R-I-A-G-E! How wonderful is the mystery of marriage! A boy is born somewhere and a girl is born at some place else. They do not know about each other's existence at all, but they are born for each other's sake nevertheless. From among countless girls, she is the one that he gets, and she too gets him from among countless young men. This was the way Leela had found Vasant, and Vasant had found her. They were able to unravel the mystery, and find the treasures for themselves. But how about this Hira? Who was the man intended for her by God? And Vimal too! To whom would she belong? If I wish, indeed, I can have her for my wife. But then, I don't want to get married, not now. What is the big hurry after all? No, no, sir, I am not getting married to Vimal, and Hira is just not the girl for me.

Dinu got up from the easy chair and sat on the bed. But he could not bear to sit on the bed. His emotions had blossomed forth in the last few days and his imagination had run riot. Garlands, flowers, saris, toilet sets—none of these were left in his room now. Hira wasn't there and Vimal wasn't there either. His room was completely vacant—deserted. He alone was there, entirely and coldly alone.

He remembered Vimal's long hair, Hira's lingering, unsteady glances. He remembered the yellow sari with the red border that had lain on the floor of his room. And the one question, that the garlands and bouquets, scents and shehnai, and many people had suggested in many ways and had even asked openly, began to echo in his ears. The question he had never seriously thought of so far, the question he had not understood in fact till now. Like a rainbow emerging clearly from the mist, the question confronted him. And its colourful mystery enchanted him, and he was restless.

Who would she be, he thought: she who would worship the marriage-idol for him, whose name he would write with his ring, who would garland him and take his hand in marriage? Well, she must be someone, the one with whom he would spend his whole life. She was going to arrive from somewhere one day, and stand before him. Who could that be? If Hira was not going to be his wife, who then was it to be? She must be there some place, but where was that place? What does she look like, what is her name? Some day, he was going to know all this. She would step into his life and she would be part of all that his life would bring. He would then be able to talk to her; she would not just remain a dream, but would be real. But how could it happen that he knew just nothing about this one person who was going to be his, who was going to give him lifelong company, with whom he would spend the days and nights, beautiful, happy and stormy, of the future?

Could she be Hira after all? Or maybe Vimal? The one who was going to change her name for his, the one among millions who was going to arrive inevitably in his life, who was she? Why should this secret about him be a secret to himself also? She might be proceeding in his direction now, at this moment in fact. Did he not after all have a right to know her?

This was the question. He was going to find out the answer to this question some day, but not now. Dinu was very disturbed and excited. He wanted to shout at the top of his voice for the girl that existed somewhere. He wanted her to come from wherever she was. 'You are going to arrive after all. I shall then be able to look at you to my heart's content. Some day I am going to feel your delicate touch on my body. I feel a great longing for you. I want to know who you are, where you are, and what you look like. How mysterious and wonderful! The partner for the rest of my life—but as yet unknown and unseen. I crave to tear off this curtain of the unknown and discover the mystery behind it. Won't you come? For a moment, at least?'

It was as mysterious as the dawn and the sunset, the morning sun and the stars, but never before had he felt any eagerness or anxiety to probe the mystery. He had just accepted its existence so far; but now he longed to solve the mystery.

His thoughts began spinning around the girl who was going to step into his life some time, though her person was still misty and unidentified. He felt suffocated inside the four walls of the room, eternally watched by the paper ghosts of Shakespeare and Ruskin. It was slowly getting dark, and the exciting mystery became more attractive as it became darker.

In a flash Dinu was out of his room. Swiftly, he walked across to where his bike was kept, leaning against the garage wall. He put on the light, and the next moment the vehicle went racing down the road.

Soon he crossed the bridge across the river, Regent Square, and the YMCA Hostel. The moon-bathed trees in the big city garden stood still like the all-attentive audience at a public meeting. The Law College building and the C.P. Club flashed past as his bike went rushing along. The fields near the club exuded cold because the water from the nearby lake had seeped in. Though there was the cosy warmth of February in the city, the winter cold was still lingering here, on the city's outskirts. The hills, fields and the lake shivered in the biting cold and the moonlight too appeared to have been frozen by it.

But Dinu wasn't himself. A heat wave was blasting through his veins, and a stormy current of blood was surging up to his head. His bike still raced down and its shadow skimmed the road as it ran.

It seemed that Dinu was not going to give up the chase until he had completely solved the mystery that had maddened him so.

Translated from the Marathi by Bal Gadgil

The Shroud

PREMCHAND

I

At the door of the hut, before the dying embers of a fire, sat father and son; inside lay Budhia, the son's young wife, in the throes of childbirth. Now and then she would wail in a heart-rending fashion.

It was a winter night. Nature seemed dumb, and the village was almost completely dark.

'Looks as if she won't last,' said Ghisu. 'It's been a long day. Why not peep in and see?'

'If she must die, why doesn't she hurry?' said Madhav, irritated. 'What can I do about it?'

'You're a heartless lout,' rejoined Ghisu. 'She made you happy for one whole year, and now this callousness!'

'Maybe, but I can't stand her writhing and wriggling.'

They were cobblers notorious in the village. If Ghisu worked for one day, he would rest for three. Madhav was such a shirker that for every half-an-hour of work he would smoke for an hour. The result was that they rarely secured work. They would not dream of working if there was even a handful of corn left at home. When this ran out and they had no food for two or three days, Ghisu would climb a tree and fell some firewood which Madhav would take to the market and sell. While the money lasted, they would loaf about. Then hunger would compel them to gather twigs or search for work.

There was no dearth of work in the village. It was a peasant community where labour was always in demand. These two, however, were sent for only when the employer was obliged to get one man's work done by two.

Had Ghisu and Madhav turned sadhus they would have been happy indeed, for they were content by nature and had great patience.

Theirs was a strange existence. All they owned were a few earthen pots in the hut. Tattered rags covered their nakedness. Thus they floated through life, indifferent to everything. They were heavily in debt, they suffered indignities, they were even beaten up. But did they care?

So acute was their poverty that people gave them petty loans even though there was little chance of repayment. During the harvest, they would pilfer potatoes and peas at night, which they baked and ate, or steal sugarcane to munch. And now too they sat before the dying embers and baked potatoes which they had pilfered from someone's field.

Ghisu had spent his sixty years in such precarious style. And, like a worthy son, Madhav followed in his footsteps. In fact, the son seemed to be outdoing the veteran father.

Ghisu's wife had died long ago, but Madhav had married only last year. Since then Budhia had tried to bring some sort of order into the household. She would grind corn or cut grass to buy a seer of wheat flour for these shameless creatures to devour. This had only made these parasites idler. They even gave themselves airs. When offered employment they would shamelessly demand double wages. And now this woman was dying of labour pains and these two were waiting for her to die, so that they could sleep in peace!

Picking a potato from the ashes and peeling it, Ghisu said, 'Do peep in and see what's happening. Must be the doing of some evil spirit. Even a witch doctor here will charge a rupee.'

Madhav was afraid that if he went inside, Ghisu would gobble up most of the potatoes. He replied, 'I'm afraid to go in there.'

'What's there to be afraid of when I am here?' asked Ghisu.

'Why don't you go in yourself?' rejoined Madhav.

'When my wife died,' went on Ghisu, 'I did not budge from her side for full three days. But yours, won't she feel shy before me? I, who have never seen her face all these days, must I now look on her naked shame? What a state she must be in! Seeing me she won't even be able to writhe and toss freely!'

'What's worrying me is what shall we do if a baby is born? We have no molasses, no oil, no dry ginger in the house.'

'Everything will come—let God give the baby first! The very people who now grudge us a copper coin will send for us and offer us silver. I had nine sons and never a thing in the house. But God somehow helped me ashore.'

In a society where the lot of the hardworking peasant

was not much better than theirs, and where only those who exploited the poor enjoyed the plums, such an attitude was nothing surprising. We might even say that Ghisu was much wiser than the peasants. Instead of following the herd of unthinking peasants, he had joined the unsavoury ranks of the idlers though he lacked the means to follow the ways and principles of the tribe. And so while others of the tribe had become leaders and headmen of the village, he was looked down upon. But he had the consolation that despite his destitution, he did not have to work half as hard as the peasants, and that no one could take undue advantage of his simplicity and his misery.

The two went on picking up the potatoes and eating them burning-hot. They had not eaten anything since yesterday and could not wait to let them cool. Their tongues were repeatedly scorched. Once peeled, the potatoes didn't seem too hot on the surface, but as soon as they were bitten into, the inside burnt their tongues, palates, and throats. There was more danger in keeping the burning balls in the mouth then in swallowing them, for inside the stomach there was ample machinery to cool them down. And so they went on swallowing fast, although the effort brought tears to their eyes.

Ghisu though of the Thakur's wedding feast he had attended twenty years ago. The satisfaction which that feast had given him had made it memorable. He remembered it to this day.

'Can't forget that feast,' said Ghisu. 'Never since then have I had a bellyful of such food. The bride's people had fed all and sundry, young and old, with puris, fried in pure ghee. Chutney, raita, three vegetables cooked dry and one in curry, curds and sweets. How can I now describe how delicious the feast was! No rationing, mind you. You had everything you wanted and as much. The people ate and ate until there was no room for a sip of water. But still the attendants went on piling hot, round, fragrant kachauris on the leaf-plates. We protested, spreading our hands over the plates, but they kept on serving. And after we had washed our hands, they gave us betel and cardamom. But how could I look at betel when I could hardly stand on my legs! I rushed straight to my bed and stretched myself out. The Thakur was indeed a large-hearted fellow.'

Savouring all these delicacies in his imagination, Madhav said, 'Nobody gives such feasts these days.'

'How can they?' replied Ghisu. 'Those days were different. Nowadays everyone thinks of economy. Don't spend on weddings! Don't spend on last rites! What, I ask them, will they do with all this money grabbed from the poor? The grabbing goes on all the same—the economy is only in spending.'

'You must have had about twenty puris?' asked Madhav.

'More than twenty.'

'I would have eaten fifty.'

'I couldn't have taken less than fifty. I was a hefty fellow. You're not even half of me.'

They finished the potatoes, drank some water and lay down near the fire, covering their bodies with their dhotis, their legs curled up beneath their bellies. Like two large pythons coiled up.

And Budhia went on moaning.

II

In the morning Madhav went inside the hut. His wife lay cold, dead. Flies hovered around her face. The stony eyes stared fixedly upwards. The body was covered with dust. The child had died within the womb.

Madhav came running to Ghisu, and the two started wailing loudly and beating their chests.

The neighbours heard the wails and hastened to offer the customary condolences to the unfortunates.

But there was little time for much weeping. A shroud had to be procured as well as the firewood to cremate her; money was as scarce in the house as meat in a kite's nest.

Father and son hurried to the zamindar weeping. The zamindar hated the very sight of them. Time and again, he had thrashed them with his own hands, sometimes for stealing and sometimes for not turning up in time for work.

'What's the matter, Ghisu? Why this weeping?' asked the zamindar contemptuously. 'You're hardly to be seen these days. Looks as though you don't want to live in this village.'

Touching the ground with his head, Ghisu said with tears in his eyes, 'I'm in great trouble, Master. Madhav's woman passed away last night. She was in great pain the whole night, Master. We sat by her and got her what medicines we could, but she has deserted us. And now there is no one to give us a hand. We're undone, the home shattered. I am your slave, Master. Who but you will now make the last rites possible? We've spent everything we had on her illness. The body can be cremated only if the Master is kind. Where else can I go but to your door?'

The zamindar had a kind heart, but doing Ghisu a good turn was like dyeing a black blanket. His first impulse was to say bluntly, 'Get out of here. You never come when sent for, and today you are fawning on me because you are in dire need. You good-for-nothing scoundrel!'

But this was no occasion for anger or punishment. Fuming silently the zamindar threw two rupees at them, without a look or word of consolation, as though casting off a burden.

Now that the zamindar had parted with two rupees, how could the village moneylenders and shopkeepers dare refuse? Ghisu knew well enough how to trumpet the zamindar's favour. Some gave him a two-anna piece, some a four-anna piece. Within an hour, he had collected a full five rupees in cash. Besides, he got some foodgrain at one place, some firewood at another.

At noon Ghisu and Madhav set out for the market to buy a shroud. Other helping hands began cutting bamboo and other wood. The kind-hearted women of the village came to have a last look at the dead body and went back shedding tears over Budhia's fate.

III

On reaching the market Ghisu said, 'We have enough firewood, Madhav, to cremate her. Haven't we?'

'Yes, we have enough,' replied Madhav. 'What we need now is a shroud.'

'Let's buy a cheap one then.'

'Yes, of course. It'll be dark by the time the body is

taken out. Who sees the shroud at night?'

'What a silly custom that she who didn't have a rag to cover her living body should need a new shroud at death!'

'Just to be burnt with the body!'

'What else? Had we these five rupees earlier, we could have got some medicines for her.'

Each had an inkling of what was in the other's mind. They went about the market from one cloth shop to another. They saw various kinds of cloth, silk and cotton, but did not select anything—until it became dark. Then, led by some mysterious power, they found themselves in front of a tavern and, as if the visit was predetermined, entered it.

For a while they stood undecided. Then Ghisu approached the counter and said, 'Sahuji, a bottle for us too!'

This was followed by snacks and fried fish. The two of them sat in the veranda and drank in peace. After several rounds in quick succession, they reached a state of exhilaration.

Ghisu spoke, 'What use would a shroud have been? It would have been burnt after all. It couldn't possibly have accompanied her!'

Looking up at the sky—as if invoking the gods as witness to his innocence—Madhav said, 'Such is the way of the world. Why otherwise would people give thousands of rupees to brahmins? Who knows whether it is repaid in the other world?'

'The rich have money, let them waste it! What have we to waste?'

'But what will you tell the people? Won't they ask, where is the shroud?'

Ghisu laughed. 'We'll tell them the rupees fell out of my waistband and got lost on the way. We searched hard but couldn't find them. People won't believe it, but they will give us money again all the same.'

Madhav too laughed at this unexpected luck. He said, 'She was a good soul, poor girl! Even in death she is feeding us.'

More than half the bottle was now gone. Ghisu ordered Madhav to get two helpings of puris, chutney, pickles, and meat from the shop just across the road. Madhav hurried there and brought back the delicacies on two leaf-plates. A whole rupee and a half was spent. They had only a few copper coins left.

They sat and ate the puris in great style, like a lion feasting on its prey in a forest. No one to answer to, no dread of public censure. They had got over such scruples long ago.

Ghisu philosophized, 'Having brought us such joy, will she not be blessed for it in the next world?'

Madhav reverently bowed his head in agreement. 'Certainly she will be. O God, you know the hearts of all! Please take her to heaven. We bless her from the depth of our hearts. Such food we never had before!'

A moment later, Madhav had a doubt. He said, 'We too shall go there one day, isn't it so, father?'

Ghisu made no reply to this naïve query. He did not want his present enjoyment to be disturbed by thoughts of the other world.

Madhav went on. 'Suppose she asks us there, "Why didn't you give me a shroud?"—what will you say?'

'Nonsense!'

'But ask she must!'

'How do you know she won't have a shroud? D'you take me for such a fool? Have I been wool-gathering all these sixty years? She shall have a shroud and a much better one at that!'

Madhav was unconvinced. 'Who will give her one?' he asked. 'You've swallowed up the money. It's me she will take to task, for it's I who put the vermilion on her head!'

Ghisu flared up. 'I tell you she shall have a shroud! Why don't you take my word?'

'Why not say who will give it?'

'The very people who would have given it now. Maybe they won't put cash in our hands . . .'

As it grew darker and the stars shone brighter, the tavern became more lively. Someone sang, another bragged, some hugged one another, or thrust glasses to their companions' lips. The atmosphere was exhilarating, the air intoxicated. There were some who got tipsy with the first round. More than the liquor, it was the air that did it. Harassed by life, they were drawn here to forget for a while whether they were alive or dead, or whether they existed at all.

And these two, father and son, continued to sip and be merry. All eyes were riveted on them. How lucky to have a whole bottle to themselves!

When they had had their fill, Madhav gave away the leftover puris in the leaf-plate to a beggar who was standing and staring at them with hungry eyes. And for the first time in his life, he felt the pride, the glory and the thrill of 'giving'.

'Take it, have your fill and bless her,' said Ghisu. 'She is dead to whom this is due. But your blessings will surely reach her. Let each hair of your body bless her. This is very hard-earned money.'

Madhav again looked at the sky and said, 'She will go to heaven, father. She will be a queen in heaven.'

Ghisu got up and, as if floating on the waves of joy, said, 'Yes, my boy, she will go to heaven. She never harassed or bullied anyone here. And in dying she has fulfilled the biggest craving of our life. If she doesn't go to heaven, will these pot-bellied ones go there—they who loot the poor right and left and pour oblations in the temple and bathe in the Ganges to wash away their sins?'

This mood of reverence underwent a swift change. Instability is a characteristic of intoxication. A fit of grief and despair overcame them.

Madhav said, 'But the poor thing suffered a lot in her life, father. How painful was her death!'

Covering his eyes with his hands, he started weeping and wailing aloud.

Ghisu consoled him. 'Why do you weep, my boy? Rather rejoice that she is freed from this web of illusion. Escaped from this tangle of misery. She is lucky to have broken loose so soon from the bonds of maya.'

The two stood up and began to sing, 'Why the witchery of the eyes, O false charmer!'

The eyes of all the others were fixed on them, while they continued singing, oblivious.

Then they began to dance. They bounced and jumped, reeled and wriggled, mimed and mimicked.

And in the end they fell down—dead drunk.

Translated from the Hindi by Madan Gopal

Prehistoric

MANIK BANDYOPADHYAY

The entire monsoon had been terrible for Bhikhu. The whole gang had been caught when they had gone to rob Baikuntha Saha's business house at Basantapur in mid-June. Of the eleven, Bhikhu alone had been able to get away, though a spear had pierced his shoulder. Running through the night he had reached the bridge with the broken headstone ten miles away, and had hidden through the day in the thick growth of bulrushes with half his body in the mud. The next night, walking eighteen more miles, he went straight to Pehlad Bagdi's house in Chitalpur.

Pehlad had not given him shelter.

Pointing at the shoulder, he had said, 'That sore's not an easy one, mate. That'll rot. The body will swell. When they come to know, where'll I be? If you hadn't murdered . . .'

'I've a mind to murder you, Pehlad.'

'Not in this life, mate.'

The forest was near—about five miles to the north.

Bhikhu had no alternative but to take shelter there. Pehlad cut bamboos and built him a raised platform in the thick overgrowth of sinjuri trees in an inaccessible part of the forest. He even made a shade of palm leaves over it.

'The tigers have all moved to the hilltop. If the snakes don't bite you, this'll be comfortable enough, Bhikhu,' he said.

'What shall I eat?'

'Why, what about the pressed rice and jaggery I've given you? I'll bring some rice every two days. People will grow suspicious if I come every day.'

Pehlad left after bandaging his shoulder with herbs and creepers, and assuring him that he would come again. Bhikhu had fever that night. He realized the next day how right Pehlad had been: the wound in his shoulder had turned septic. His right arm was terribly swollen and he had lost the power to move it.

In that condition, drenched in the rain, braving mosquitoes and insects, pulling out a leech from some part of his body every hour, panting with fever and the pain of the wound, Bhikhu spent two days and two nights on that narrow platform in a forest which even tigers shun during the rains. He was drenched when the rainwater came pelting down at a slant. When the sun shone, he gasped for breath in the intense, almost palpable humidity. He did not find a moment's respite from the tyranny of the insects. Pehlad had given him a few bidis. He had smoked them all. There was no jaggery left, but the red ants that had come swarming for it were still crowding the platform. Bhikhu was feeling the sting of their frustration all over his body.

Wishing Pehlad's death, Bhikhu still fought for his

life with all his might. By the morning when Pehlad was supposed to come, his water pot was also empty. After waiting for Pehlad till the afternoon and then unable to bear his thirst any longer, he took the water pot to the narrow stream some way down. Having filled it, he climbed back to the platform again. His suffering then cannot be described in words. When he was blind with hunger, he chewed some pressed rice to fill his stomach. He crushed the ants continuously between the fingers of his one good hand. Catching hold of leeches, he pressed them around his wound so that they might suck the poison out. At one point, seeing a green snake peeping out from the foliage near his head, he sat with a stick in his hand for two whole hours looking in that direction; and after that, at an interval of an hour or two, he noisily beat the bushes all around with the stick and made as much noise as he could with his mouth to scare the snake away.

He would not die. He would never die. In such conditions a wild animal cannot live; but he—a human being—he would certainly live.

Pehlad had gone to a wedding at a distant relative's house in another village. He did not come even the next day. At the wedding festivities, he had drunk a great deal of toddy and was lying in a stupor. In the three days that he spent there, not once did he think how Bhikhu's days and nights were passing in the forest.

In the meantime, gangrene set in into Bhikhu's wound and a reddish ooze started trickling out. His body was slightly swollen. His fever went down a little, but the unbearable, suffocating pain all through his body overcame him and threw him into a torpor exactly like the intoxication of toddy wine. He did not feel hunger and thirst any more. He did not even feel it when the leeches sucked his blood and, swelling like tender little palwals, fell off from his body themselves. A sudden jerk of his foot made the water pot fall down and break. The pressed rice inside the bundle, wet by the rain, started rotting. Attracted by the reek of his wound, foxes hovered around below his platform.

In the afternoon, Pehlad returned from his relative's house and went to find out how Bhiku was. He shook his head solemnly at what he saw. He had brought with him a bowl of rice, a few small fried fish and a little cooked saag for Bhikhu. Sitting near Bhikhu till the evening, he himself finished them by and by. Then, returning home, he made a small stretcher from bamboo and came back with Bharat, his brother-in-law.

Putting Bhikhu on the stretcher, the two of them carried him to Pehlad's hut. They made a bed of straw in the loft and laid him there.

And so strong was Bhikhu's grip on life that with only this shelter, no medical treatment and almost no nursing to speak of, he hovered on the threshold of life and death for a month, till he gradually won a victory over death. But his right arm did not heal. It withered like the dead branch of a tree, and turned inert and useless. At first, he could, with great difficulty, move it ever so slightly, but in the end, even that ability was lost to him.

When the wound in his shoulder started healing, using his one arm, Bhikhu began to go down the bamboo ladder when no outsider was present at home. And one evening he made a blunder.

Pehlad was not at home at the time. He had gone out with Bharat to drink toddy. His sister had gone to the river. Pehlad's wife came into the room to put her little son to bed. Seeing the look in Bhikhu's eyes, she was about to run off quickly when Bhikhu caught hold of her arm.

But Pehlad's wife was a Bagdi woman. It was not easy to overpower her with only his left hand and in his weakened condition. Freeing her arm with a violent push, she left the room, hurling abuses. When Pehlad returned, she told him everything.

In his state of drunkenness, Pehlad felt that it was his duty to make short shrift of this ungrateful wretch. After giving his wife a blow with the stout bamboo staff in his hand, he went to break Bhikhu's head with it. However, he realized, even in his intoxication, that however great a duty it might have been, it was a practical impossibility. In his left hand, Bhikhu was holding his chopper tightly. Therefore, instead of bloodshed, there was an exchange of obscenities between them.

At last Pehlad said, 'I've had to spend seven rupees on you. Give me the money. Give it, and then get out of my house—get lost!'

Bhikhu said, 'I had an armlet tied at my waist. You've pinched it. Return my armlet first—then I'll go.'

'Who knows anything of your armlet?'

'Give me back my armlet, Pehlad, if you don't want trouble. This I'm telling you, if I don't get my armlet, I'll slit your throat open, just as I did to Saha babu. Give me my armlet—I'll go right now.' But Bhikhu did not get his armlet back. Bharat arrived in the middle of their quarrel. The two of them cornered Bhikhu. Weakened and crippled, Bhikhu could not do much more than get a bite at Pehlad's armpit. Pehlad and his brother-in-law beat him half-dead and turned him out of the house. Bhikhu's healing wound opened and started bleeding. Wiping the blood with his hand and panting with fatigue, he went away. Nobody could fathom where he went in the darkness of the night. But in the small hours, Pehlad's home caught fire and created total chaos in the Bagdi locality.

Pehlad beat his forehead and kept uttering, 'Oh hell! Oh hell! The devil had come to my house, oh hell!'

But the poor man dared not utter Bhikhu's name for fear of the police.

The second phase of Bhikhu's primitive, uncivilized life began that night. A river ran beside Chitalpur. After setting Pehlad's house on fire, Bhikhu stole a fisherman's boat and let it sail along the current. He did not have the strength to push the pole; holding a flat bamboo like a rudder, he somehow managed merely to steer the boat straight. He was not able to sail far before daybreak.

Bhikhu had a fear that Pehlad would let his name out to avenge the burning of his homestead. In his anger he would not pay heed to his own danger. The police had long been looking for him. After the murder at Baikuntha Saha's house, their efforts had been redoubled. If Pehlad turned informer, the police would search the entire neighbourhood. It was dangerous for him to surface within the radius of twenty to thirty miles. But, by then, Bhikhu was desperate. He had had nothing to eat since the previous afternoon. His feeble body was still stiff with pain after the tremendous thrashing from two strong young men.

At dawn, he reached the landing stage of the subdivision town and tied his boat. He bathed, dipping himself again and again in the river to wash the bloodstains off his body, and entered the town. He was faint with hunger. But he did not have a single pice on him to buy some puffed rice. He put out his hand to the first man he met in front of the market and said, 'Please, babu, give me two pice.'

The gentleman looked at his thick, rough, matted hair, the mud-coloured dirty strip of torn cloth wound around his waist and the limply-hanging arm as thin as a rope, and perhaps felt compassion. He gave him a pice.

Bhikhu said, 'Just one, babu? Give me another.'

The gentleman got angry and said, 'Gave you one—and that wouldn't do? Go—scram!'

For a second, it seemed that Bhikhu would hurl some horrible abuse at him. But he controlled himself. Instead he looked daggers at him with angry red eyes, and then moving on to the adjacent shop, bought puffed rice with the pice and started swallowing it greedily.

That was his first lesson in begging.

In a few days, he had learned all the codes of this department of the oldest business in the world. He mastered the gestures and language of appeal as if he were a beggar by birth. Now he did not even clean himself. His hair was soon matted into clumps and many a family of lice kept increasing their numbers in it. At times, Bhikhu madly scratched his head with both hands, but he was scared to cut off his ever-growing hair. He earned a torn coat from begging and wore it on the muggiest of days to hide the mark on his shoulder. The withered arm was the strongest advertisement he had when begging; he could not afford to cover up this limb. So he tore the whole right sleeve of the coat from the shoulder. He also got hold of a tin mug and a stick.

From morning till night, he sat begging under a tamarind tree by the side of a road near the market. He breakfasted on a pice's worth of puffed rice. At noon he entered a deserted garden a little further away from the market. Under a banyan tree, he cooked rice in an earthenware pot on an improvised fire. He sometimes cooked small fish or vegetables in an earthenware bowl. His stomach full, he leaned against the tree and pulled contentedly at a beedi. Then he again went and sat under the tamarind tree.

All day long he cried in a gasping whine, 'Please, sir, one pice. God will give you if you give me. Please, sir, one pice . . .'

Like many another ancient proverb, the shloka, 'Nothing will ever be gained by begging' is really untrue. Between a thousand to fifteen hundred persons passed Bhikhu throughout the day and, on average, one person out of every fifty gave him one pice or a half-pice coin. If the number of half-pices was more, he earned five to six annas a day, but usually his income was nearer eight annas. The village market was held there twice a week. His income was never less than a whole rupee on market days.

The monsoon was over now. Both sides of the river were white with catkins. For eight annas a month, Bhikhu rented the broken shed attached to Binnu Majhi's cottage. He lay there at night. He got hold of a dilapidated but thick blanket which had belonged to a man who had died of malaria. He spread the hay gathered from people's houses, spread the blanket on top and slept soundly. During his occasional forages for alms from householders in the town, he had been given some torn clothes. He rolled them into a bundle and used it as a pillow. If at night, there was a nip in the damp air rising from the river, he opened the bundle and wrapped himself in a piece of clothing.

The life of ease and satisfying meals soon brought back the health that he had once had. His chest expanded. The muscles on his arms and back started rippling with each movement of his limbs. The excitement of suppressed strength gradually made him arrogant and impatient. He still begged, piteously reciting the jargon he was used to, but his anger knew no bounds if he was refused. If the street was deserted, he hurled obscene abuse at the man who had refused him alms. If the shopkeeper did not give him an extra helping when he bought something for a pice, he was almost ready to beat him up. When the women went down to bathe in the river, he went and stood at the edge of the water, pretending to beg. If the women were alarmed, he was happy. If they asked him to go away, he did not budge but bared his teeth in an impertinent grin.

At night he was restless in the bed he had made himself.

He was becoming tired of this joyless life lacking the touch of a woman. His mind yearned for his past reckless action-packed life.

In those days, he would raise a real racket after drinking cup after cup of toddy at the shop. He would walk into Basi's room with unsteady steps and spend a drunken night there; and, occasionally, at dead of night, they would go in a gang to a household and create bloody havoc. They would loot the money and ornaments and disappear in the darkness. The indescribable expression on the face of a wife when her husband was bound and beaten up in front of her eyes, the wails of a mother when blood spurted out of her son's body—what more exciting addiction was there than to watch those expressions in the light of the flaming torches or to hear those moans and wails? It seemed he had been happier then—even though because of the police he had to abscond from one village to another and hide in forests and jungles. Most of his gang had been caught and sent to prison many times, but the police had not been able to get him more than once. That was the time when, with Rakhu Bagdi, he had abducted Sripati Biswas's sister. He had been sentenced to seven years' imprisonment; but nobody had been able to keep him locked up for more than two years. One rainy evening he had scaled the walls of the jail. After that, all by himself, he had cut openings in fences and burgled households; he had clapped his hand over the mouths of young women alone at the waterside and robbed them of their bangles and the chains round their necks in broad daylight. Stealing Rakhu's wife from him, he had run away with her to Noakhali, and from there, across the sea to Hatia. Six months later, he was back, having deserted Rakhu's wife in Hatia, and then he had become the leader of three gangs in succession and had committed robberies in so many villages so far apart—he did not remember all their names. And then, only the other day, he had slit the neck of Baikuntha Saha's second brother at a stroke of his chopper.

What a life that had been, and what it had come to now!

He, who loved killing men, could merely vent his frustration by sneering at the traveller who refused him alms. His physical strength was still at its peak; only the means of applying that strength was lost. In so many shops, shopkeepers sat at dead of night, checking their balance sheets with bundles of notes in front of them. In so many houses, the men went abroad on work, leaving their women behind. And, instead of becoming rich in a night by merely bounding down in front of them with a sharp weapon in his hand, he lay quietly in Binnu Majhi's shed.

Feeling his right arm in the darkness, Bhikhu's regret knew no bounds. He, with his spirit and his strength, was yet a non-entity like the innumerable cowards and weaklings on this earth, only for want of an arm! Did ever man meet such a fate?

Yet he could bear this misfortune. Regret brought its own anodyne with it. But Bhikhu could no longer live alone.

Right at the entrance of the market sat a beggar woman. She was young. Her body was tight. But on one leg, right from under the knee to the foot, she had an oily, weeping sore.

It was this sore of hers that brought her more alms than Bhikhu received. That was the reason why she took such care that the sore did not heal.

Occasionally Bhikhu went and sat with her. 'That sore—it won't heal, will it?' he would say.

The beggar woman said, 'Why not? Just a matter of putting medicines!'

Bhikhu eagerly said, 'Then heal it. Put the medicine and heal it quick. You don't have to beg once that sore's healed—you know that? I'll keep you.'

'Who said I'd stay with you?'

'Why? Why won't you stay? I'll feed you, keep you in comfort, you won't have to do a thing. Why d'you say no?'

The beggar woman was no fool. She pushed some tobacco leaf into her mouth and said, 'And then, after some time, when you drive me away, where shall I get this sore from?'

Bhikhu promised to remain faithful until death. He tried to entice her with rosy pictures of happiness. The beggar woman would not bend. Bhikhu left disappointed.

The moon rose in the sky. The tides flowed in the river. There was a hint of abandon in the bracing air of winter. The clusters of bananas growing in the orchard beside Bhikhu's shed were gone. With the money earned from the bananas, Binnu Majhi bought his wife a silver waistband. The ferment in the palmyra juice gradually strengthened and deepened. Bhikhu's repulsion evaporated in the heat of desire. He seemed unable to control himself any longer.

Waking up one morning, he went straight to the beggar woman. 'Well, then, come along. Come with your sore and all,' he said.

The beggar woman said, 'Couldn't you come earlier? Go to hell now. Go and eat cinder from the brazier.'

'Why? What's all this about eating cinder?'

'You thought I was pining for you? High hopes! I'm living with him there.'

Looking that way Bhikhu saw that a lame, bearded

beggar, of about his own age, had found a place for himself at some distance. Like his own right arm, this man's leg had withered from the knee down. He had set it in front of himself very carefully, and was calling upon Allah to attract the compassion of all around.

A short wooden leg lay by his side.

The beggar woman said, 'Don't you dare sit down! Move on, run . . . I tell you he'll kill you if he gets an inkling.'

Bhikhu said, 'Oh, beat it, every bastard talks of killing! I can kill ten like him single-handed—keep that in mind.'

The beggar woman said, 'If that is so, go and dare him. What are you doing here with me?'

'Give him up. Come to me.'

'Oh my darling! Have a fag! My sore had put you off—why should I have anything to do with you, you scum? Why should I give him up? Do you earn like him? Do you have a room? Be off, or else I'll raise hell.'

Bhikhu retreated for the time being, but he did not give up. He came and stood near the beggar woman whenever he found her alone. Making an effort at intimacy he asked, 'So what's your name?'

So devoid were they of identity that they had not even thought it necessary till now to ask each other's names.

The beggar woman grinned, showing her black teeth.

'After me again? Go to that hag there.' Bhikhu squatted down near her. Since many people gave rice instead of money, Bhikhu had now taken to slinging a bag from his shoulder. He took out a big, plump banana from his bag and said, 'Here, eat it. I stole it for you.'

The beggar woman at once peeled her lover's gift and

gobbled it up. Pleased, she said, 'Want to hear my name? Panchi they call me—Panchi. You've given me a banana, I've told you my name. Now get going.'

Bhikhu did not show any sign of budging. It was not for the mere luxury of hearing her name that he had made an offering of a big banana like that. He squatted on the dust as long as he could and exchanged pleasantries with Panchi. It was only at their level of communication that these could be considered pleasantries. To others, it would seem that they were abusing each other. Panchi's man was Bashir. One day Bhiku even tried to strike an acquaintance with him.

'Salaam, mian.'

Bashir said, 'What are you up to? Why do you keep coming this way? Salaam mian, indeed! I'll crush your skull with one blow of this stick.'

This was followed by a verbal war of the coarsest kind. They did not come to blows for Bhikhu had a stick in his hand and Bashir carried a stone.

Before he returned to his tamarind tree, Bhikhu said, 'Wait, I'll do you in.'

Bashir said to Panchi, 'I'll kill you, by Allah, if you talk to him again.'

Bhikhu's income fell at this time. New travellers did not travel down the same road every day. In two months the number of newcomers lessened in proportion to the number of regulars. Many of those who had given alms to Bhikhu once did not feel the need to help him a second time. There is no dearth of beggars in the world.

Bhikhu could barely make ends meet. Except on market days, he could not save a pice from his income. Worries beset him.

Living in an open shed would be difficult in winter. He needed walls of some kind round him, wherever that might be. No young beggar woman would consent to live with him unless she had a proper shelter and two meals a day. And yet, if his income fell as it was falling, he would perhaps not be able to provide even himself with square meals in winter.

He would have to raise his income by hook or by crook.

He could not think of any means of increasing his income as long as he stayed here. He had no means of taking to burglary; he had no means of turning into a labourer; it was impossible to snatch money unless he committed murder. He had no wish to go away from this town leaving Panchi behind. Bhikhu's heart rebelled against his own fate. The happy family life of Binnu Majhi right next to his shed caused him to burn with envy. Sometimes the desire to set Binnu's house on fire gave him no rest. Wandering by the riverside like a madman, he sometimes thought that he would find no peace till he owned all the food and all the women in this world.

Bhikhu spent some more time in such torment. Then, one night, putting all his valuables in the bag and tying all his savings tightly in the inner end of his dhoti, Bhikhu left his shed. He had one day picked up an iron rod about a cubit long by the side of the river. By rubbing it against a stone in his free time, he had made one end of it sharp and pointed. He put this weapon in his bag too.

In the darkness of the new moon, the stars were glittering all over the sky. There was silence and calm on

God's earth. Having come out after long years to prowl in the deserted world of midnight with a terrible plan in his mind, Bhikhu suddenly felt an unspeakable joy. He suddenly muttered to himself, 'If only God had taken the left and spared the right!'

Walking down the riverside for half a mile, he entered the town through a narrow path. Keeping the market to his left, he wandered through the narrow lanes and by-lanes of the sleeping town till he reached the other end. It was here that the metalled road to the town ceased to follow the path of the river. After going by a different route for about two miles, the river then turned and flowed a mile or so alongside this road before changing its course again to the south.

For a part of the road, a few isolated houses could be found on either side. After that there were paddy fields and occasional plots of fallow land covered with undergrowth. It was by the side of such a cluster of bushes that some wretched people had cleared some space and had erected a few hovels. One of these hovels belonged to Bashir. Waking up at dawn each day he clattered off on his wooden leg to beg in the town and returned in the evening. Panchi set dry leaves on fire and cooked rice. Bashir smoked his hookah. At night Panchi wrapped strips of cloth round her sore. Lying side by side on a bamboo cot and conversing in their sharp filthy language, they fell asleep. A rancid, rotten stink rose from their nest, their bed and their bodies and, emerging through the holes of the thatched roof, mingled with the air outside.

Bashir snored in his sleep. Panchi muttered in an undertone.

Bhikhu had followed them one day and marked their hovel. Now in the darkness, he carefully went to the back of the room, and putting his ear to the bamboo wall, stood for a while in the clumps of yam. Then he came around to the front of the room. Panchi had merely closed the door without bolting it from inside. Stealthily moving the loose door to one side, Bhikhu took the rod out of his bag and clutched it tightly. He entered the room. There was starlight outside but in the room even that meagre light was lacking. He could not light matches with his one hand. Standing in the room Bhikhu calculated that it would not be possible to estimate the position of Bashir's heart in the darkness. If the left-handed blow did not find its mark, Bashir would have time to raise a hue and cry. That would be terribly inconvenient.

Pondering for a few moments and moving towards Bashir's head, he pushed the sharp end of the rod about two inches into the crown with one thrust. There was no way of knowing in the darkness whether or not the blow had been fatal. Bhikhu thus could not feel assured even after knowing that the rod had gone into the head. With all his might he clutched Bashir's throat with his one hand.

'Silence! One sound and I'll finish you off too,' he told Panchi.

Panchi did not shout; she only whimpered in terror.

Then Bhikhu told her again, 'No noise! Silence, if you care for your life!'

When Bashir's body became inert, Bhikhu removed his hand from his throat.

He paused to regain his breath and then said, 'Light the lamp, Panchi.'

When Panchi lit the lamp, Bhikhu looked at his handiwork with deep satisfaction. His pride knew no bounds for having finished a strong man like that with his single arm. Turning to Panchi he said, 'Look! See who brushes off whom! I pleaded with him again and again, mianbhai, you can't overshoot the mark—give up the idea. Mianbhai was piqued. Says, I'll bash your head in! Have it your own way—bash my head in, mianbhai.' Bowing with great sarcasm to Bashir's corpse, Bhikhu bobbed his head this way and that, and roared with laughter. Suddenly enraged, he said, 'Why has madam lost her speech? Come on, talk, you slut. Shall I do you in too—what?'

Trembling, Panchi said, 'What will you do now?'

'See what I do! Where does he keep all his savings—tell me that first.'

Panchi had discovered with great trouble the place where Bashir hid his money. At first she pretended ignorance. But her resistance gave way as soon as Bhikhu stood over her and clutched her hair.

The amount Bashir had saved in his entire life was not very small. It came to more than a hundred rupees in rupee and eight-anna coins. In the past Bhikhu had earned much more than this after having killed a man. Yet he was pleased. He said, 'Make a bundle of whatever you want to take with you, Panchi. Then let's start while the night's still deep. The crescent moon will rise in a little while. We'll be able to see our way from here.'

Panchi tied her bundle. Then taking hold of Bhikhu's hand, she limped out of the house and on to the road. Looking at the eastern sky, Bhikhu said, 'The moon will rise in no time, Panchi.'

'Where are we going?' Panchi asked.

'To the district town. I'll steal a boat from the landing. We'll hide in the rushes opposite Chhiptipur during the day. Then at night—straight to the district town. Now, put on speed, Panchi, we have to walk two miles.'

Panchi was finding it difficult to walk with her sore leg. After a while Bhikhu suddenly stopped still. 'Does the leg hurt a lot, Panchi?'

'Yes, it hurts.'

'Shall I take you on my back?'

'But how can you do it?'

'I can. Come.'

Clinging to Bhikhu's neck, Panchi hung on to his back. Bent forward by the weight of her body, Bhikhu took to the road with long strides. The paddy fields on both sides lay languorous in the hazy light. The thin crescent moon came up in the sky from behind the trees of the distant village. There was silence and calm on God's earth.

There is perhaps a history of that moon and this earth. But the inherited continuum of darkness that Bhikhu and Panchi had gathered from their mothers' wombs, that had been stowed away in their bodies when they came to this earth, the darkness that they would leave hidden inside the fleshly contours of their own children—that darkness is prehistoric. The light of the earth has not been able to reach it till this day—it will never be able to.

Translated from the Bengali by Nandita Datta

In the Flood

THAKAZHI SIVASANKARA PILLAI

The temple was situated at the highest point in the area. There the deity stood in water reaching up to the neck. Water! Water everywhere! Only the watchmen were left in those houses where householders owned a boat. All the inhabitants of that village had gone in search of dry land. There were sixty-seven children in the three-roomed upper storey of the temple. There were also three hundred and fifty-six adults, and domestic animals like dogs, cats, goats and fowl. All lived in amity. There was no discord.

Chennan, the untouchable, had been standing in water for a whole night and day. He had no boat. His master had fled for his life three days back. As soon as the water seeped into the house, Chennan had built a platform with coconut stems and twigs. He spent two days sitting on it hoping that the water would recede soon. Moreover, there were four or five bunches of bananas and a haystack. If he left the place, there would be people to snatch them away.

Now there was knee-deep water above the platform. Two rows of coconut leaves on the thatch of the roof were already under water. Chennan shouted from inside the house. Who would hear that call? Who was there nearby?

There were some creatures with him whose lives depended on him—a pregnant wife, four children, a cat and a dog. He was sure that it would take only less than twelve hours for the water to flow over the roof, and that the end was drawing near for him and his family. It had been raining for three days now. Somehow he broke open the roof, got out and looked in all directions. There was a large boat moving to the north. Chennan hooted at the boatmen in a loud voice. Luckily, the boatmen understood the situation. They turned their boat towards the hut. Chennan pulled out the children, his wife, the dog and the cat through the opening in the frame of the roof. By then the boat had drawn near. The children were getting into the boat. 'Hey! Chennacha,' someone called from the west. Chennan turned back. 'Please come here!' That was Madiyathara Kunjeppan. He was shouting from his rooftop. Chennan caught hold of his wife and hurriedly got her into the boat. The cat also jumped into the boat. No one remembered the dog which was wandering on the western slope of the roof. The boat moved away.

The dog returned to the topmost point of the roof.

Chennan's boat was already far away. It seemed to be flying swiftly. The creature howled in death's agony. He produced sounds like the cries of a helpless man. Who was there to hear them? He ran along the four slopes of the thatched roof. Stopping occasionally to sniff at certain points, he howled on.

'Dhudeem!' Frightened by this unexpected commotion

a frog that had been sitting comfortably on the rooftop plopped down in front of the dog. The dog drew back in fear and stood there for a while staring at it. He walked around it sniffing here and there in search of food perhaps. The frog urinated into his nostrils and jumped into the water. The disturbed dog sneezed, blew his nose again, fiercely shaking his head and wiped his face with one of his forelegs.

The terrible torrent started again. The dog bore it sitting hunched up. His master had already reached Ambalappuzha.

It was dark. A huge alligator floated by slowly brushing against the hut half-sunk in water. The dog barked in horror, with his tail lowered. The alligator floated on, not aware of him.

Sitting on the rooftop, that miserable creature howled, staring into the dark and cloudy skies. The pathetic cry of that dog reached far-off places, which the merciful god of wind, Vayu, carried to the distant shores. Some of those tender-hearted men who had undertaken a vigil over the houses might have said, 'Oh! That dog is howling all alone from the rooftop!'

His master might be having his supper on the shore. Today, as usual, he might leave a ball of rice for the dog after his meal.

The dog howled loudly and uninterruptedly for some more time. The noise grew feeble and then died into silence. A watchman was heard chanting the Ramayana from a house in the north. The dog stood looking towards the north as though listening to it. He moaned a second time as though his throat would give way.

The melodious recital of the Ramayana flowed on

once again in the perfect silence of that night. Our dog remained still for quite a long time listening to that voice till the quiet and sweet song was dissolved in the sweep of a cold breeze. There was no other sound to be heard except the roar of the wind and the beating of the waves.

Chennan's dog climbed up to the rooftop and lay there. He breathed heavily and muttered something in despair. A fish was seen jumping up. The dog got up and barked. The frog leapt up in another part of the flooded lake. The dog whimpered in disgust.

It was morning. The dog started howling in a low heart-rending tone. The frogs stared at him. He looked dispassionately at them jumping into the water, sliding across the surface of the water and finally sinking down.

He looked hopefully at those thatched roofs which could be seen above the surface of the water. All of them were empty. There was no fire or smoke anywhere. He snapped at the flies that gluttonously bit into his body and munched. He tried to drive the ones in his fur away by scratching with his hind leg.

The sun shone for some time. He slept in that mild sun. The shadows of the banana trees swaying in the slow breeze kept moving on the rooftop. He jumped up quickly and barked at them.

The sun disappeared with the arrival of clouds. The entire place grew dark. The wind stirred the waves. The carcasses of animals floated in the water. The waves swept them away. They moved about freely, without fear. He looked at them with envy.

A small boat moved fast in the distance. The dog got up and wagged his tail and observed the direction of the boat. It disappeared into the coconut grove.

It began to drizzle. The dog looked in all directions squatting on his hindlegs, his forelegs supporting him. In his eyes was reflected the helplessness that would make anyone weep.

The rain stopped. A small boat from the northern house came forward and moored under the coconut tree. The dog wagged his tail, yawned and then howled. The boatman climbed onto the coconut tree, plucked tender coconuts and got down. He pierced the tender coconuts, standing inside the boat, drank the juice and rowed away.

A crow came flying from a far-off tree and swooped down on the rotting body of a huge buffalo. As Chennan's dog kept barking greedily, the crow pulled at the flesh and ate it nonchalantly. Satisfied, it flew away.

A green bird twittered, sitting on the leaf of a banana plant near the house. The dog was disturbed and started barking. The bird flew away.

An ant's nest that had been swept by the flood reached the roof. The ants had survived, unhurt. Our dog gave it a kiss, probably taking it to be an edible thing.

His soft snout was inflamed and reddened by continuous sneezing.

In the afternoon, two men came that way in a boat. The dog barked gratefully, and wagged his tail. He said something in a language very close to the human language. He came down into the water and got ready to jump into boat. 'Look! There is a dog!' one of them said. He groaned as an indication of his thankfulness, as though he understood the man's compassion. 'Let him be there,' the other man said. The dog opened and closed his mouth, making a noise as though he was eating something with relish. He prayed. He tried to jump twice.

The boat moved away into the distance. The dog groaned once again. One of the boatmen turned back. 'Ayyo!' That was not the boatman's cry. It was the dog's voice.

'Ayyo!'

That tired and heart-moving wail merged with the distant breeze. The endless sound of the waves again. No one turned back towards the dog. He remained like that until the boat disappeared from sight. Then he climbed up the roof, muttering as though he was bidding farewell to the world. Perhaps he meant to say that he would never again love a human being.

He lapped up some cold water. That pathetic creature looked at the birds which were flying about. A water-snake rushed towards it, playing about in the waves. The dog jumped up and climbed on to the roof. The water-snake crawled into the house through the hole which Chennan and his family had used to get out. The dog edged around that hole and peeped in. Suddenly alert, he began to bark. His voice fully expressed his hunger and his fear for his life. A speaker of any language or even an inhabitant of Mars would understand its meaning. It was a language comprehensible to all.

It was night. Rain started pouring heavily, accompanied by a terrible storm. The rooftop was swaying amidst the beating of the waves. Twice, the dog was about to fall off the roof. A big head emerged above the surface of the water. It was an alligator. The dog began to bark in fear. The sounds of fowls crying together in unison was heard from nearby.

'Where is the dog barking? Haven't the people moved

from this house?' A boat loaded with hay, coconut and bunches of bananas stopped near the banana tree.

The dog started barking, turning towards the boatmen. He barked angrily, standing near the water with his tail lifted up. One of the boatmen climbed on to the banana tree.

'Hey, the dog is likely to jump down.'

The dog did jump forward. The man who had climbed up the banana tree fell into the water. The other fellow caught him and dragged him into the boat. By then, the dog had reached the rooftop swimming through the water, and continued to bark angrily.

The poachers cut all the banana bunches. The dog barked louder and louder as though his throat would burst. The men shouted at him, 'Hey, you will be sorry for this later.' They then carried away all the hay into the boat. The last one in the group climbed on to the rooftop. The dog promptly jumped at his feet and bit him. He got a mouthful of flesh. The man jumped into the boat, screaming aloud. The one who was standing in the boat struck the dog's belly with the punt. 'Miawo, miawo, miawo,' the dog's cry died down into a frail wail. The man who was bitten by the dog started crying in pain. 'Keep quiet,' the other fellow consoled him. Both of them then left. The dog kept barking fiercely looking in the direction in which the boat had gone for a long time.

It was about midnight. A big, dead cow came floating and remained inside the house. The dog stood at the top watching this. He did not step down. The carcass was moving slowly. He scratched and tore up the thatch, and wagged his tail. When the carcass began to move away beyond reach, the dog slowly stepped down and pulled it towards him. He then started eating the flesh with relish. There was food in abundance to meet his great hunger.

'Tup.' A resounding whack. The dog disappeared. The cow squirmed once, went down and then floated away.

Then there was no sound except the roar of the storm, the croaking of the frogs and the beating of the waves. There was no sound of the living. The kind house-watcher in the neighbourhood did not hear the helpless cries of the dog any more. Rotting carcasses floated here and there in that vast expanse of water. The crow sat on some of them and fed itself. No sound disturbed its composure. There was no hindrance to the activities of the poachers either. There was emptiness everywhere.

After some time, the hut collapsed and sank into the water. Nothing was seen above the endless stretch of water. That faithful dog had watched its master's house till his death. He was no more. The hut too reciprocated by remaining aloft above the water till the moment the dog was snatched away by the alligator. Then it sank. It disappeared into the water.

The water began to recede. Chennan came swimming towards his hut in search of his dog. He saw the dead body of the dog lying at the foot of a coconut tree. The waves kept moving it slowly. Chennan turned the dead body over with his toe. He was not sure that it was his own dog. One ear had been bitten off. Even its colour could not be recognized as the skin had rotted away.

Translated from the Malayalam by Jancy James

Ardhanari

C. RAJAGOPALACHARI

Ardhanari was a Harijan boy from the village of Kokkalai in Salem district. He went to Delhi with Sri Malkani, Secretary of the Society for the Service of the Untouchables. Sri Malkani was very pleased with this boy, whom he met at Salem, and immediately decided to take him to Delhi with him. There he put him in a school and looked after him. He spoke to a well-known firm of traders in Delhi and got him a job in their office at Rs 60 a month. As Ardhanari was honest, diligent and had personality, he got on well. He was getting Rs 150 a month before he was twenty-four; and when, some time later, a place in a big mill belonging to the same firm fell vacant in Bangalore, they sent Ardhanari there on a salary of Rs 200 a month.

He spent two happy years in Bangalore. His immediate senior, Govinda Rao, had had training in Manchester for two years. He and Ardhanari were of about the same age, and as he liked Ardhanari's disposition and manners, they became close friends.

Govinda Rao had a sister called Pankaja. Brother and sister loved each other very much. Their parents had died when the girl was just ten years old, and she was now twenty and unmarried. She and Ardhanari often met, as she accompanied her brother when he visited Ardhanari and also when the latter came to see her brother. When Govinda Rao found that his sister and Ardhanari seemed to like each other, he was glad. He often asked himself: 'Why should not these two marry and settle down here?'

One day Govinda Rao asked his sister, 'Pankaja, have you ever thought about marriage?'

'I have no strong feelings on the matter,' she replied.

'Then, what about marrying our Ardhanari?'

Pankaja showed no objection to being thus questioned, but she evaded the question by talking about something else. Some weeks later, the same matter was broached again, casually.

'Why, Gopy, are you tired of me already? Am I a burden to you?' she said at first, and laughed. Then she began to cry. Girls, especially those who have lost their mothers, are very sensitive.

'Stupid, don't talk of being a burden or of my getting tired of you. Just tell me if you care for the idea of marriage. If you say no, that will please me, because then I can always have you with me,' he said, and wiped her eyes. Then he said again, 'Mother is dead. Who else is there to ask you what you feel about it?'

'If it comes about, I shall go through it. But what is the point in discussing it now?' asked Pankaja.

'You two seem to like each other. And as we have stopped caring about caste or family, why should you not marry him?' he asked.

'What indeed have we to do with caste? But we do not yet know what he feels about it,' said Pankaja.

'Don't worry about that. He must think himself very lucky if he gets someone like you for his wife,' said Govinda Rao. He was sure there was no one to compare with his sister in the whole world.

When Ardhanari was told about this, his joy knew no bounds. But a minute later his face fell. 'But how can that be, Govinda Rao?' he asked.

'Why? What is the trouble?' asked Govinda Rao.

'What is my caste and what is yours?' said Ardhanari.

'Oh! The question of caste! Nonsense!' Govinda Rao exclaimed and laughed. 'What is a brahmin? What is a non-brahmin? We stopped thinking about such things long ago. If you like each other and finally decide to marry, we need not worry about caste.'

'I belong to the Coimbatore district. I am a Saiva Mudaliar.' That was what Ardhanari had told them. A Saiva Mudaliar is a vegetarian high-caste non-brahmin. Having said this on some occasion out of fear and snobbery, he was unable to retract it afterwards. He was ashamed to confess the truth about his caste. In Delhi a few people knew his antecedents, but none in Bangalore.

'What is Pankaja's wish?' asked Ardhanari.

'Pankaja seems to like you. Her replies to my questions show that she is willing.'

'Is it not proper that I should ask her and find out for myself?' said Ardhanari.

'Yes,' said Govinda Rao.

Thus the affair was put off. He resolved that he would tell Pankaja the truth, whatever might happen. But later his resolution failed.

'Why should I go out of my way to tell her this? If I do, Govinda Rao and Pankaja will both hate me. They say that they do not care for caste distinctions. But yet if they come to know that I am a pariah, they will never give their consent. Besides, I shall be considered a liar,' he thought.

The next day he thought the matter over again and went to Govinda Rao's house, intending to disclose the truth. But on the way he again debated with himself. 'When we love each other, what reason is there to consider this caste question? Why should we give any quarter to this injustice? Who created caste? Is it not all a lie? Why should I make so much of it and speak to her about it? Why should I spoil the whole business? They have told me distinctly that they do not care about caste. Why then should I refer to it at all?' He made up his mind to suppress the truth.

'Pankaja, do you really like me? Shall we get married and live together?' he asked.

'But do you want to?' said Pankaja.

Ardhanari's father Muniappan, brother Ranga, and mother Kuppayee lived in the pariah quarters of Kokkolai. While he was in Delhi and later in Bangalore, Ardhanari used to send them twenty rupees regularly every month. They did not know what their son was earning. It was a princely allowance for them, and they lived on it very happily. Unfortunately, Muniappan was in the habit of drinking. When he began to get money regularly every month, this became worse. Ranga did not like this but could not prevent it. He was the teacher in a village school and unmarried. When his mother pressed him to find a wife, he would say, 'Not now, wait for some time more,' and always put off the matter.

Ardhanari, after his transfer to Bangalore, used to visit his people twice a year. When he found his father addicted to alcohol, he felt ashamed beyond measure. He could not bear the dirt and untidiness of the house. He would stay there for only a day or two and then return as soon as possible.

'We will go with you, Ardhanari,' his father would say whenever Ardhanari got ready to return to Bangalore.

'No, indeed. If they see you with me, they will dismiss me,' Ardhanari would reply.

'Yes, father, we should not go there,' Ranga would say.

Because he sent them money regularly, they would not argue much more about it. Thus it went on for some time.

Ardhanari thought it would be best for him to go somewhere far in the north again once he was married.

'Though they are very kind to me, if they know that I am a pariah, things would certainly go wrong. Even if they do not mind that, when they see the life and habits of my father and my people . . . Pankaja would certainly be disgusted. She would not even look at me afterwards.' Ardhanari would talk to himself in this strain again and again, and further strengthen his resolve to hide the truth. He decided to marry as soon as possible and go away to some place in the north. He wrote letters to the directors of the company he served and asked for a transfer to some other mill in north India.

One day Pankaja quite unexpectedly said, 'Ardhanari, I want very much to see your mother. We have both decided that you should take leave for a week and all three of us should go and visit Coimbatore, Ootacamund, and other places. What do you say?'

Govinda Rao also said, 'There is not much work in the office now. The first week of next month will suit us all very well.'

Ardhanari's heart beat fast. 'Oh, yes, we could do that. But I have a letter today that there is a severe epidemic of cholera in our village,' he said.

Pankaja was all anxiety on hearing this. 'Cholera! Have you asked your people to move elsewhere? Why not ask them to come over here?' she said.

'I was just thinking of doing so,' said Ardhanari.

After three days Ardhanari got a letter from Ranga:

Blessings to younger brother Ardhanari,

There is severe cholera here. There have been many deaths. We are afraid. Father continues as before. He does not listen to our advice. The money that you sent this month is all spent. If you can send us thirty rupees, we are thinking of locking up the house and going to Salem to stay there till this fear of cholera is over.

Yours affectionately,
Ranga

Ardhanari was surprised and shocked. 'What is the meaning of this? What I said in deceit has turned out to be true. God is trying me perhaps,' he said to himself, and was undecided as to what he should do. He resolved to send the money the very next day.

Ardhanari got no sleep that night.

Bad thoughts, shameful thoughts, kept stirring in his

mind. Whenever he thought of his father, he felt disgust. The wish often arose in his mind that his father would die of cholera and relieve him of all this misery. The next moment, he would censure himself for this thought. He tossed restlessly on his bed all night, and in the morning he took a cold bath. The postman brought letters. As he had expected, there was another letter from his village. With trembling hands, he opened it and read:

> Father is suffering from cholera. We are greatly afraid. The mother goddess must save us. We have not a pice with us.
>
> Ranga

When he read the letter Ardhanari's face grew dark. He remained seated in his chair for quite a long time. He did not send any money that day.

Nor did he send any money the next day.

'How is the cholera in your village?' asked Pankaja.

'Still very bad, I'm afraid,' said Ardhanari.

'Is there enough sugar in the coffee?' asked Govinda Rao.

'Oh, yes! It is very good,' said Ardhanari.

When he returned home, there was a letter waiting for him.

> Mother too has cholera symptoms. You have not sent us any money. We are helpless. Come at once.
>
> Ranga

Ardhanari sent no money that day either. He had turned his heart into stone. 'This disgraceful aspect of my life will now disappear forever. This release looks like God's kindness to me. There is no Dharma or justice higher than His will. Why should I try to circumvent it? If father and mother die, then there will be nothing left to prevent my marriage with Pankaja.'

Suddenly, 'Tut! Tut! What a sinful thought, you wicked man,' someone reprimanded him. When he turned his head around, he saw Pankaja standing behind him. He was alarmed that his secret was out. Then his mind cleared again. No one had spoken. It was just an illusion of his mind.

'How did you come in without making any sound?' he asked.

Pankaja laughed. 'I knocked on the door three times and then entered. You are worried about something, so you did not hear me come in,' she said.

'I must go to my village. It appears the cholera is worse there now. My father and mother are there and I must make some arrangements for them,' he said.

'Yes, that should have been done long ago. If you go there now, you must be very careful. You must neither eat nor drink while you are there,' she said.

Ardhanari left for Salem the same night. But instead of going straight to Kokkalai, he delayed on the way, and only reached it after four days. His mother was already dead and poor Ranga had followed her. Only his drunkard father had escaped, and was alive and well.

'Please take me to Bangalore. What shall I do here after this?' he begged Ardhanari. Ardhanari would not hear of it. He was adamant. 'I will send you enough money. You must remain her. Do not ask to come with me for I cannot take you,' he said.

The father entreated the son like a helpless child. 'I can't stay here,' he sobbed. Ardhanari refused to be moved by his weeping. 'How can I give up Pankaja?' he said to himself, and would not listen to his father's lamentations. The next day he placed a ten-rupee note in his father's hand and left for Salem.

'Alas! What have I done? I have killed my mother and brother. Why did I do this? Is there another villain like me in this world? How can I forsake my father like this? What shall I tell Pankaja?'

Immersed in such thoughts, he could not sleep in the train. When he arrived at Bangalore, he walked the whole way to his house in a dazed manner. There he bolted the door and lay down. He did not send word to Govinda Rao or Pankaja about his return, nor did he go to the office.

The same night he took his luggage and again went to the railway station and bought a ticket for Salem.

At Salem, he heard that an untouchable had drowned himself in a well in Kokkalai. When he got to Kokkalai, he learned that the man was his own father.

Someone said that they were holding an inquest at the police station over Muniappan, the drunkard. He did not go there, but, unnoticed by anyone, returned to Salem and took a train to Bangalore.

'Pankaja, you must try to forget me,' said Ardhanari.

'I shall do that afterwards. Tell me the news from Salem,' said Pankaja.

'They are all dead. They are dead because I did not do what I should have done. I have lost all interest in life now. I am going to resign my job and go to my village. Please forget me,' he said.

She looked at him two or three times. Then she got alarmed and ran to call her brother.

Ardhanari had fever. At first the doctor said it was typhoid, then he said it was brain fever. He had to stay in bed for over a month. Govinda Rao and Pankaja remained at his bedside without rest until, after the fourth week, the fever reduced.

'There is no more cause for anxiety,' said the doctor. Very soon Ardhanari was well enough to sit up in bed.

'I am a pariah, a sinner. I am really an untouchable, a liar. I renounce marriage. For God's sake, forget me,' said Ardhanari.

Pankaja laughed, 'What do I care what caste you are? Why should we part from each other?' she said, trying to soothe him.

Ardhanari did not agree. 'You do not mind my caste, I know. But I am a murderer. I have killed my father and mother,' he said, and told them the whole tale.

When he was quite well, he resigned his job and returned to Kokkolai. He is now the ascetic, who runs the school in the Mariamman temple.

Translated from the Tamil by C.R. Ramaswami

Exchange of Lunatics

SAADAT HASAN MANTO

A couple of years or so after the partition of the subcontinent, the governments of Pakistan and India felt that just as they had exchanged their hardened criminals, they should also exchange their lunatics. In other words, Muslims in the lunatic asylums of India should be sent across to Pakistan; and mad Hindus and Sikhs in Pakistani asylums be handed over to India.

Whether or not this was a sane decision, we will never know. But people in knowledgeable circles say that there were many conferences at the highest level between bureaucrats of the two countries before the final agreement was signed and a date fixed for the exchange.

The news of the impending exchange created a novelty situation in the Lahore lunatic asylum. A Muslim patient who was a regular reader of the *Zamindar* was asked by a friend, 'Maulvi sahib, what is this thing they call Pakistan?' After much thought he replied, 'It's a place in India where they manufacture razor blades.' A Sikh lunatic asked another man, 'Sardarji, why are we being sent to

India? We cannot speak their language.' The Sardarji smiled and replied, 'I know the lingo of the Hindustanis.' He illustrated his linguistic prowess by reciting a doggerel.

Hindustanis are full of shaitani
They strut about like bantam cocks.

One morning a mad Muslim yelled the slogan 'Pakistan zindabad' with such vigour that he slipped on the floor and knocked himself senseless.

Some inmates of the asylum were not really insane. They were murderers whose relatives had been able to have them certified and thus saved from the hangman's noose. These people had vague notions of why India had been divided and what was Pakistan. But even they knew very little of the complete truth. The papers were not very informative and the guards were so stupid that it was difficult to make any sense of what they said. All one could gather from their talk was that there was a man of the name of Mohammed Ali Jinnah who was also known as the Qaid-i-Azam. And that this Mohammed Ali Jinnah, alias Qaid-i-Azam, had made a separate country for the Muslims which he called Pakistan.

No one knew where this Pakistan was or how far it extended. This was the chief reason why inmates who were not totally insane were in a worse dilemma than those utterly mad: they did not know whether they were in India or Pakistan. If they were in India, where exactly was Pakistan? And if they were in Pakistan, how was it that the very same place until recently had been known as India?

A poor Muslim inmate got so baffled with the talk about India and Pakistan, Pakistan and India, that he got madder than before. One day while he was sweeping the floor, he was suddenly overcome by an insane impulse. He threw away his brush and clambered up a tree. And for two hours he orated from the branch of this tree on Indo-Pakistan problems. When the guards tried to get him down, he climbed up still higher. When they threatened him he replied, 'I do not wish to live either in India or Pakistan; I want to stay where I am, on top of this tree.'

After a while, the fit of lunacy abated and the man was persuaded to come down. As soon as he was on the ground, he began to embrace his Hindu and Sikh friends and shed bitter tears. He was overcome at the thought that they would leave him and go away to India.

Another Muslim inmate had a Master of Science degree in radio-engineering and considered himself a cut above the others. He used to spend his days strolling in a secluded corner of the garden. Suddenly a change came over him. He took off all his clothes and handed them over to the head constable. He resumed the preparations without a stitch of clothing on his person.

And there was yet another lunatic, a fat man who had been a leader of the Muslim League in Chiniot. He was given to bathing fifteen to sixteen times during the day. He suddenly gave it up altogether.

The name of this fat Muslim was Mohammed Ali. But one day he proclaimed from his cell that he was Mohammed Ali Jinnah. Not to be outdone, his cell-mate who was Sikh proclaimed himself to be Master Tara Singh. The two began to abuse each other. They were declared 'dangerous' and put in separate cages.

There was a young Hindu lawyer from Lahore. He

was said to have become unhinged when his lady-love jilted him. When he heard that Amritsar had gone to India, he was very depressed: his sweetheart lived in Amritsar. Although the girl had spurned his affection, he did not forget her even in his lunacy. He spent his time cursing all leaders, Hindu as well as Muslim, because they had split India into two, and made his beloved an Indian and him a Pakistani.

When the talk of exchanging lunatics was in the air, other inmates consoled the Hindu lawyer with the hope that he would soon be sent to India—the country where his sweetheart lived. But the lawyer refused to be reassured. He did not want to leave Lahore because he was convinced that he would not be able to set up legal practice in Amritsar.

There were a couple of Anglo-Indians in the European ward. They were very saddened to learn that the English had liberated India and returned home. They met secretly to deliberate on problems of their future status in the asylum: would the asylum continue to have a separate ward for Europeans? Would they be served breakfast as before? Would they be deprived of toast and be forced to eat chappatis?

Then there was a Sikh who had been in the asylum for fifteen years. And in the fifteen years he said little besides the following sentence: *'O, pardi, good good di, anekas di, bedhyana di, moong di dal of the lantern.'*

The Sikh never slept either at night or in the day. The warders said that they had not known him to blink his eyes in fifteen years. He did not as much as lie down. Only on rare occasions he leant against the wall to rest. His legs were swollen down to the ankles.

Whenever there was talk of India and Pakistan, or the exchange of lunatics, this Sikh would become very attentive. If anyone invited him to express his views, he would answer with great solemnity, *'O, pardi, good good di, anekas di, bedhyana di, moong di dal of the Pakistan government.'*

Some time later he changed the end of his litany from 'of the Pakistan Government' to 'of the Toba Tek Singh government'.

He began to question his fellow inmates whether the village of Toba Tek Singh was in India or Pakistan. No one knew the answer. Those who tried got tied up in knots when explaining how Sialkot was at first in India and was now in Pakistan. How could one guarantee that a similar fate would not befall Lahore and, from being Pakistani today, it would not become Indian tomorrow? For that matter how could one be sure that the whole of India would not become a part of Pakistan? All said and done, who could put his hand on his heart and say with conviction that there was no danger of both India and Pakistan vanishing from the face of the globe one day?

The Sikh had lost most of his long hair. Since he seldom took a bath, his hair had matted and joined with his beard. This made him look very fierce. But he was a harmless fellow. In the fifteen years he had been in the asylum, he had never been known to argue or quarrel with anyone. All that the older inmates knew about him was that he owned land in village Toba Tek Singh and was a prosperous farmer. When he lost his mind, his relatives had brought him to the asylum in iron fetters. Once a month, some relatives came to Lahore to find out how he was faring. With the eruption of Indo-Pakistan troubles, their visits had ceased.

The Sikh's name was Bishen Singh but everyone called him Toba Tek Singh. Bishen Singh had no concept of time—neither of days, nor weeks, nor months. He had no idea how long he had been in the lunatic asylum. But when his relatives and friends came to see him, he knew that a month must have gone by. He would inform the head warder that 'Miss Interview' was due to visit him. He would wash himself with great care; he would soap his body and oil his long hair and beard before combing them. He would dress up before he went to meet his visitors. If they asked him any questions, he either remained silent or answered, '*O, pardi, anekas di, bedhyana di, moong di dal of the lantern.*'

Bishen Singh had a daughter who had grown into a full-bosomed lass of fifteen. But he showed no recognition of his child. The girl wept bitterly whenever she met her father.

When talk of India and Pakistan came up, Bishen Singh began to question other lunatics about the location of Toba Tek Singh. No one could give him a satisfactory answer. His irritation mounted day by day. And now even 'Miss Interview' did not come to see him. There was a time when something had told him that his relatives were due. Now that inner voice had been silenced. And he was more anxious than ever to meet his relatives and find out whether Toba Tek Singh was in India or Pakistan. But no relatives came. Bishen Singh turned to other sources of information.

There was a lunatic in the asylum who believed he was God. Bishen Singh asked him whether Toba Tek Singh was in India or Pakistan. As was his wont, God adopted a grave mien and replied, 'We have not yet issued our orders on the subject.'

Bishen Singh got the same answer many times. He pleaded with 'God' to issue instructions so that the matter could be settled once and for all. His pleadings were in vain; 'God' had many pressing matters awaiting 'His' orders. Bishen Singh's patience ran out and one day he let 'God' have a bit of his mind '*O, pardi, good good di, anekas di, bedhyana di, moong di dal of wahi-i-guru ji ka khalsa and wahi-i-guru di fateh! Jo boley so nihal, sat sri akal!*'

This was meant to put 'God' in his place as God only of the Muslims. Surely if He had been God of the Sikhs, He would have heard the pleadings of a Sikh!

A few days before the day fixed for the exchange of lunatics, a Muslim from Toba Tek Singh came to visit Bishen Singh. This man had never been to the asylum before. When Bishen Singh saw him, he turned away. The warders stopped him. 'He's come to see you; he's your friend, Fazal Din,' they said.

Bishen Singh gazed at Fazal Din and began to mumble. Fazal Din put his hand on Bishen Singh's shoulder. 'I have been intending to see you for many days but could never find the time. All your family have safely crossed over to India. I did the best I could for them. Your daughter, Roop Kaur . . .'

Fazal Din continued somewhat haltingly, 'Yes . . . she too is well. She went along with the rest.'

Bishen Singh stood where he was without saying a word. Fazal Din started again. 'They asked me to keep in touch with you. I am told that you are to leave for India. Convey my salaams to brother Balbir Singh and to brother Wadhawa Singh . . . and also to sister Amrit Kaur . . . tell brother Balbir Singh that Fazal Din is well and happy. Both the grey buffaloes that they left behind have calved—one is a male, the other a female . . . the female died six days later. And if there is anything I can do for them, I am always willing. I have brought you a little sweet corn.'

Bishen Singh took the bag of sweet corn and handed it over to a warder. He asked Fazal Din, 'Where is Toba Tek Singh?'

Fazal Din looked somewhat puzzled and replied, 'Where could it be? It's in the same place where it always was.'

Bishen Singh asked again, 'In Pakistan or India?'

'No, not in India; it's in Pakistan,' replied Fazal Din.

Bishen Singh turned away mumbling *'O, pardi, good good di, anekas di, bedhyana di, moong di dal of the Pakistan and Hindustan of dur philley moonh.'*

Arrangements for the exchange of lunatics were completed. Lists with names of lunatics of either side had been exchanged and information sent to people concerned. The date was fixed.

It was a bitterly cold morning. Busloads of Sikh and Hindu lunatics left the Lahore asylum under heavy police escort. At the border at Wagah, the superintendents of the two countries met and settled the details of the operation.

Getting lunatics out of the buses and handing them over into the custody of officers of the other side proved to be a very difficult task. Some refused to get off the bus; those who came out were difficult to control; a few broke loose and had to be recaptured. Those who were naked had to be clothed. No sooner were the clothes put on them than they tore them off their bodies. Some came out with vile abuse, other began to sing at the top of their voices. Some squabbled; others cried or roared with laughter. They created such a racket that no one could hear a word. The female lunatics added to the noise. And all this in the bitterest of cold when people's teeth chattered like the scales of rattlesnakes.

Most of the lunatics resisted the exchange because they could not understand why they were being uprooted from one place and flung into another. Those of a gloomier disposition were yelling slogans like 'Long Live Pakistan' or 'Death to Pakistan'. Some lost their tempers and were prevented from coming to blows in the very nick of time.

At last came the turn of Bishen Singh. The Indian officer began to enter his name in the register. Bishen Singh asked him, 'Where is Toba Tek Singh? In India or Pakistan?'

'In Pakistan.' That was all that Bishen Singh wanted to know. He turned and ran back to Pakistan. Pakistani soldiers apprehended him and tried to push him back towards India. Bishen Singh refused to budge. 'Toba Tek Singh is on this side,' he cried, and began to yell at the top of his voice, '*O, pardi, good good di, anekas di, bedhyana di, moong di of Toba Tek Singh and Pakistan*.' They did their best to soothe him, to explain to him that Toba Tek Singh must have left for India; and that if any of that name was found in Pakistan, he would be dispatched to India at once. Bishen Singh refused to be persuaded. They tried to use force. Bishen Singh planted himself on the dividing line and dug his swollen feet into the ground with such firmness that no one could move him.

They let him be. He was soft in the head. There was no point using force; he would come around of his own—yes. They left him standing where he was and resumed the exchange of other lunatics.

Shortly before sunrise, a weird cry rose from Bishen Singh's throat. The man who had spent all the nights and days of the last fifteen years standing on his feet now sprawled on the ground, face down. The barbed wire fence on one side marked the territory of India; another fence marked the territory of Pakistan. In the no-man's land between the two barbed-wire fences lay the body of Bishen Singh of Toba Tek Singh village.

Translated from the Urdu by Khushwant Singh

The Curds-seller

MASTI VENKATESHA IYENGAR

Mangamma has been supplying curds to us for several years now. Our relations are of the kind usual in this city. In other places, the curds-seller supplies the curds you require every day and takes payment at the end of a month. Here, supply and payment take place on the same day and you are not bound to take any quantity every day. The curds-woman passes by our house most days. She comes into the house and asks if we want any curds. We buy if we need some and pay at the rate prevailing on the day or, at the latest, pay her the following day.

Her village is close to Avalur, I forget its name: Venkapur or something like it. As I talked sympathetically, Mangamma sometimes visited me both on her way to the city and back to her village. She would sit in the yard and chat about one thing or another, chew paan-supari or ask for it, and after resting for some time, start for her village. If I had time, she would tell me of the troubles in her household and ask me to tell her of mine. What trouble had I to report to her? By God's grace, everything is well with me. The worst I can report would be that the cat came and drank up the milk or that the rats ate the cucumber overnight. When I told her of such things, Mangamma would say, 'Alas, that is the way of the world,' and that would start her on a discourse about her experience, with hints for how to cope with refractory ways of this world. Mangamma and I thus came to be very intimate companions.

One day about a month ago, Mangamma came and called out as usual asking if I wanted curds. I was within. My little boy said, 'Yes. We want curds.' Walking up to her and stretching his hand out, he said, 'Give it.' Mangamma sat down and took out some good thick curd and put it in his hand. 'Ask mother to come soon,' she told him, 'I have to go.' By that time I had come out. Mangamma said, 'Amma, you have a child as good as gold. You are so good and your child is worthy of you. But, amma, what is the use of all this? It lasts only till he grows up. Then some creature comes along to own him. The boy who calls one "mother, mother" so prettily will not ask then whether the mother is alive or dead.'

I said, 'Something seems to have happened, Mangamma. Surely your son treats you with respect?'

'Oh well, I suppose I am foolish to expect anything else. My husband deserted me. I can expect nothing better from my son.'

'Why Mangamma, I thought you were happy with your husband.'

'You see, amma, I never bothered about wearing good saris and looking pretty; another woman did, and she drew my husband away from me. I thought it best to bear it without a murmur. I let him feel that he had his home and his wife to come to any time he chose. I shouldn't grumble, amma. They say we shouldn't sell milk and curds—they are amrita. I sinned that way and paid the penalty. I lost my husband. That is my fate. But look, amma, you must be careful. Wear pretty saris when your husband comes home. Men are inconstant. You must snare them with a pretty sari or blouse. Buy flowers and perfume, and make yourself attractive.' Then she glanced at the sari I was wearing and shook her head. 'This is all right when you are alone and working in the kitchen. But you must change in the evening. Wear something pretty.'

I laughed. It was sound sense all right. But it was a pity that she should have acquired her wisdom through suffering.

'You are right, Mangamma,' I said.

'Look, amma, there are four ways of keeping husbands true to us. Some people will tell you to administer this herb or that root. You might as well take them to the cremation-ground straightaway. Don't you listen to such advice. Give him something nice to eat every now and then; whatever your difficulties at home, dress well, look desirable, and keep smiling; get all the groceries you need once every month so that you don't need to worry him about marketing; save a little money and give him a rupee or two when he asks for it. This is all the herb and root needed. Let a woman do this, and her husband will follow her like a dog. Forget this, and his thoughts begin to wander.'

'Here is a wise woman,' I thought as I bade her goodbye.

One morning, about a fortnight ago, Mangamma came in a very dejected mood.

'What is the matter, Mangamma?' I asked.

'Nothing pleasant, amma. Why talk about it?' she said, wiping her eyes with the end of her sari. 'I don't seem to be wanted by anybody.'

'What has happened? Had words with your son?'

'Words enough, amma. I have told you of that little child, my grandson. He did something and his mother beat him. I couldn't stand it. "You are brutal," I said, "to beat that child like a rakshasi!" She turned round to me, bold as brass, and abused me roundly. "Is this the language you use to me who gave birth to your husband?" I said, "Let him come home. He will have something to say about it." When he came home I told him of what had happened: "She thrashes that poor darling mercilessly, and when I protest she has the temerity to abuse me. Can't you put some sense into her?" "Put sense into me indeed!" she intervened. "Have I no right to bring my own child to order? Didn't I give him birth even as you did to your son?"

'Well, she is his wife; I am only his mother. She can turn round on me any time, and I can do nothing. "Well, mother," he said, "after all it is her own child. Why should you interfere? If you *must* call somebody to order, here I am."

' "Then you think I am wrong?"

' "I don't know about right and wrong. But you cannot very well deny her the right to punish her own child."

' "I see. You are completely under her thumb. She may beat her child, and heap abuse on me, and it is all right with you. Tomorrow she will ask you to drive me out, and I shouldn't wonder if you do it."

' "Well, mother, what would you have me do? Suppose you tell me that you will not stay here if my wife does, and that she should not stay if you do. If I am to choose . . . well, she is a helpless woman . . ."

' "And I am not helpless? Who will look after me?"

' "Well, you have money laid by; you have cows and calves; you are not dependent on me."

' "So you would have me set up house by myself?"

' "That is as you please. If you insist on setting up house separately, I wouldn't say no. I have had enough of these bickerings."

' "Very well then. From this afternoon I live apart from you. May you and your wife be happy."

'I said this and came away with the curds.' Mangamma burst into tears as she ended her narrative. I did what I could to comfort her. 'Forget it, Mangamma. I know you will go home and live with them as before. These things adjust themselves.'

The next day she appeared to be a little more composed, though certainly not her old cheerful self. I asked her if she had made peace with her son. 'Peace! Do you think this daughter-in-law of mine would permit mother and son to be on good terms? By the time I went home yesterday she had kept my pots and pans, an earthen vessel full of ragi and another of rice, some salt and chillies, all on one side. She and her husband had finished their meal and she was lolling on the mat without a care in the world. Apparently they were waiting for an excuse to put me out, and I supplied it. All right, I won't thrust myself on them. I now live by myself. You see how far they go, amma? I used to give some curds to the child every day before going out. Today she took the child away just at that time. Clearly she doesn't want me to speak to her child.'

I was surprised that what was after all a trivial incident should have assumed such proportions. But of course there was nothing I could do about it. After a few commonplaces I sent her away.

For a day or two after that, Mangamma did not mention the subject again. I took it that she was living separately. And then one day she asked me what the velvet jacket I wore cost me.

'Why this interest in it, Mangamma?' I asked.

'You see, amma, hitherto I was saving up money for my son and grandson. I see no point in my doing so any longer. I thought I might buy myself a velvet jacket.'

'It might cost seven or eight rupees.'

She left and apparently ordered the jacket on her way home. She wore it when she came the next day.

'You see this finery, amma? When my husband was with me, I never bought a good sari; and he went after another woman. I saved money for my son, and you know what happened. Now I am flaunting velvet!'

I wondered whether the shock of being turned out by her son had unsettled her mind. Extreme passion sometimes has that effect. I said nothing however.

The story of the velvet jacket did not end there. It led to quarrels with some people in the village. One of the boys of the village was studying in Bangalore. He affected western dress—collar, tie and all. When he met Mangamma, he said jocularly, 'Well, Mangamma, what is the festive occasion? I mean, the velvet jacket . . .'

Mangamma flared up, 'You imperinent youngster! Hold you tongue, will you? If you can choke yourself with that thing around your neck, why grudge me my velvet jacket?' Hot words passed, a dozen people gathered, and there was laughter at her expense.

This was duly reported to me the following day. The daughter-in-law made this the occasion for adding her own comments—in Mangamma's hearing. She said to her neighbours, 'My mother-in-law cannot buy me a blouse. But did you see hers?' At the time of her son's wedding, Mangamma had given the bride a necklace, earrings, bangles, pendants and a waistband. Every year she had also been buying her some ornament or other. The daughter-in-law forgot all this.

Mangamma took no notice of her comments the first couple of times and then complained to her son, 'Your wife has been making biting remarks about my jacket. She has been going about saying that I never bought her any present. Haven't I given her bangles, necklace and earrings?' Before the son could say anything, his wife snapped, 'I suppose the old widow wants to wear earrings and bangles. She can have them and flaunt them.' 'Less sauce, my girl,' said the husband in mild rebuke and, turning to his mother, said, 'Mother, I have had enough of these quarrels. If you want the jewellery you gave my wife, you can take them back.'

'You see, amma?' Mangamma asked. 'He does not ask his wife to stop saying things about me to our neighbours. He offers me the jewellery, putting me in the wrong! I am sick of life.'

I felt very sorry for her. She was old and this son was her only child. Surely his wife could be more considerate to her mother-in-law? And all this because the old woman asked her not to beat the child! Why can't people be more sensible? But then this is how quarrels generally develop. If two people do not like each other, any trivial incident is enough to touch off a quarrel; and there is endless pain for everyone concerned.

Some time after this, Mangamma came to me with a request, 'Amma, you are good people and I can trust you. I have some money laid by. Could you put it in that place they call a bank? It is attracting people's attention.'

'What happened?'

'There is a man called Rangappa in our village, a dandy and a gambler. Yesterday as I was coming along with the curds, he joined me and said, "I hope you are keeping well, Mangamma."

' "So, so," I said, "you know how things are with me."

' "Yes, Mangamma, I know. You are right. With people behaving as they do, how can anybody be happy? These young people cannot keep their tongues in leash and we older people wonder that such things should be. But that is how the world goes, Mangamma."

'We walked on. I grew uneasy wondering why he was following me—there is a deep well near that grove, and I had some money in my purse. But nothing happened. He asked me for some lime, took it and went his way. Today he was there again. He talked of this and that and then said, "Mangamma, I am badly in need of money. Could you lend me some? Come harvest time, I shall sell my ragi and pay you back." "Money!" I said, "how should I have any?" "O, we all know. What is the good of keeping money buried, Mangamma? You can help me, and earn some interest on it." And after a while he added, "I would not have asked you if you and your son and daughter-in-law lived together. Naturally you would have liked to give them presents now and then. But now that you are living away from them . . ."

'You see, amma, when a woman lives alone she draws attention.'

I said that I would speak to my husband about it.

The next day she said, after measuring out the curds, 'Shall we go in, amma? You can count the money.'

'I haven't mentioned the matter to my husband, Mangamma. Some other time.'

'But I am feeling frightened, amma. Rangappa waylaid me again this morning near the grove. "Sit down, Mangamma," he said, "you are not in a hurry?" I sat down—I was afraid he might use force. He talked of all things and sundry and then took my hand and said, "How nice you look, Mangamma!"

'Amma, even when I was young, my own husband would not hold my hand. No other man has ever held it. And now this has happened! I drew away at once and said curtly, "Enough of this nonsense, Rangappa. You are not my husband, and it is no business of yours how I look." Yesterday he wanted my money, and today my honour. The man who sat by my side on my wedding day, had the auspicious rice showered on him, and called me wife—he left me in my youth. Another woman would have sought consolation elsewhere. But I preserved my honour. And today this rascal dares to seize my hand!'

Mangamma's affairs seemed to be taking a serious turn. 'Look, Mangamma, you are heading for trouble. Tell your son about this. Why don't you forget the past and go back to him?'

'And give my daughter-in-law a chance to spread

rumours about me and make me an outcast? . . . Well, it is getting late, amma. Please mention the matter to your husband and tell me tomorrow.'

She was back again an hour later. 'A strange thing happened today,' she began.

'What?'

'I bought some sweets for the child . . .'

I didn't understand this. She had told me that her grandchild was not allowed near her.

'What child?'

'Why, my grandchild, of course. What other child could it be?'

'But you told me that he was not allowed to come to you?'

'True, his mother forbids it. But would the child keep away from me? He runs up to me when his mother is not looking, drinks some milk, asks for curds, and dances about when I give it. When he upsets things, I tell him that his mother will take him away, and that keeps him quiet. It is a delight to watch children's pranks, amma. So today I bought some sweets for him and put them in my basket. Near Shankarpur a crow swooped down from a mango tree and carried off the packet.'

'That is nothing to worry about. You can buy some more.'

'Of course I can. It is not that, amma. But they say it is a bad omen, being touched by a crow.'

'Why, what happens if it does?'

'They say it means death. That is why I was perturbed. But after a minute, I told myself it was as well. Mine is a life nobody values. The sooner I touch the feet of God, the better. Anyway, that is what happened.'

'Don't be silly, Mangamma. You put a packet of sweets where any sensible crow would go for it, and when the packet is carried off, you say it is an omen of death! Go home, and don't be absurd.'

'Then you think it does not mean anything?'

'Nonsense. Go home and forget it.'

It is strange, the way this woman's thoughts run, I thought. She wants her son, her daughter-in-law and her grandson; she wants to be respected as the head of the household. All that is natural enough, quite human. Now that she is denied what she wants, she is tired of life; and yet she is afraid of death! And she wants to conceal that fear. We say that village folk are simple and unsophisticated. But how complex her mind and thoughts are—layer on layer, fold on fold! It is a queer game, this thing we call life.

Mangamma reported fresh developments when she came next. Her grandson had come to stay with her. She was delighted. 'The courage of the child!' she said. 'He is such a little fellow, hardly that high, and yet he leaves his mother and comes to me! He used to come on the sly, but yesterday he came and said he would not go back to his mother. She came, threatened to thrash him, made a scene—but the child clung to my knees and would not budge. Of course I urged him to go back, and his father also coaxed him. But the child would not listen. It is strange, amma, these ten days I have been a little scared of sleeping alone in the house. But the presence of this little child has given me courage—I feel I have male protection. My grown-up son will not have me with him, but my grandson tells me he will stand by me. It must be God that put it into his head. My daughter-in-law raged throughout the night. But it had no effect on the child. This morning I felt that the child should not be left alone when I was away selling curds. I took him to her door, and he went in.'

'But suppose she beats the child?'

'No, she won't. She might beat him sometimes when he is always with her. But now she will be happy that the child will be with her at least for half a day. It is this way, amma; you see, when we lived together I had never noticed how pretty my daughter-in-law was. Of course she does look queer when she frowns. But now I see her from a distance, as you might say. She does look pretty, and that is why my son is her slave. I also took my son for granted. I never noticed when he came in and when he went out. Now I sit at the door of my house and wonder why he is so late in coming or why he leaves home so early. She must feel the same about her child. If she beats him, he would come away to the city with me tomorrow. Would she give up the child she has borne?'

'Perceptive woman,' I said to myself. I felt that their differences would soon be amicably settled.

And that is what happened. The child spent two mornings with his parents and, on the third, he insisted on accompanying his grandmother on her rounds in the city. The old woman could not, of course, carry both the child and the basket with the pot of curds. This presented a problem. Then her son and daughter-in-law came to her and said, 'Amma, granted that we were in the wrong; should you carry your anger so far?' The neighbours also spoke for them. Mangamma went back without loss of face, as she was longing to do. But taking the child to the city with her was still a problem. So they came to an arrangement. Mangamma had so far kept the milk-and-curds business in her own hands. The ostensible reason was that the daughter-in-law had to do the cooking; the real reason was that Mangamma wanted the purse strings in her own hands. Now that the child insisted on staying with her, things had to change. The daughter-in-law said, 'Why should you, in your old age, go out every day in the hot sun? It is time you stopped working. You are the head of the family and it is right that you should be at home to see that everything is in order. I shall do the curds-selling.' Mangamma agreed. 'You may take it over,' she said, 'I shall go one or two days in the week when I feel like it.'

One day Mangamma and her daughter-in-law came together. One of them had the child in her arms and the other carried the basket. 'This is my daughter-in-law, amma,' Mangamma said. 'She does not want her old mother-in-law to work any more. She has taken me back home. She says that at my age I should not walk all this distance in the hot sun. She will bring you curds henceforth.'

And so Mangamma handed us over to her daughter-in-law. I spoke to them for some time, exhorted them to treat each other well and dismissed them with paan-supari.

So far I had heard only Mangamma's version of the quarrel, and I was curious to hear the other side. So one day, I asked the daughter-in-law, 'You seem to be a good and a sensible woman, Nanjamma. How could you drive out your own mother-in-law?'

'I would never do so, amma. I am not a rakshasi. But you see, she insists on having her own way in everything and makes a non-entity of my husband. If he is not respected as the man of the house, what sort of husband would he make? What sort of wife would I be, and how can I run the house? I stood it for some time—after all she was his mother and had brought him up. But when she started saying I shouldn't beat my child, I thought it was time to protest. Have I no rights as a mother?'

I smiled. 'So your way of asserting your rights as a mother is to beat your child?'

'I beat him and I fondle him too. She who objects to my beating him may also object to my fondling him. She would hold me accountable for anything I may do. My son is *my* son, and my husband is *my* husband. If I do not have the right to say a word to my husband or to slap the child when he goes wrong, what sort of life would I be leading?'

If Mangamma had sounded sensible, so did her daughter-in-law.

'Now you have won your freedom?'

'Things look better. After all, it is a question of adjustment. If I push the matter to breaking point, some designing person may wheedle her money out of her. There is a fellow called Rangappa. When mother-in-law lived separately he asked her to lend him money, and I heard she was willing. He said so. Then I told my son, "Go to your grandma. She will give you sweets. Don't come back till I tell you to." I wanted to end the quarrel and thought of this device.'

'So the child did not go to her of his own accord?'

'He did, but I suggested it to him.'

'Did you tell your husband of this?'

'You may be sure I did not. Men don't understand these things.'

Nanjamma was certainly not inferior to Mangamma in common sense. The struggle is still going on in that household. That woman's son and this woman's husband—it is for him the battle is being fought. The mother is determined not to give him up and the wife is equally determined to capture him. It is difficult to speak of victory or defeat in a matter like this. The daughter-in-law is like the crocodile, safe under the water, catching hold of the leg of the child. The mother is on the bank and is pulling at the hands of the child hoping to save him. The plight of the child is far from enviable. The same battle goes on in the house of Mangamma the curds-seller in the village, and of Thangamma the curds-buyer in the city. The last act of this play will never be written.

Translated from the Kannada by
N. Moorthy Rao and the author

Womenfolk

KIRIT DOODHAT

'Jadu, are all preparations over?' asked Savaji-ata. Jadu uncle responded, 'Yes, ata'—'ata' was what we called grandfather and his brothers.

'How are things in the kitchen?'

'There are reservations, but they are from the womenfolk. Mother and aunt are still not prepared to send Manju.' That made Savaji-ata wild. 'These women, they will never learn! I told them not to insist, but do they understand? Now, if they don't, I must straighten them out.' Having expressed his opinion, he left the office and walked towards the kitchen.

'The womenfolk have gone a little overboard,' said Jadu uncle and started drawing squares for hopscotch on the office floor. Then he noticed me and said, 'Boy, tell your grandmother to keep you ready first thing in the morning so that you don't delay the others.

Meanwhile in came Ramaji-ata, Jadu uncle's father. He enquired, 'Where is Savaji-bhai, and how far has the matter progressed?' 'Mother and aunt are still not willing;

he has gone to the kitchen.' 'Does it mean that tomorrow's Amreli visit has to be called off? In fact, that Batako chap left for Medi today and I sent word with him confirming tomorrow's plans.'

'Mother says, "Forget this proposal. We will find many willing families apart from the Viranis. Does everything hinge around this?" '

'Mother is silly. Is the Virani family so beneath ours that the proposal should be turned down for a flimsy nothing? I have already told Magan the tailor to set up his machine in this office from Thursday. Our gifts to Manju must fill an entire room of the Virani house. After all, she is the only daughter among all the children of us four brothers.'

Suddenly Savaji-ata entered the office, fuming with anger. He hit at the bed with his turban and said in exasperation, 'Oh, this husbandry business!'

'What's the matter, bhai?' Ramaji-ata asked.

'. . . Had to make Mother cry, what else? I told her clearly, "Mother, you and these four women can leave this house. We need none of you." Then she started crying and said, "In that case, do what you like and drown the girl in a well. We will keep her ready early tomorrow." . . . Jadu, oh, this husbandry business!'

By this time Vaghaji-ata and Mathur uncle had returned with the tractor. Vaghaji-ata was Manju's father, but was not interested in the fact that it was his daughter whose affairs were being discussed. He followed a simple policy: worldly affairs were Savaji-bhai's responsibility and he should sort them out. But Savaji-ata's son, Mathur uncle, was very active. Even as he was jumping off the tractor, he asked, 'So, Jadu, what is the view of the women-generals?'

Jadu uncle said, 'They have somehow been made to accept. We can breathe again once tomorrow's visit passes off.'

Vaghaji-ata came inside and sat down quietly in the office. Bhagat too sat there silently as if he did nothing but chant prayers the whole day. Bhagat used to be a man of this world like his three brothers; but by now he had come to be known as Bhagat. Earlier, he was involved in family life; but one day he called his wife, Chanchalma, and told her, 'From now on leave me to myself and to God. You will be my wife in the eyes of the people, but I am beginning a new life from tomorrow. From now on, no wordly activities for me.' And then he became an ardent devotee. People said that Bhagat had become one with God, though on this matter a different view prevailed too. Before he became a devotee, Bhagat used to borrow beedis from the low-caste villagers. Those people believed that his brain was affected by the smoke of borrowed beedis, that his devotion was mere pretense. Bhagat refused to talk to anybody beneath the status of God. However, occasionally he would seek me out for a conversation since I was a child. As I played about in our courtyard, he would call out, 'Come here, nephew.'

I would go close to him and he would tell me that he had just completed composing a Mirabai bhajan. He would very often compose a Mirabai bhajan or Narsimh Mehta bhajan. He asked me, 'Want to hear?'

After I nodded 'yes', he sang his bhajan keeping beat on the rusty tin lid of some wooden box. Then he would ask me, 'Makes sense?'

I would shake my head to say no. He would bare his teeth in agreement and say, 'How can it? This is devotion;

what? Devotion.' Then I would repeat, 'Devotion.'

The important thing was that he used to offer me a ten-paisa coin after subjecting me to his bhajans. So, as long as I got the money, I did not mind his singing, whether it was devotion or nonsense. That mattered very little to me.

'It wasn't proper that you made Mother cry,' Mathur uncle remarked. He was right. Mathur uncle's grandmother, Jakal-ma, was revered by everyone in the village. Her word was respected, her advice sought by everyone. The womenfolk refrained from using foul language while beating children if she was around. Even Savaji-ata used to ask for her advice whenever he felt confused in his transactions. So this was a new turn to events.

Manju's betrothal with Dinesh, the son of Medi's sarpanch, Ratibhai, had been fixed while she was still a child. Dinesh was his father's only child. His mother died in his infancy. Matters had gone well all these years. But when the wedding was barely three or four months away, somebody managed to convince Dinesh that Manju had spots on the secret parts of her body. In the past, two or three girls of their community had been driven out by their husbands when such spots were detected on the night after the wedding. So Dinesh wanted to have a check-up done in time to avoid any future embarrassment. He sent a message saying either he would go to Manju's place for getting her check up-done, or she should be sent to his place.

On summer afternoons I used to go to Savaji-ata's house to play after completing my homework. I would meet Manju drying her hair after her bath, after completing her household work, or writing letters to Dinesh at a table by the poor light of the room. I would climb up the table and ask, 'What are you doing, Manju?' She used to blush a little and reply, 'You see, I am writing to Dinesh.'

'Have you mentioned me in the letter?' I always insisted that I be mentioned in letters sent or received. Manju would pretend to frown, 'You will certainly be mentioned when your wife writes to you.' But I placed the practical difficulty before her. I did not have a wife yet. Manju said, 'You will have a wife someday. If you are so desperate, go home and try some magic.' I used to go back to ask my father, 'Father, when will I get a wife?'

Father would give his consent at once, 'If you like, we can bring one home tomorrow itself. Tell me, you want a wife with a single ponytail or with two tails?'

This confused me so I asked grandmother what the difference was. And she would explain to me that a wife with a single tail is hard-working whereas one with two will work only when she finds time from her make-up and fashion. Then, after giving some serious thought to this matter, I used to say, 'We must get a wife with a single ponytail. What use is a wife if she does not work?'

Manju sported two ponytails, and she did not do much work at home. Her mother used to tell her frequently, 'You lazy brotherless girl, learn something useful while you are here with us; otherwise, at your in-laws' we too will get abused with you.' But Chanchal-ma, Bhagat's wife, maintained, 'Manju is the family's Laxmi. The family could pay off all debts after she was born. How could she be asked to slog?'

Nobody argued against this, especially because, among other things, Chanchal-ma was not considered as sophisticated as the other women in the family. Savaji-ata frequently used to say, 'She is a peasant girl, how else will she talk?' She worked the whole day like a beast of burden and drank cups of boiling tea that burnt her innards. 'Because her grandfather and our father were close friends from childhood, Father did not turn down the proposal.'

So Chanchal-ma was indeed a little less sophisticated but once she started speaking, she did not spare anybody. Except that she always respected Jakal-ma. Moreover, if occasionally her childhood culture surfaced, she did not mind using a foul word or two. Then Jakal-ma used to scold her, 'Chanchal-bahu, this isn't right.' And, as if she wanted to touch the words of the old woman to her forehead, Chanchal-ma would pull her pallu down her forehead. But when she heard Dinesh's story of spots, Chanchal-ma let her tongue loose, lashed at him and expressed her desire to finish him off as well as his father. She cursed, 'Manju is my daughter. Let anybody come to have her check-up done, I, I will show . . . !'

All women of the family were united on this issue. Even the prudent Jakal-ma had lost her equanimity.

All women said that it would not matter if the betrothal had to be broken but Manju should not be subjected to the check-up.

Savaji-ata immediately went to Medi. He said to Ratibhai, 'We have known each other for so many years; how could you think that I was trying to pass off a pebble for a pearl to you?' But Ratibhai offered no other reply but: 'Dinesh's mother died when he was a baby. He has been brought up like a prince. If he says it is day, it is day; when he says it is night, it is night.'

When this reply was brought back, the men all sat together to decide the future course of action. Ramaji-ata said, 'There is only one way out now. We must accept the demand Dinesh has made.' Savaji-ata asked Jadu uncle to inform his mother, 'Keep Manju ready tomorrow morning. We have to send her to Amreli to Dr Khokhar's hospital. If anybody asks, say Manju's aunt is unwell and has been admitted to Dr Khokhar's hospital. Say that you are going to visit her. And let Dinesh verify what he wants to. Go, let us now get over this whole affair.'

Jadu uncle left, but returned with great speed. 'The womenfolk say that this engagement must he broken.' Savaji-ata was more surprised by this than he was by Dinesh's demand. 'Look at this, they say cancel the betrothal! And when another proposal is made, the first question that will be asked is, "why did this one fall through?" '

Vaghaji-ata's face started glowing with energy like *maryada purushottam* Ramachandra's. He said, 'Jadu, get the cart ready and take your aunt back to her parents.'

Vaghaji-ata said again, 'Brothers, let us stop doing our men's work from tomorrow and start cooking in the kitchen.' Jadu uncle said, 'Nephew, women always run upto their wits' end.' The word 'end' was in English. 'We will be fools if we get into any further exchange of words with them. When you grow up, never forget this. What?'

Savaji-ata said, 'This is what will happen when you face the ghagra-clad army.'

Then everybody took a deep breath and broke into laughter. They had not experienced this kind of joy even when they watched Bhavai performances where the drummer would play a prank on gentlemen as dignified as Savaji-ata: instead of saying 'Give alms, gende-folk, we are your sweepers', the drummer used to say 'Give alms, kende-folk, sweepers'. Even that disguised cursing had not made them roar so much with laughter. It was good I was present there. Otherwise, if some outsider had come in and seen them in that state, one would have thought that they were bemoaning Jakal-ma's demise.

It was decided that Manju would go to Amreli the next day. It was decided that Jadu uncle should go in his cart and return in the evening after the business was over. I said that I wanted to see *Jesal-Toral* which was showing in some cinema hall in Amreli at that time. So it was decided that I too would be included in the party. Manju had been crying since the morning and was reluctant to get up from where she sat, in a room. So, Savaji-ata got wild, 'Go, it is getting late. Why not get over the whole business fast?'

Jakal-ma's eyes filled with tears. She held Manju by the arm, 'Get moving, lazy brotherless girl, what will you gain by not going?' Except for Manju's sobs and the heavy breathing of the bullocks, everything else was quiet. Only Bhagat said something, as if he had raised his brows in order to talk to God, 'Sister, Manju is still immature, that is why she is weeping. Otherwise, everyone has to pay for one's karma. How said, God?' So saying, Bhagat gave his consent. One felt that God had nodded in consent. Between her sobs, Manju said to Jadu uncle, 'If you love my bhabhi, brother, let us return home.' Finally, in irritation, Jadu uncle said, 'I may re-marry if your bhabhi dies, but this cart will not turn back.' After this, Manju did not plead with Jadu uncle at all until the end of the journey.

When we all reached Dr Khokhar's hospital, Dinesh's motorbike could be seen parked outside. Jadu uncle said to me, 'Boy, I am off to buy tobacco. You stay here.' About the same time, Dinesh emerged out of a room and, pointing towards another room, he said to Manju, 'Come this way.' Manju clutched my hand, 'Stay with me.' Dinesh said, 'He is not required.' Then he said to me, 'You stay here.' He led Manju into the room and then within a few moments rushed out of the room, whistling, got onto his motorbike and left. Manju followed him out of the room. I asked, 'What happened, Manju?' She replied, 'It is better to die than to live a life like this.' I probed further; but she gave no reply, just wept and wept.

After a while Jadu uncle returned. He asked me about what had transpired. I told him that Dinesh had left and Manju had been crying. 'It is all right, let's be quick otherwise we will be late for the movie.'

On our way back, Manju continued weeping throughout the journey. Back home, everybody started enquiring, 'What happened, what happened?' Jadu uncle said, 'Dinesh Kumar left even before I returned there, and Manju has done nothing but cry.'

The next morning at ten, Jadu uncle brought home a palmfruit and sweets, and he brought the news that Ratibhai had agreed to the marriage. He carried the palmfruit to the kitchen where Manju had been sitting and sulking. 'Take this palmfruit and break it open on Manju's head. In fact, it should be broken on every woman's head. The lot, all those who had got together and had been crying!'

Then everyone from Vaghaji-ata to Ramaji-ata started

going to the kitchen to rebuke the womenfolk and blame them for nearly causing disaster. 'No sense at all. If we had followed your advice, we would have become the laughing-stock of the community.' In the end, Savaji-ata came in too, saying, 'When there is a difficulty, one must use one's brain. It is not good to shout every time you see water. Do you follow? But what is the use of talking of wisdom before you, and what is the use in not talking either? It is like pouring a lot of water on dry stones. These women, really they are . . .'

Jakal-ma had been quietly telling beads sitting in a corner. She said nothing. But as Savaji-ata turned his back on them and took a step towards the office, Chanchal-ma stood up from near the fire where she was making millet rotis. She held a burning stick in her hand and she spoke venomously, 'Masters of your mother, you talk of wisdom now? Your bottoms should be burnt with this stick . . . Look at this gem of a girl . . . ' She banged the burning stick on the blackened crackling wall. The sparks flew in all directions. Then Chanchal-ma sat down and started crying loudly. She sobbed and sobbed, while the millet roti in the baking pan turned dark like coal.

Translated from the Gujarati by G.N. Devy

Redemption

Pudumai Pithan

It was the children who knew her best. They called her Murukku-patti Muthachi. To them, she had always been old like their own grandmothers. She made a living by selling murukku or gram-flour savouries which she made herself. So she became Murukku-patti. There was nothing dramatic or spectacular about her life. She never shot into affluence as people like her often do in novels. Nor did a long-lost brother, prosperous and rich, appear in her life from far-off Rangoon. Her wares brought her no more than a meagre living. In poverty and want she was elder sister to that proverbial embodiment of indigence, Kuchela. The wonder of it was that in this work-a-day world long past the age of the legerdemain of the orthodox which goes by the name of miracles, this penniless old woman, who was barely able to eke out a living day by day, should make plans to celebrate the wedding of her only daughter. But that was what Murukku-patti did.

As we know, only the poor and the downtrodden

remain slaves to the withered old customs and compulsions of our Hindu society even to this day. This society of ours does not permit grown-up girls, especially of her class, to remain unmarried for long. In this respect the state of the unmarried girl is even more pathetic than that of the child-widow. The latter may, at the worst, feel humiliated and unwanted, but a maid is tortured on the cross of scandal and public condemnation. The tyrannies of social taboos have no hold on the rich, for they are the gods beyond the pale of laws of society. Not that the old woman Muthachi was sensitive to all this. But somehow she had realized that it was imperative that her daughter should be married and had arranged to give her in marriage to Madasami, a pankha-puller in Mr Windle's bungalow. The wedding was to take place the next morning.

At five-thirty that evening, Murukku-patti was sitting on the payal of goldsmith Thangvelu Asari's house. The grey-haired old woman sat leaning against the wall, her legs outstretched before her, each wrinkle on that lined, aged face eloquently proclaiming a whole history of care and hardship all its own. She wore no *pampadam*, the traditional pair of earrings, and the empty holes in her ears hung down large and gaping, dangling like rings of dried snake-gourd. Two lengths of white cloth—at least it must have been white once—did duty for a sari and proclaimed her humble status in life. She stuffed a withered betel into her mouth and followed it up with a strand of black tobacco. She then wiped her fingers on the floor and asked, 'What about it, Asari? Come on, do finish the job quickly. Don't let me down.'

'Achi, don't be afraid. Before the sun goes down your

job will be finished,' assured the goldsmith as he went on with the job of polishing the pair of earrings he was working on. It was doubtful if the old woman found his words reassuring. For three months she had been entreating him to do this small job for her. And that day since morning she had been literally sitting on his doorstep, refusing to go home without her earrings. Poor Muthachi had not eaten all day. She sighed.

A little later she tried again. Smiling ingratiatingly, she said, 'I have to return to Kalisavaram. The path lies through lonely woods, as you know. When I get back home, I have to complete all the arrangements for tomorrow. There is so much to do.'

'I would have finished your earrings if that other job of Sirukulam Subbaier's had not come,' said the goldsmith. 'He would not leave me in peace until I had finished what he wanted yesterday, when he came to take it away. Or else your rings would have been ready by this time. It is not such a big job, after all.' Having allayed her anxiety, he continued, 'Oh well, that is all right then . . . But, tell me, Achi, this is the first wedding in your house, isn't it? How much will it cost?' The smith was trying to make conversation.

'Oh, something . . . according to my humble means,' said Muthachi cautiously. 'Maybe, all told, a couple of hundred.'

'And the jewels? How much would they be?' asked the goldsmith.

'How much, eh? These jewels are nothing more than what my late husband gave me. A couple of rings. And this pair of earrings which you are making. The rest of the expense comes to, say, fifty. But let that be. You tell me, when will this job be finished?' Muthachi was becoming anxious about her earrings.

'Look! Can't you see I am working? Do my hands have wings or what? I am trying to work as fast as I can. Don't be in such a hurry.' And he continued soothingly, 'But tell me, have you heard this? Times have become bad, I must say. There is no safety anywhere. Nothing but theft and robbery all over the place. The other day there was a burglary in our landlord's house. They lost nearly two thousand rupees. And you know that Chettiar who has a pawn shop? He had gone to Pattamadai a few days ago to collect the interest from his clients there. When he was returning with the money tied round his waist, he was waylaid near Malapperambu and robbed. The poor man reached home in a frenzy of grief, beating his breast. This is what we have come to. Would such things have happened in the days of our Kattappa Raja?'

'And who was it that perpetrated all these atrocities and escaped?' enquired the old woman.

'Oh, who else but that Sangu Thevan! We have had such goings on only after these Company people came.'

'May the Lord of the Bamboo Reed protect me! Well, have you finished?'

'Just a minute. A little finishing here and it is done,' said the goldsmith, and presently he wrapped the pair of earrings, as well as the gold dust left over, in two separate pieces of red tissue paper and handed them over to the old woman. Muthachi undid the knot in her sari-end and taking out a Company rupee placed it near the goldsmith.

'What is this? I have been working for you since morning without even stopping to eat my meal, and is this all I get?'

'You know me, brother. A poor, old woman.'

'So you will deprive the labourer of his honest wages? You will make him work for nothing?'

The old woman knew she had no time to argue. She gave the goldsmith what he asked for, tied the earrings carefully in her sari-end, tucked the small knot of cloth safely at the waist, and started on her homeward journey walking as fast as she could.

However fast one walked, a human body is not a motor car, after all. What is more, she was an old woman. The hour of twilight, which poets describe so enthusiastically, soon passed and night came swiftly. The road was a mere deserted footpath through dense woodland, full of trees and shadows. Soon it grew darker and darker until one couldn't see the palm of one's own hand.

Muthachi had never been afraid till now—either of thieves or of evil spirits—but today was different. She seemed to see a Sangu Thevan behind every tree; on every branch overhead crouched a Sangu Thevan ready to spring down on her. Passing each tree became a kind of victory. And so Murukku-patti hurried along, trying to escape from the Sangu Thevans that her imagination had created.

As she walked thus, tormented by fear, a dark shape appeared before her. The old woman's lips murmured the dreaded name of Sangu Thevan in a frightened whisper, though she was hardly aware of it. She trembled from head to foot. Then, paralysed with terror, she stood there unable to take a step forward. She tucked in the knot at her waist more securely and prayed, 'Dear Lord of the Bamboo Reed, you alone must protect me!' When, in a little while, she saw the dark form disappear ahead of her in the same direction as she was taking, it occurred to her that he could be a traveller like herself, hurrying home on foot. Pinning her faith on the Lord of the Bamboo Reed, she went forward and called, 'Who is it, please? Stop sir, sir!'

'Who is it shouting there?' The deep voice of a man came through the darkness.

'Please wait. I am also coming,' called the old woman as she walked briskly forward. The dark shape became clearer. She could see the man's big turban, long side-whiskers, his short dhoti tied tightly round his sturdy waist, and the stout stick he was carrying under his arm. When she saw how tall and powerfully built he was, the old woman felt relieved and confident that now she would reach home safely.

'Look here, old woman; where do you think you are going in this pitch-dark night?' asked the stranger.

'Not far, but how fast can an old woman like me walk? Is it very late? I have to go home and finish the rest of my work. What time is it?' The old woman walked on asking many questions.

'Time? It is not very late. Where exactly are you going?' asked the man falling into step beside her.

'What does it matter where I am going? I have to see someone in your village.'

'What caste are you?'

'We are Vellalas. You?'

'We are Thevars.'

'So you are a Thevar, are you? Then may I ask how you can permit this state of affairs? When someone of your community turns bandit and plunders the countryside, how can honourable men like you keep quiet? Is this behaviour a sign of the age of sin in which we live?'

'Don't be so angry, dear old woman,' chided the man, laughing. 'After all that is our traditional occupation, don't you know? . . . True. This is the age of sin. But you talk without understanding. The man you speak of belongs to one branch of our community, I to another. That scoundrel is one of the Kondayam Kottai Thevars. I belong to Veeram Mudithangi. Now tell me, old woman,' he asked with curiosity, 'why are you so frightened?'

'That is because I am worried about my millions,' mocked the old woman, trying to hide her true thoughts.

'Don't lie to me. If your waist is not heavy with gold, why be afraid of anyone on the way?' the stranger taunted her.

'All right,' said old Muthachi confidentially. 'Why shouldn't I tell you the truth? Tomorrow is my daughter's wedding. I have to reach home and get everything ready. I have obtained a pair of earrings on hire. Even the poor must try to impress people with such things or else who will respect us?'

'Oh, you have that pair of earrings with you. How many children do you have? Is your daughter the eldest?' His eyes watched her, though she did not know it, and his mind also.

'Only one.'

'I see.'

They walked on in silence. The Thevan seemed preoccupied. He repeatedly glanced at the old woman as he continued on his way, lost in his own thoughts.

A little later the old woman said, 'At last ! There I see

the temple. Now I can go home by myself.'

'Achi! Wait. I have something for you,' said the stranger. 'Take this. Let your first grandson bear my name.'

'God bless you, sir. May you prosper ever more!' murmured the old woman and, happy at this unexpected piece of good fortune, put out her hand to receive the gift. 'What name shall I give him?'

'Sangu Thevan.'

The bag of coins Muthachi had received fell from her hand, and she whispered in terror, 'Spare me.'

'Achi, don't be afraid. No harm will come to you.' And the man picked up the bag and put it back into her hand. The old woman, too frightened to speak or protest, hurried away, only turning to look at him again and again. Soon she was lost in the darkness of the night.

Sangu Thevan sat down on a rock nearby. He was no longer feeling confused. He could think clearly again.

'Yes, the poor woman was taken aback,' he chuckled to himself. 'Naturally. It was not a rupee or two. It was a hundred rupees. A fine joke, indeed: Sangu Thevan and the old woman. What a story!' Murmuring to himself, he rose and walked off briskly along a footpath leading away from the village and its temple, back into the woods.

Translated from the Tamil by Santha Ranga

Must Visit Eluru

CHAASO

In the small inter-class compartment of the train, I lay snugly with my holdall spread on the upper berth and my luggage tucked under my head. Around eleven—or was it twelve?—someone tugged at me insistently and woke me. Yawning, I opened my eyes; there stood below a widow. She was a stranger; quite fair, past forty, who had not shaved her half-grey hair.

I composed myself and sat up. There was no one else in the compartment. I looked out; it appeared to be Nidadavole station.

'Who are you, please?' I asked.

Her face quite split in two with laughter.

'Get down first, she said in a tone of singular familiarity. The light from the compartment lamp lit up her mouth right up to the pomegranate bud of an uvula. When she smiled, her rosy cheeks, swelling like apples, crinkled up her eyes. Her soft full lips, like scarlet spring beetles, had grown slack, but within were well preserved pearl-like teeth.

'Who are you, please?' I repeated my question.

'Get down first, I say,' she said, with the same easy tone of close acquaintance.

I jumped down. The rear end of my dhoti was loose and the dhoti almost came undone. She laughed and held up the plaited end of the dhoti, saving my honour. Taken aback, I snatched it from her hand, dressed myself right and proper and took another look at her. She was clad in an ochre-coloured Mysore silk dhoti of the kind widows use as a sari, with an appropriately broad black border sprinkled here and there with a thread of zari. Rather rotund, about five feet tall, the golden skin of her plump arms merged with the ochre of her dhoti-sari and gleamed brilliantly.

'It has been a long time, looks like you have forgotten!' she said.

I was baffled. I could not remember any such lady-like widow, and one claiming such intimacy, among my relatives. I stood staring at her.

'Your son has gone to eat his meal—why do you look shocked?' she said.

Who was this woman? Who was 'my son'? My son was just three months old. My wife had gone to her mother's place to deliver the child and was still there. Who was this, this divine-looking devil? I grew rather alarmed.

'You have not seen me after I suffered this fate. True, how can you recognize me? The last time you saw me was nine years ago. I look so different now,' she said and started weeping.

'There must be a mistake. You have mistaken me for someone else,' I said.

'Am I mistaken? Didn't you go to school in Vizianagram?'

'Yes, I did.'

'Your name is Purushottam, isn't it?'

'Yes!'

'Now do you recognize me?'

I racked my brains. I couldn't recall her. Meanwhile she was saying, 'Yes. Men have hearts of stone, no room for love and affection there. They won't remember certain things. But do women carry these things in their hearts? Good heavens, someone might enter the compartment. Won't you sit with me and chat for a while before anyone comes, please?'

'What is your surname?'

'So! things have come to such a pass! Now I need to recite my caste and gotra? By God's grace we have met after all these years and I am so happy. There has not been a day when I didn't think of you. You have provided me with a little sustenance, and that is more than enough! So you still cannot remember me?' she said, and irrationally started crying again. What a predicament! Too shocked for words, I stood before her like a lifeless log. Between sobs, she resumed, 'I recognized you the moment I saw your face. Confirmed it when I read your name on the box: "T. Purushottam, BA", and I rejoiced that you had passed the BA examinations. Have you forgotten me so completely? All right then, do you remember the auditor next door?'

At that, my heart felt as if it would burst.

'Manikyamma garu! How changed you are!' I slapped my mouth and forehead, bemoaning all that had happened.

I was eighteen at that time. I was doing my Intermediate at college. The auditor garu, an old man of sixty, used to live upstairs in the house next door to us. Manikyamma garu had married this widower and she was about thirty or thirty-five years of age. Having borne no children, she looked shapely, slim and delicate like a porcelain doll. Our two families grew very intimate.

Her widowhood, this rather obese body, the half-grey hair, had all happened later.

One day, I was returning from the college around two o'clock. Manikyamma garu hailed me and I went to their house.

'Make yourself comfortable,' she said, gesturing towards the folding chair. It was rather sultry, so I picked up the palm-leaf fan.

'Let me fan you,' she said, snatching the fan from me.

'Of course not,' I said.

'Nothing wrong!' She began to fan me.

'I must have my coffee and rush back to the college,' I said, getting up.

'Can't you have that coffee here?' she said. She went in and returned with a couple of rasgollas in a plate and water in a silver tumbler.

'Got them from a hotel?' I asked.

'I made them myself!' she said.

I had never imagined that our womenfolk were capable of making such delicacies. She continued fanning me and observed, 'It is time for you to start shaving.' Soft fine hair had just appeared on my chin. I had felt too shy to go to the barber.

'You have grown up. We must find a bride of marriageable age for you,' she said.

I was abashed. I concentrated on eating, quiet as a mongoose. The second rasgolla cloyed. She went in and promptly brought a hot mango chutney as relish and some coffee. I finished the food and stood up.

'I am feeling bored. Keep me company for a few more minutes please,' she said.

'But the college?'

'Skip it for the afternoon!'

'Oh, no. I have my optionals class now.'

'Be a good boy!' she said, leading me by the arm into their room.

'Have some betel,' she said.

Over the years we had grown so familiar with each other. Jokes and pranks were the normal thing between us. But now, all alone with her, her teasing behaviour confused me acutely. I put the betel in my mouth and got up to leave. 'Skip the college for today,' she said, tweaking my cheeks, and slipping her hands onto my shoulders, she pulled me to herself and seated me on the bed.

I grew suddenly hot all over. I could sense the drift of what she was doing all along, but now it hit me like a thunderbolt. I had of course come to feel the urges natural to my age, but I had never looked at Manikyamma garu from that angle. I was then eighteen; and she, almost double that. I was filled with apprehension, but still I did not leave the room. I sat feeling like a bride on her wedding night.

'Tomorrow, first thing, shave. Your face should feel smooth like a flower, not rough like a bittergourd,' she said fondling my beard. She continued, 'The first beard feels soft.' She lifted my face and, opening her eyes wide, she looked deep into mine. 'Don't tell anyone what I am doing—don't think ill of me—we are close enough, that is why I am taking liberties—don't think otherwise,' she said. 'I shall buy a bicycle for you—get a gold ring for you,' she said saturating every inch of my face with kisses.

You cannot catch the thief within the house or the bandicoot in the granary, they say. The auditor garu stayed on in the town for five more months. That period I cherish as one long amatory epic in the prabandham tradition. Those one hundred and fifty days were one hundred and fifty golden leaves in that epic, each moment filled with heavenly nectar. In its tempo and flow, it far outshone the renowned art of the best of our prabandham poets, Allasani. Though my life has been misery itself, like a drumstick tree infested with caterpillars, those five months are like ambrosial honeycombs on the branches of that wretched, wasted tree.

Our separation can only be described as a tragedy. I went to our village for the vacation and when college reopened, I returned to find that they had been transferred and had left for some other place. Not a word about them, or their whereabouts since then. If I can describe my pangs of lovesickness for her, it will be an epic of romantic separation; some day I must compose it carefully.

When I passed my BA examination and made it in the Service Commission tests, I secured a government job and married a girl of my choice. In the nuptial chamber when I glanced at my bride, her face lowered with acute shyness, I remembered my own plight with Manikyamma garu. I took my bride into my arms, still thinking of Manikyamma garu, and suffered quietly.

Now, when after all these years she appeared before

me—to think of it!—I could not even recognize her.

'How changed you are!' I said.

'It has been nine years. Everything has changed now. God's will. And we have met again like this. Where are you going?'

'Bezwada.'

'Why?'

'I work there.'

'Good. You are close to us. Are you married?'

'I have two children. A daughter of one and a half years and a boy of three months.'

'So your wife has two children by you. You actually have three children in all.'

'Three children?'

'Yes, you have given me a handsome boy.'

It gave me gooseflesh to hear that.

'Nine years old now. Absolutely your likeness. You will see when he returns. Somehow you have been my saviour. Your divine gift has helped me inherit my husband's earnings and patrimony. Without it, my brothers-in-law wouldn't have thought twice before shaving my head as a widow and brushing me aside and doing me out of the cash and property.'

'Where are you settled now?'

'Eluru is my native place. I built a two-storeyed building there. Your son is fortunate. We have ten thousand silver rupees. We get fifteen thousand coconuts and ninety *puttis* of paddy. Come home, you can see for yourself.'

Having eaten puris and drunk coffee, the boy returned.

'Mother, won't you at least eat some fruit?' he said, climbing into her lap.

Undoubtedly my son, exactly my likeness. Born to me when I was eighteen and to a woman some eighteen years older than me, born to me without my knowledge, not knowing me, not in a position to know me ever as his father, this son of mine had been growing up in Eluru for the last nine years!

'Have you seen the boy?' she said.

Of course I had. With all my life and being, I gazed my fill at him, I looked at my son and the paternal affection quite overwhelmed me.

'Come here, dear boy,' I beckoned to him.

Without feeling bashful at all, readily and familiarly he came over to me. I took him in my arms and experienced all the joy of filial embrace. Manikyamma garu covered her mouth with the hem of her sari and wept bitterly.

'In which class are you?' I asked him.

'Second form,' the boy said.

'Can you converse with him in English?' she said. 'For the last three years, I have engaged a Christian tutor to coach him.'

' "I am below ten". Is this right or wrong?' the boy asked. I was in real trouble. The statement appeared to be correct; but I was also worried that there was some error in it somewhere. What is the use of passing the great BA exam? Are our professors able to teach us well in college?

'You tell me, dear boy,' I said.

'Absolutely wrong. You should say "I am under ten". My tutor did not know even this much,' he said, giggling happily.

'Tomorrow I have to attend the office. I shall come on Sunday.'

'I shall come to the station!' the boy said.

'Of course, come!'

The boy yawned, became sleepy. I lowered the holdall from the upper birth, spread it on the lower berth, put the boy on it and sat by him, with my hand resting on him reassuringly. Until we reached Kaikaram, we chatted about this and that, and I enjoyed it. By the next station, Pulla, the boy had started snoring. Then the train reached Dendulur, the last station before Eluru.

'We are almost there. You must come on Sunday,' she said, her eyes sparkling, her whole face glowing.

Before we knew it, in just seven short minutes, we reached Eluru. I escorted them to the gate and handed them over to the cartman.

'See you,' she said.

'Are you coming on Sunday?' said the son.

'Must visit Eluru!'

Translated from the Telugu by V.P. Ranga Rao

Death of a Banana Boat

Jogesh Das

Krishna, Krishna! Dhaniram stopped at the gate. Such a huge house, sitting solemn and silent in broad daylight! Better keep quiet. It was an old two-storeyed wooden house; the chest-high wall had gathered moss, the wooden staircase had cracked and all the doors and windows were wide open. But there was no sign of life anywhere. There were the plants, looking fresh and lively, but the flowers seemed dead. There was no whisper of a breeze. The massive gate had splintered and looked as if it were grinning. A bad omen? The heart started thumping. Krishna, Krishna!

Still, he had to go ahead. No dilly-dallying. He must see the old man, the landlord. If he was not in, then the Burrababu. The landlord was a nice man, though a bit miserly. He would not spend a paisa without reason. But he was too old now, and the Burrababu was managing the estate. Burrababu was a short-tempered man. He was the one who threw him out of the house. One day while smoking a beedi, he set his own mosquito-net and pillows on fire. God, how he flared up! Once a cow strayed into the garden, and the thrashing he gave the cow . . . God! Another morning, Dhaniram could not wake him up and he missed his train. When he returned from the station, a sharp slap was in store for Dhaniram, as well as one month's pay and the notice to depart.

Burrababu's anger, in fact, was due to a different reason and Dhaniram knew it. But he had not told anybody. Dhaniram wanted to marry Rupeyee, or Rupeshwari. He had brought the orphan Rupeyee from a nearby village to look after Burrababu's children. Months went by and Rupeyee grew up and blossomed into a beautiful woman; soft hands, silken legs, big shining eyes and a sweet smile. Dhaniram felt like fainting away at the sight of her smile. Dhaniram desperately wanted to marry her. But one day Burrababu called him and warned, 'Look! I will kill you if you ever lay your hands on Rupeyee.'

Dhaniram crept cautiously by the side of the wall, out into the veranda, wondering if Burrababu would ever be kind to him. Chhotababu would surely have helped him. He used to give him money whenever he needed. But, he had gone abroad—er—to America. So now Dhaniram had to see the old man to get him to agree to a reduction in rent. Otherwise he would be in trouble. He had an ailing widowed sister and her two kids to look after. Mother was too old; she couldn't move without a walking stick. The sister mostly remained bedridden. She couldn't attend to the kitchen. So what could he do? Couldn't possibly throw her out. She was only a kid a few years ago, a little girl crying to her mother for dolls. What had he given her? Nothing. And when he came back home finally, after the slaps and all, she had gone off to her husband's place. What a shame!

This time the flood had destroyed his paddy crop. He had, of course, grown some kharif paddy. God willing, it could be a good crop. But he couldn't pay the land revenue from selling it. He had also exhausted all his savings on doctor's fees. He had little imagined that the flood would wash the crop away. If he did not get a few days' grace, he would be in real trouble. Burrababu could no doubt get him a tax relief.

He had put both the kids—Mani and Tuni—in the school. Could they be asked to attend the school on an empty stomach? Mani couldn't be send to the fields. With some money, however, their mother could be cured. He had left Rupeyee at Burrababu's disposal. He could not win her hand. Burrababu wanted Rupeyee. He had often seen them having fun together. When he would go in to give the newspapers to Burrababu, or take money for shopping or fetch Madam's sandals for repairing, he would see them. When they saw him, Rupeyee would go red, pulling the sari quickly over her bosom, and Burrababu would smile sheepishly. And his heart would pound in pain.

Nobody was there in the veranda. Strange! He had worked here for eight years, but the house hadn't changed a bit. The long wooden poles, the creaking staircase, the smoke-filled kitchen, the same laundry wire stretching out to the main house. But something seemed missing.

Dhaniram reached the veranda and tapped the railings nervously. No response from inside. The silence perturbed him. The balcony could be seen from the veranda. Nothing up there except the green and thick window screen, the colour of a banana leaf, hanging in front of Burrababu's room. He kept standing, holding on to the railing and facing the courtyard. He would have to see someone anyhow. Kharif paddy . . . ailing sister . . . Mani . . . Tuni . . . land revenue!

Ah, somebody was coming from behind the kitchen . . . a girl. She saw him and stopped, and then quickly backed off behind the house. Was it Rupeyee?

At the back of the house, there was a dish-washing pit, an ash-heap and a water tank. Beyond these were a straw-house, a kitchen garden and an orchard full of trees like jackfruit, lichi, betelnut and mango.

It must be Rupeyee. She had gone pink; no wonder. She was living in all comfort. Her bosom had also become bigger. That he could see, even if she was wearing a blouse. She seemed to have put on some weight.

She was avoiding him. She had to—she was scared of Burrababu. The same Rupeyee used to flirt with him, teasing and giggling. One day she was cutting betelnuts under the gulmohar tree when he had held her hands. She had pulled away from him and blushed. Another time he had said that he would take her away in a horse cart. In reply, she threw a staff at him. Madam, Burrababu's wife, who was watching the scene from the kitchen window, just smiled it off. That day Rupeyee had felt very ashamed and she had left the place in a huff. But Dhaniram could never bring himself to propose to her, for Burrababu had threatened him. He had paid the salary and sacked him. Forget it. No use fighting a rich man over a girl. There were many girls around—as beautiful, less beautiful and even more beautiful than Rupeyee. When he had left his job and gone back to the village, he had found that there just wasn't enough time to think about girls. The house was in shambles, Father was dead and Mother was too old to walk. And then the widowed sister had moved in with him, bringing along with her illness, hunger and the children. He decided to start farming. No more domestic service. He would get back the land he had leased out for share-cropping. Where was the time to think about girls? It could wait.

But Dhaniram couldn't get Rupeyee out of his mind. Girls were funny that way. Once you saw them, you got stuck, you kept on staring at them even if you were deep in trouble or you didn't have any time.

Somebody was coming down the stairs. Dhaniram turned around and was startled to see Madam standing there. Both exchanged glances. She pulled the chaddar round her head and threw a long look at him. He wanted to say 'Madam!' But words stuck in his throat. He felt his lips drying. Her round face was looking pale and grave. She didn't speak or smile. After leaving his job, Dhaniram had come here quite often and she had always greeted him with a smile and offered him fried rice, tea or betelnut. She had even advised him to get married and settle down. Something was wrong today. She looked sad. Her long lashes were wet and the big eyes red. She must have been crying. He felt very bad. He had great respect for her.

When she reached downstairs, he managed to cry out 'Madam!' She tried to smile. 'How are you, Dhani?' she asked. No, no, that couldn't be Madam's smile. Oh God! What was wrong? He could not even ask.

She said slowly, 'Take a seat. When did you come?'

Dhaniram sat down on the bench. 'Not very long ago,

Madam, came just now. Nobody seems to be around.'

Madam fell silent, staring blankly at the door.

'Madam,' he called again.

'Ah, yes, Dhani,' she seemed to fumble for words, 'all the family are there. Any problem?'

Dhaniram was startled. She sounded strange. He didn't know what to say. He had already forgotten what had brought him here. Suddenly, he remembered the kids. 'Ah, Madam, where are the children? I don't see them around.'

'The sister-in-law had come yesterday. The kids have gone with her. Want some betel? It's there. Let me go and inform Father.' She swept a look from Dhaniram to the betel-pot and went upstairs.

Cutting betelnut, Dhaniram reflected, the kids had stayed out since yesterday! Well, they are grown up now, they can stay out, and their uncle's house is not very far. He finished cutting the betel and chewed it. But nobody turned up! Usually the old man would send for him or Burrababu would show up and call him upstairs. Today Madam also didn't return! Rupeyee too seemed to have disappeared. Nobody washed dishes that long. She couldn't be working in the wood-shed or in the garden. Was she out picking mangoes?

Suddenly, Dhaniram heard footsteps upstairs and stood up. The old landlord, tall and handsome, wearing thick glasses and a long white shirt, and waving a curved stick came down few steps and halted. He threw a quiet long look at Dhaniram. Dhaniram bowed in salutation for the first time. He didn't have to salute his master when he was working here. Today, the house seemed to crash on him. Madam's voice was strange—and Rupeyee was perhaps hiding somewhere for fear of Burrababu. He had picked a very bad day to come to plead for relief in revenue.

The landlord asked him to come upstairs, and left. Dhaniram could hear the heavy steps receding into the drawing room where the old man discussed only business. He followed him fearfully. The old man was known to be a grave person. But today he sounded unusually cold and curt. He looked around before climbing the stairs. He was sweating visibly. No, Rupeyee was not to be seen anywhere. On reaching upstairs, he found the door to Burrababu's room closed. Where was Madam? Was she in Burrababu's room? It was painful without kids around, felt Dhaniram. They help ease tensions.

He stood at the door of the landlord's drawing room. The old man was sitting in the cane chair, staring straight out of the window. The walking stick was resting in his lap. 'Sir,' he said softly. There was no reply for a minute. He stood there holding his breath.

'I was expecting you, Dhani,' replied the old man. 'What's the matter?' Dhaniram gathered himself up and slowly narrated the whole story. The old man is very calculating, he thought, one does not know how he will react. Dhaniram felt panicky after he finished his tale of woe. Both sat into silence for a few minutes. Finally, the old man, without turning to him, said, 'So your sister is ailing. Are you consulting a doctor?'

Rubbing his hands together, Dhaniram said, 'I have spent whatever little money I had on the treatment. But she needs more medicines. I never thought the crop would be washed off. Otherwise I'd have saved something to pay the land revenue.'

'Get me the pad and pencil,' directed the landlord. Dhaniram nearly stumbled as he went over to the table and brought a pencil and a thick writing pad. He had performed this ritual umpteen times during his eight years in this house. The landlord would write while he would remain standing, waiting.

But why the pad today? he wondered. The old man never conveyed any message to Burrababu in writing; it was always oral. And why did he say that he was expecting him? Dhaniram felt mystified.

Folding up the letter, the landlord said, 'Go, give it to Burrababu.' Dhaniram put the pad and pencil back on the table. 'Dhani,' he added, 'see me before you leave.'

But how was he to meet Burrababu? The door was closed. Ah . . . now it had opened. Strange! As if the door had been waiting to open for him. The thick green screen was swaying; the door must have been opened just now. Oh God, gasped Dhaniram, as the screen swung into the room. Burrababu was seated in a corner of the huge bed. As he entered the room, Burrababu lifted his head: dishevelled hair, five days' growth of beard and eye-sockets looking hollow and black. He was wearing a purple khadi kurta without buttons and a shabby dhoti. Oh God! What had happened to this handsome dashing man? Dhaniram had always been scared of this man, but today he felt like pitying him. 'Eh . . . come Dhani, come here.' Burrababu's voice had become so soft! Why not? Madam herself was the goddess incarnate, wasn't she?

'Sir, are you all right?' inquired Dhaniram, handing him the letter. 'Well, it's nothing, Dhani . . . take a seat.' Burrababu offering him a seat in his bedroom! Was Dhaniram dreaming? He didn't accept the offer. That was something he could not possibly do.

Burrababu read through the letter. The room was looking as gloomy as Burrababu's face. All the screens, except one, were hanging down. Burrababu finished reading the letter and looked up at Dhani. He gave Dhaniram a long look and waved him to sit down.

He pulled a stool away a little and seated himself. Burrababu looked at him and read the letter again. Dhaniram wondered if the old man had written about the relief. What could it be then? He repeated the story . . . paddy . . . crop . . . flood . . . sister . . . Mani–Tuni . . .

Finally Burrababu announced, 'Dhani, your sister's case sounds quite serious. Don't neglect the treatment. These days there is no dearth of diseases. And as for the land revenue, something will be done.'

Dhaniram was overwhelmed. The old man seemed to have written down everything! No, he never wrote in such detail. Then how did Burrababu know the details?

It was getting darker. The sun had mellowed. Burrababu went near the window, and said, 'Dhani, did Father talk about Rupeyee?'

Dhaniram was stunned. How did Rupeyee come into the picture? 'No, he did not mention her name,' he said.

'Dhani,' pleaded Burrababu, 'save me. Only you can save me. Don't worry about the land revenue. And as for your sister's treatment, take two hundred rupees. That ought not to worry you at all.'

Dhaniram could not believe his ears. He was hearing such words for the first time in his life. Rich people are a strange lot.

'Dhani,' Burrababu pleaded again, 'take Rupeyee away from here. She is pregnant, four months now.'

Dhaniram got up sharply, shocked. Rupeyee pregnant! Now he knew why she was looking heavy and ran off seeing him, why the house had fallen silent, why the children had been sent to the uncle's house; why Madam was crying; why the old man and Burrababu knew everything; and why Burrababu was expecting him!

'Dhani,' Burrababu continued, 'if you don't help me, I will die. Only you can save us, Rupeyee and me.'

Burrababu came up to him and shoved a bundle of ten-rupee notes into his hands. Two hundred? He felt relieved touching the notes. He could do lot of things with two hundred. Fifty rupees were enough for his sister's treatment. With the rest of the money, he could buy clothes for Mani and Tuni. But how could he maintain Rupeyee, the pregnant princess? When Burrababu said his name again pleadingly, he said, 'Let me please talk to the master, Burrababu.' As he left the room, he saw the man standing, helpless and miserable. He felt sorry for him again.

Just outside the room, he almost ran into Madam, who was coming up the stairs. Her eyes swollen, she said, 'Dhani, don't go away, wait downstairs. I'm making tea for you.'

The old landlord came up to him. 'Dhani,' he said, 'if you take Rupeyee, it will be good for all of us and her. She will lead a better life. Of course, you have to be careful. Rupeyee can be useful to you too. How will you manage your home without a woman? Take her, Dhani, and all of us will be saved.'

Dhaniram did not reply. The old man, Burrababu, Chhotababu of America, Madam, Rupeyee—all of them would be saved. He too would be saved, as the old man said. Well, sounds all right, reflected Dhaniram. It will do good to one and all, and he would get a wife too!

It was already evening when Dhaniram finished the tea and sweets served by Madam downstairs. The rooms upstairs were already lit. Madam had often offered him tea in that very brass glass and sweets wrapped in papers. This was not her special treatment. Dhaniram looked at the lady with renewed respect and affection. She never tries to please anyone with selfish motives, not even today. He put the glass in the kitchen and took a betel.

He was about to ask, 'Where is Rupeyee?' But there she was, standing in the dark with a bundle. Since there was no talk of Rupeyee, he did not feel like mentioning it to Madam. Then he smartly bowed, touched the lady's feet and started off without saying anything.

Rupeyee was standing near the door in the dark. 'Rupeyee,' he said, 'come along.' She followed him, walking along the wall. He did not look back, nor said anything.

A horse cart was parked near the gate. Burrababu was standing there in the dark. Dhaniram held the cart door open for Rupeyee. Both of them climbed in. Then he closed the door. Burrababu waved and the cart pulled out of the gate. He forgot to wish his master. He was now thinking about Rupeyee whom he had once teased under the gulmohar tree, that he would take her away in a horse cart.

Translated from the Assamese by Harish C. Pradhan

Notes on Authors

Gurzada Apparao (1861-1915), poet, playwright, academic and administrator, is considered the first Telugu short story writer, who exercised great influence on his successors. Many of his stories deal with contemporary social problems, especially women's issues, and all of them are written in a colloquial style and with delicate humour.

Manik Bandyopadhyay (1908-56) was the greatest Bengali realist writer and the first Marxist novelist in India. His work offers a penetrating insight into the changing times that saw the disintegration of colonial rule, the loss of traditional values by the urban middle classes and the ruthless exploitation of the rural masses, against a backdrop of riots, famine and peasant uprisings. His most famous works include the novels *Padma Nadir Majhi* and *Putul Nacher Itikatha*, and the short story collections *Pragaitihasik* and *Sarisrip*.

Vaikom Mohammed Basheer (1910-94) was an acknowledged master of the short story in Malayalam and lived a life as varied as the stories he wrote. He participated in the freedom struggle, was imprisoned several times and travelled widely through India. Along with other writers, he evolved a new literary language which derived from the spoken idiom. His novels, such as *Balyakalasakhi* and *Nduppoopakoranandarnnu*, have been widely translated and won many awards.

P.B. Bhave (1910-80) was one of the most prolific of Marathi authors and one of the pioneering short story writers in that language. His works include thirty-one collections of short stories, sixteen novels, fourteen collections of articles and seven plays. Influenced by the Ramayana, Mahabharata and the poetry of Kalidasa, his works celebrate ancient Indian culture in all its glory.

Chaaso was the pen name of Gudipati Venkatachalam (1894-1979). He was a social crusader, novelist and perhaps the first Telugu writer to espouse the feminist cause. Many of his works rebelled against deep-rooted customs and views, and attacked the caste system. He was an active participant in the reformist movement, and also wrote books on the education of children and women. His contribution to the evolution of a new colloquial Telugu prose style is considerable.

Krishan Chandar (1914-77) was perhaps the most prominent participant in the progressive movement in Urdu literature, noted for his experiments with abstract writing and with a new poetic prose style. His most famous novels include *Ghaddar*, *S'hiksat* and *Ek Gadhe Ki Sarzugast*. He also wrote plays, film scripts and satires. He was awarded the Padma Bhushan. His work has been widely translated.

Jogesh Das (1927-99) was one of the most distinguished Assamese novelists and short story writers. Six collections of his short stories and fifteen novels have been published, perhaps the most famous of which is *Dawar Aru Nai*, a unique experiment in Assamese literature. His work is an exposé of the problems of lower middle class life. He received several Sahitya Akademi awards. His work has been widely translated.

Dhumaketu (1892-1965) was the pen name of Gaurishankar Govardhandas Josh, a prolific writer, who is considered one of the pioneers of the Gujarati short story. He published twenty-four collections of such stories, as well as thirty-two novels on historical and social subjects, and plays and travelogues. His writing is characterized by a poetic style, romanticism and powerful depiction of human emotions.

Kirit Doodhat (b.1961) is a member of the parishkruti movement in Gujarati literature, which is concerned with the revival of the traditional culture which is being lost as a result of economic and social changes, and cultural and linguistic aggression. He is currently the deputy collector of a district, and in close contact with the rural mileu. His short stories have been widely published.

Gangadhar Gadgil (b.1923) is the initiator of the navakatha movement in Marathi literature. He is a prolific writer who has published over fifty works, including novels, short stories, travelogues and plays. His writing emphasizes urban complexities and psychological tensions, and he depicts the inner life of common men and women with great perception and immediacy.

Masti Venkatesha Iyenger (1891-1986) is considered the pioneer of the short story in Kannada, and it is on these stories that his fame largely rests, though he wrote some great novels, poems and plays. A distinguished civil servant, he won many awards as an author, including the Sahitya Akademi award and the Jnanpith award. The best of his short stories are found in the two volumes of *Sanna Kathegalu*, and his novels include *Cheena Basava Nayata* and *Chika Vira Rajendra*.

Amin Kamil (b.1924) began his career writing poetry in Urdu, but later switched to Kashmiri. He also writes short stories, plays and novels, and does translations. His collection of short stories *Kathi Manz Kath* and the novel *Ghati Manz Gaash* have won many awards. He writes in the everyday language of common people but crafts his creations with meticulous care.

Saadat Hasan Manto (1912-55) is regarded as the greatest of Urdu short story writers though his career was tragically brief. His work, marked by its unsentimental realism, questions ethical codes and explores the delicate nuances of human nature under extreme stress.

Godavarish Mohapatra (1895-1965) was a poet, journalist and short story writer. He was the founder and editor of the widely-read satiric journal *Niankhunta*. He won the Sahitya Akademi award for his collection of poetry *Phula O Kanta*.

Thakazhi Sivasankara Pillai (1914-99) was one of the most prolific and eminent of Malayalam writers. The most famous of his thirty-nine novels is *Chemmeen*, which won the Sahitya Akademi award, and *Kayar*. He also published over five hundred short stories, which are characterized by their social and romantic realism.

Pudumai Pithan (1906-48) was the pen name of Cho Vriddhachalam, a pioneer of Tamil literature in his brief writing career. He belonged to the Manikkodi group, named after the periodical which published new and experimental work. He wrote poetry and criticism as well as short stories. His short stories often retold ancient tales and fables in a form relevant to the contemporary age. His collections of short stories include *Kanchanai*, *Annirabu* and *Kalyani*.

Premchand (1880-1936) was the champion of progressive literature in India. His early writing was in Urdu. Under the influence of Mahatma Gandhi, he started championing the cause of the masses and writing to promote social justice and bring in a new social order. He published over three hundred short stories and twelve novels, the most famous of which is *Godan*.

C. Rajagopalachari (1878-1974), the eminent statesman, was also one of the foremost Tamil writers. His interests in law, social reform and the independence movement permeate his fiction. He translated the Ramayana and Mahabharata. His collections of fiction includes *The Fatal Cart and Other Stories* and *Way Out*.

Fakir Mohan Senapati (1843-1918) was the first Oriya writer to write novels and short stories, which are powerful portraits of the social history of his state. He began to write only at the close of a varied career which included teaching, journalism, administration and participating in the freedom struggle. His works include four novels, including the satirical masterpiece *Chha Maan Atha Guntha*, and numerous short stories.

Kulwant Singh Virk (1923-87) was an eminent Punjabi short story writer whose work encapsulates the lives of rural society in central Punjab. His collection of short stories *Naven Lok* won the Sahitya Akademi award.

Krishna Sobti (b.1925) is noted for her powerful writings on feminist and gender-related issues which challenge established social norms. Her most famous novels include *Hitromirjani, Dar Se Bichri* and *Jindaginama*.

Rabindranath Tagore (1861-1941) was perhaps Bengal's greatest writer, whose eminence is yet unchallenged and whose ceaseless innovations in poetry, prose, drama and music won him great renown all over the world. He was awarded the Nobel Prize for literature. His most acclaimed novels include *Gora* and *Ghare Baire*, while *Galpaguccha* is his most famous collection of short stories.

K.P. Poornachandra Tejasvi (b.1938) is an important exponent of the post-navya stream of fiction in Kannada. He has published two collections of short stories, *Huliyurina Sarahaddu* and *Abachurina Post Office*. His short stories are characterized by a fluent narrative style and his protagonists are often victims of social or political forces which they are unable to comprehend. His novel *Chidambara Rahasya* won the Sahitya Akademi award.